Marked by Moonlight

a magical, mysterious shapeshifter/vampire romance

Château Nocturne
Book 2

Anna Lowe

Contents

Free Books

Get your free e-books now!

Sign up for my newsletter at *annalowebooks.com* to get three free books!

- *Desert Wolf*: Friend or Foe (Book 1.1 in the Twin Moon Ranch series)

- *Off the Charts* (the prequel to the Serendipity Adventure series)

- *Perfection* (the prequel to the Blue Moon Saloon series)

Chapter One

MINA

I tapped my fingers on the steering wheel, looking at Auberre's public park through the windshield. Honestly, how hard could this be?

My heart pounded and my fingers tapped faster, but my nerves were still on edge.

You can do it, I tried telling myself.

What if I couldn't? What if I failed?

If Marius were around, I would have been eager to prove to him what I was capable of. But my dragon shifter lover was away on another job with his colleagues Roux, Bene, and Henrik — their second trip since we'd returned from Mallorca. Only three days this time, but it already felt like an eternity.

To avoid moping over Marius like a love-sick puppy, I'd assigned myself a list of tasks to accomplish in that time. So far today, I'd gone for an early morning run, scraped peeling paint in the west wing of the château, and set out on an epic shopping trip in anticipation of the guys coming home — er, coming back — soon.

Now it was time for the next item on my list. Shadow-walking, right here in the public park, where everyone could see — or rather, *not* see.

All my life, I'd been brushed by magic that came and went as it pleased — little relics of my mixed ancestors' much greater abilities. The way normal people vowed to master knitting, gardening, or a foreign language, I'd made halfhearted resolutions to learn magic. I hadn't ever actually accomplished much, though.

But the past few weeks had shown me I had to sharpen every tool in my box if I wanted to survive another brush with ruthless supernaturals.

Shadow-walking was tool number one — making myself invisible, in a sense. To do that, I had to maintain an illusion of myself in one place while sneaking over to another. I'd succeeded a few times in the past, but I needed to do it reliably. Confidently. Hence, this visit to the park.

But now that I was here, my resolve faded away like moonlight on a stormy night.

You can do it, I pictured Marius saying.

I pushed the car door open, strode to the park, and plopped down on a bench, rubbing my hands nervously. I could do this. I could definitely do this. Once I started, it would all come naturally. Right?

I looked around. No one in sight. I settled into as natural a position as possible, gazing solemnly at the tricolor flags flanking the village war memorial. I carefully noted every detail, from the angle at which my ankles crossed to the way one hand rested over the other. I catalogued the length of my shadow and the way the autumn breeze flowed around my body. Then, recreating that exact scene, I inched silently away, checking the illusion I'd left behind.

Sad gaze aimed at the war memorial — check. Body and shadow unchanged — check. I was there, but I wasn't there.

At the same time, I had to conceal every trace of the real me. That meant erasing my shadow, rearranging the breeze, and creating the illusion of untrampled grass under my feet.

Intense didn't begin to describe the process. It was like painting two different scenes at the same time, keeping one eye and one hand on each. But the consequences of an error now weren't merely a smudged canvas. It was smudging myself right out of existence.

My head started to throb, but I kept it up, maneuvering farther away with every step. Then, for practice, I turned away, because an illusion was that much harder to maintain without visual feedback. Had my illusionary head tipped to a strange angle? Was my nose migrating over to my mouth like a warped Picasso portrait?

A cloud covered the sun, dimming every shadow. I hurried to correct the faux shadow at my fake double and the too-bright spot I'd been mind-casting over my real shadow. Then the sun emerged again, and I reversed the process.

Whew. I made a mental note to stick to indoor shadow-walking — if I had to shadow-walk at all.

I paced from side to side, trying different distances and checking for another cloud. Luckily, the sky looked as if it would remain clear for the next few minutes.

I was just congratulating myself on a job well done when someone called from the street.

"Oh, Mina! *Bonjour!*"

It was Madame Fontaine, the retired schoolmistress, approaching the park.

The good news was, she was focused on fake me. That proved the illusion was working. Yay, me!

The bad news was, she was closer to the bench than I was, and my illusion was about to be exposed.

Oh shit.

I sprinted over, desperately trying to keep myself masked. A damn good thing no one was around to notice the details I lost track of in my rush, like my footsteps in the grass or the shadow I cast.

"Mina! Yoo-hoo," Madame Fontaine hollered when fake me didn't turn.

I made a mental note to try more realistic, moving illusions in the future — if I ever worked up the nerve to try this again. Because damn, was I cutting it close.

At the last possible second, I jumped into the space occupied by the illusionary me and released the spell.

Madame Fontaine did a double take, and I winced. I hadn't resumed exactly the same position, making my image skip like a badly edited video.

"Oh *bonjour*, madame," I panted.

Her brow furrowed. "Are you all right, dear?"

I nodded quickly. "Fine, thank you. I guess my mind was somewhere else."

My body, too, but no need to mention *that*.

Glancing at the war memorial, she patted my hand. "It's good to know young people still remember their sacrifice."

I often did, but my motives today were entirely selfish, making me feel terribly guilty. I made a mental note to lay a wreath the next time Armistice Day came around.

"It's so sad," I said, and I meant it.

She patted my hand again. "All we can do to honor their memory is to make the best of the time we've been gifted with."

Her wise words prompted another round of soul-searching. Was I doing my best with the time I'd been gifted? Shouldn't teaching fifth graders rank higher than renovating a crumbling building and carrying on with a dragon shifter I might not have a future with? Or was it just as important to hold true to my heart and my family's legacy?

A legacy that involved magic. Was I a fool to play with fire, or was I justified in trying to rekindle it?

Berating myself for another *me, me, me* moment, I silently read the names on the war memorial. Then I took a deep breath and offered Madame Fontaine my elbow.

"Does a trip to the *boulangerie* qualify as making the best of the time we've been gifted?"

She chuckled and stood, wrapping her arm around mine. "Always. Especially when there are éclairs involved."

Off we went, arm in arm, and for the first time, I felt she and I had something in common other than both being teachers and residing in the same peaceful corner of Burgundy.

"It's so lovely to have young people back in town," Madame Fontaine said along the way. "You...Clement..."

She meant my childhood buddy turned local hottie/police officer/overprotective wolf shifter. A man I loved like a brother, but only as a brother.

She didn't exactly waggle her eyebrows, but *Why on earth aren't you two already married?* came through loud and clear.

"It's lovely to be back in town," I said diplomatically.

That also saved me from trying to explain how Marius's soulful eyes and gritty determination more than made up for his slightly sketchy background. She would never understand anyway.

I endured another few minutes of hinting and matchmaking, but the éclair was worth it. And, oh! The splitting headache that always plagued me after magic-making had dissipated already.

I said my goodbyes and walked back to my car, making a mental note to always, always follow up magic practice with a pastry. For mental health purposes.

Then my phone rang, and I lit up in anticipation of a call from Marius. Was his mission finished? Was he safe? Was he on his way home to me?

I yanked my phone out of my pocket and hurried to my car, heart pounding in giddy elation.

Chapter Two

MINA

My fingers shook as I checked the display. I was that excited —
and pathetic. For the three days that Marius had been away,
I'd practically kept my nose pressed to a window like a faithful
mutt, waiting for his return. Every time my phone rang, my
figurative tail wagged, and every time someone else spoke on
the other end of the line, that tail drooped again.

Like now, with caller ID showing *Geneviève*. I loved my
sister, but talking to her didn't give me all the feels talking to
Marius did. Either I was infatuated... or *destined mates* really
was a thing.

I slid into my car and answered the call, trying to sound
chipper.

"Hi, Gen."

"Hi. How are you?" she asked sweetly.

Red flags flapped in my mind. Gen rarely used that tone
with me.

"Good. How are you?" I braced myself.

"Good." She hesitated. Another red flag, because Gen
blasted through conversations the way she blasted through life
— unencumbered by the thought process, as our favorite radio
talk show hosts liked to say.

"I need a favor," she finally said.

"Pick you up at the airport? Any time," I declared.

I'd inherited Château Nocturne together with Gen and our
cousin, Dora, and we'd agreed to devote all our resources to
turning the neglected estate into a viable business... somehow.

But so far, I'd been the only one on-site dealing with cobwebs, cracked walls, and leaks.

Finally, Gen dropped her bombshell. "Unfortunately, I've been delayed."

"Again?" I screeched.

Originally, Gen had been scheduled to fly to France a week after I had, way back at the beginning of the summer. Now, it was late September, and I was still dealing with the place alone.

Well, not quite alone, because I had taken in three shifters and a vampire as boarders — a game changer as far as renovation work was concerned...and in other ways. But I still shouldered sole responsibility for the place, and every nerve-racking decision, no matter how small or how big, was up to me.

"I'm really sorry. I promise I'll be there as soon as I can."

"I need you here *now,* Gen."

"I know, I know. And I'm *really* sorry. I just have to sort out a few more things..."

A few more things meant *her life*, and, much as I loved my sister, I had my doubts.

"Gen..." I grumbled, torn, as always, between sisterly support and tough love. Tough love was definitely winning.

"I swear, I'll rebook the ticket soon."

I clenched my jaw. She'd probably paid more in rebooking fees than the original ticket by now.

Then again, I was the lucky one not to have blazed through a string of toxic relationships. Maybe I should be more understanding...if I didn't scream into the phone first.

And, ha. What a stir that would cause in sleepy little Auberre! Mesdames Fontaine and Martin would burst out of the *boulangerie* to investigate. Curtains would be yanked aside as folks in the surrounding houses eagerly listened in. The houses that were still occupied, at least, and by people whose hearing was still sharp. No great danger, because Auberre, like most of rural France, had seen a demographic shift over time, with a heavy tilt toward the over-seventy end of things.

"The problem is, Gordon asked me to meet some people, and now I can't make the date," Gen said.

Whooping alarms joined the red flags in my head.

"Hello?" Gen said when I didn't reply. "Can you hear me?"

I swallowed hard. "Say that again, please. I didn't quite catch it."

"I said, Gordon asked me to meet some people for him," Gen hollered. "And I won't be able to make it now, so I was hoping you could."

The breeze making those red flags flap increased to force 10. Why would Gordon ask Gen when I was much closer?

"What people? Where? When?"

"Next week, in Paris. I think they're amateur art collectors or something. I didn't ask."

I could have screamed, *You didn't ask? How can you be so gullible?* But until recently, I would have done the same. Anything for Gordon, our kind, generous godfather. No questions asked.

That was before I learned that the "bodyguards" he'd sent to board at Château Nocturne were mercenaries and that his "business interests" included shady backroom deals.

My stomach churned as I thought back to the little favors Gordon had asked of me in the past. Parties he'd asked me to attend, packages to pick up or drop off. I'd never stopped to think there might be something dubious at work, and I still struggled to believe that now. But after recent events... Well, I'd learned all was not as it seemed with dear old Gordon.

"Why did Gordon ask you instead of me?" I asked.

"Gordon didn't want to bother you with it. He knows how busy you've been."

He also knew I was the responsible one — and the one on his side of the Atlantic. Clearly, he wanted to keep this a secret from me.

"Who are you supposed to meet? Why?" I asked.

"Gordon was going to give me the details later. But don't worry. I'll call him to say I couldn't make it."

That wasn't the part I worried about.

"Unless..." she hinted.

"Unless I offer to help instead of you?" I filled in.

I had no intention of offering any such thing, and yet I already knew I would. Better me than my gullible, trusting sister.

"What else do you know about this?" I asked.

Not a hell of a lot, as it turned out, making for a short conversation.

"But don't worry—"

Ha. The more she said that, the more I did.

"—I'll call Gordon and explain," she finished.

"Don't!" I practically shouted, then cleared my throat and tried again in a normal tone. "Don't. I was planning to make a trip to Paris later this week. I'll discuss it with him then."

I'd been planning no such thing, but it bought me time to think.

"You think he'll be mad?" Gen asked.

I could see her sad-puppy face now. It didn't work on me, but it would work on Gordon.

"No," I sighed.

Not only would Gordon not be mad, he would go to great lengths to console her. Tickets to the opera... VIP entry to the opening of a new art exhibit... Gordon was incredibly generous in that way.

"I'm really sorry," Gen went on. "I know the château is taking every minute you have—"

Mostly, yes, but I'd also been shagging Marius every spare moment I found. I'd never really believed in destiny, but since *insatiable lust* was one of the signs, well...

"—and I swear I'll make it up to you."

"You *will* make it up to me," I said firmly. "The second you get your ass over here." Then inspiration hit me, and I sweetened the deal. "Clement is back in Auberre, you know. And single."

"He is?" Her voice rose.

I sighed. Gen had harbored a crush on the wolf shifter since she was five and Clement about nine. A painfully unrequited crush, but you never knew.

"Yes, and he's asked about you."

"He did?" she squealed.

I held the phone away from my ear, contemplating my fib. I'd mentioned Gen to Clement, and he'd made a noncommittal sound in reply. Close enough?

"Just another reason for you to get over here ASAP," I said.

"I will. I promise. It's just that this run of *Peter and the Wolf* got extended by a few weeks."

Right, and the hot new percussionist was probably perfect for a rebound fling — Gen's favorite cure for a relationship gone sour. She designed sets for the Children's Theatre of New England, and her love life had a way of mirroring the dramas that played out on the stage.

I ended the call and gazed over the town park. French horns played the wolf's menacing tune in my mind as I considered what Gen had said.

A car passed, then a minivan, but I was too absorbed in my thoughts to notice until they were two blocks away. Only then did I fumble with my keys and start my car, because that was Henrik's sports car and the minivan Roux drove with Marius and Bene. They were coming home!

My battered old Citroën sputtered to life on the second try. I raced off, sparing it no mercy in my eagerness to catch up with my man. I did limit myself to just a shade over the speed limit, lest I give the police an excuse to ticket me. And not just any police officer, but Clement. I loved him, but it was strictly platonic. From my side, at least. From his…

Well, that was where things got a little complicated.

The minute I passed the town limits, I revved the Citroën's poor, straining engine. Not long after, I swung left onto a country road that led to the château's long, tree-lined driveway. I screeched into the wide arc area in front of the building, scattering gravel, then leaped out to greet them.

"Oh hi, Mina," Bene said, looking uncharacteristically guarded.

Usually, the blond lion shifter was as sunny as can be. Not today, though.

Roux's eyes were rimmed with dark lines, and he greeted me with a flat, "*Bonjour.*"

The man was a tiger shifter and a dead ringer for David Beckham — without the smirk. But, my, did he look tired.

Henrik, a dark-haired vampire, bent into the slightest hint of a bow, avoiding my eyes. "Hello."

"Hi," I chirped, more to the van door than any of them, because surely Marius would exit next.

I pictured him extending his long legs and arms and stepping out, then wrapping those arms around me. Arms that could turn into wings, plus midnight eyes that had a way of peering deep into my soul. Hair the color of a chocolate lover's dreams, and a bad boy expression that masked how much more there was to him.

I waited. Any minute now, I would get treated to all that. Very, very soon. . .

I waited another few seconds, then stuck my head inside the vehicle. But Marius wasn't snoozing in the back or finishing a call or dealing with luggage. He wasn't there at all.

I whirled to the others. "Where's Marius?"

Bene looked at his feet, while Roux and Henrik looked at each other.

Oh God.

Marius was a kick ass dragon shifter who could look out for himself. But he took part in highly secretive and dangerous missions for my godfather, Gordon.

My voice rose along with my pulse. "Where is Marius?"

Chapter Three

MINA

"He's…um…" Roux scratched his ear.

"He's all right," Bene filled in quickly.

Good old Bene. The only socially intelligent being in this bunch of growly supernaturals.

My panic subsided slightly. "Totally all right?"

Bene shot me a crooked smile. "As all right as a dragon shifter will ever be."

Roux pinned him with a hard look, and Bene's humor vanished.

"Uh…I'd better unpack," Bene mumbled, trotting toward the west wing.

I stared. What was there to unpack in that tiny sports duffel of his?

It was all I could do not to shake Roux. A damn good thing I didn't, because he looked edgy. Well, even edgier than usual. And you didn't go shaking a testy tiger.

"Marius is all right, but he's not here?" I asked.

Roux stuck his hands in his pockets. The top pockets, because he loved cargo pants, an echo of the military life he'd once led. Henrik looked around awkwardly, then thrust something at me, not at all his usual, bored, aristocratic self.

"A gift," he murmured then hurried up the stairs.

I stared at the small flat can. Caviar?

Henrik, of all people (er, vampires?), had brought me a present?

13

Something was definitely wrong. That, or I was reading too deeply into old-world manners that required him to bring a gift to the lady of the house, as he insisted on calling me.

Old-fashioned manners didn't prevent Henrik from avoiding me, though. Only Roux stuck around, compelled, no doubt, by his tightly wound sense of honor.

"What's going on?" I demanded.

He rubbed his chin, then finally came up with, "Marius had to…take care of a few things."

His tone suggested innocuous trifles like a dental checkup or mowing his grandmother's lawn.

Much about Marius remained a mystery to me, but if there was one thing I'd learned about the dragon shifter, it was that he didn't do *innocuous* or *trifles*. This was the guy who'd torched half an acre of forest in pursuit of an intruder. A man whose idea of a diversion was a fire big enough to burn a Mallorcan villa to the ground. Everything Marius did, he did big.

"Take care of a few things," I echoed, showing my disbelief. "Like what?"

"I didn't ask," Roux mumbled. "Now, if you'll excuse me…"

He grabbed his bag and headed into the house.

I stared at the door he disappeared through. The guys and I had had a rough start, but we'd gradually moved on to more cordial relations and even bonded, especially after that mission in Mallorca. Now, we were suddenly back at square one. Why? What had happened?

I trailed Roux into the house, a little forlorn. His footsteps echoed through the massive entry hall and up the stairs. Then everything went quiet, until *Bam!* The breeze slammed the front door shut.

I stood alone in that vast space, feeling small and hurt. Had I been kidding myself about forming genuine friendships with the guys? Was I stupid to think of a group of dangerous supernaturals as anything more than clients?

I squeezed my hands into fists. No, dammit. We'd laughed and cried together. (Well, I'd cried.) Roux had carried me out of a burning building. Bene had given me a touching birthday present. Henrik had...um...refrained from sucking my blood. If that wasn't friendship, what was?

So where the hell was Marius?

Turning on my inner detective, I studied the caviar. It looked like the real deal, with Cyrillic script and everything. I stared at the hallway leading to the men's quarters. Whoa. Had their mission taken them to Russia?

But, no. The sticker on the base of the can was printed in French, English, and German, and marked *Noir Impérial Importateurs SRL, Bruxelles.*

I looked back up at the empty stairway. Brussels, maybe?

Then again, that can could have been resold anywhere in Europe.

I stood, lost and confused, for another few minutes. Then I peered outside, willing another car to come down the drive. Marius would hop out, throw his arms around me, and everything would be all right again.

But there was no car. No Marius. No explanation. Just the vast, echoing space of the front hall.

I trudged toward the kitchen, then veered off to my apartment in the east wing, unable to face Madame Picard. She was busy preparing dinner for five, not four, but not busy enough to hold back from a barrage of questions I couldn't answer.

Once in my apartment, I went straight to a window and stared at the driveway while my emotions churned.

I didn't have Marius's number, because I'd never needed it, with him living at the château. I'd learned to live with radio silence whenever he was on a mission for Gordon, but his latest mission was over now. So where the hell was he?

Celeste jumped into my mind. Was his succubus ex somehow involved in this?

The thought made me sick, but what could I do?

Get much-needed work done instead of sitting around fretting, I chided myself.

I detoured to the mini fridge in my apartment, broke off a chunk of dark chocolate, and headed for the door. Then I stopped, turned back, and grabbed another chunk. I was in the midst of an emotional crisis, and I deserved it, dammit!

Then I headed for the upper level of the opposite wing of the château — the rooms corresponding to mine, where my guests lived. I'd originally assigned them rooms on the ground floor, but Marius had immediately moved to the upper floor, while Henrik had moved in to the attic. I'd been furious at the time, but that was before... Well, before Marius and I had...

I trailed off there, trying to fill in that blank. Before he and I had fallen in love, or before he and I had started our ill-fated affair?

In any case, my latest renovation project focused on the four upstairs rooms in their west wing, because the plan was to rent out accommodations in addition to hosting weddings and other events someday.

I snorted under my breath. High-paying, *human* guests, I hoped, not temptingly dangerous dragon shifters who messed with my heart.

Work was the last thing I felt like doing, but the château wouldn't renovate itself, so I pulled on my work overalls, headed to the west wing, and started scraping paint from a window frame. My focus was only half there, however. The rest had me peeking around the room, spying the few possessions Marius had left behind. Wondering. Wishing.

But there were no love letters revealing a secret affair, no map pinned with locations of murders to investigate — or carry out. No duffel bag full of weapons, and certainly no album of childhood memories to give me some insight into the man I loved.

Time dragged. The shadows of the forest that fringed the château stretched and crept across the lawn. Roux and Henrik paced outside, deep in conversation. I watched them from the corner of my eye then checked the clock. Five p.m.

I worked straight through till six, though my mind spun with conspiracy theories the whole time. Habit drove me to shower and into the dining room for dinner afterward. A decision I regretted the instant I walked through the door.

Roux, Bene, and Henrik were there, and Marius's absence loomed large. They stood silently by the windows, and the atmosphere was very much that of a wake. My heart hammered. No one was dead, right?

"Any news?" I asked, trying to sound matter-of-fact.

Roux shook his head grimly.

My phone pinged, and they all tensed. I fumbled in my haste to answer, then grimaced.

"Oh hello, Gordon. How are you?"

All three men paled. Even Henrik, who looked more ghostly than usual.

Gordon responded with the usual pleasantries, but I could sense an undertone to his words.

"Yes, all's well here, thank you. I got a lot of work done on the west wing. You should come visit and see the progress for yourself."

Roux's eyes went wide, and Bene made a cutting motion with his arms.

I turned the screws a little tighter, watching the men as I spoke into the phone. "Maybe next weekend?"

Roux joined Bene in making frantic *stop* gestures.

"Oh, that's too bad," I said when Gordon politely declined, citing work.

Bene exhaled, and Roux rubbed his chest, right over his heart.

Then Gordon asked about my houseguests, as I'd guessed he would.

"Are they back?" I echoed his question to my three guests.

Roux and Henrik nodded like a couple of those toy dogs with bobbing heads people kept in their cars, while Bene put his hands together in a pleading motion.

"Yes, they're here now. Roux, Bene, Henrik..." I said, then paused.

"And Marius," Roux hissed.

So, whatever Marius was up to, it wasn't a job Gordon had assigned. Interesting. No, infuriating. I glared at the men.

Bene flapped imaginary wings, miming a dragon, while Henrik went for a threatening approach, letting his long vampire fangs extend.

I flashed him my middle finger.

"And Marius," Roux repeated, pleading this time.

I considered for another split second, then spoke into the phone. "And Marius, of course."

I jabbed a finger at Roux, mouthing, *You owe me.*

Henrik turned to the drinks cart, poured a scotch, and handed it to Roux.

"Would you like to speak to him?" I asked Gordon.

Roux nearly spat out his drink. I shot him a fake smile, though I trembled inside. What if Gordon called my bluff?

"Not necessary," Gordon said.

I exhaled.

"I just wanted to check in," my godfather added.

Funny, how that always coincided with the comings and goings of my houseguests. Or not funny at all, because I hated being used. And I hated the new truths these not-strictly truthful men had unveiled to my naive eyes. I'd thought my godfather had done me a huge favor by paying for his team of "bodyguards" to board at the château, but he was actually using it as a base from which to conduct nefarious business deals.

"I appreciate it," I said, not as enthusiastically as I had in the past.

"I'm sorry I can't make it, but please come visit any time," Gordon said.

I made a mental note. Maybe I would, dammit. Maybe I would.

"Thanks so much. Talk to you soon?" I said, summoning what cheer I could.

"*À bientôt,*" he echoed.

I hung up, pinning the men with my best teacher look. The one that said, *I know you're guilty, and I'm giving you a chance to confess before I really explode.*

Bene rubbed his hands nervously and glanced at Roux — a classic tell pointing to the ringleader of the bunch.

"What. Is. Going. On?" I gritted out, one syllable at a time.

Roux puffed out his cheeks, then fessed up. "Marius left at the end of our mission."

"In Brussels?" I tried.

"I'm not at liberty to say."

I rolled my eyes, then pressed on. "Where did he go?"

"I don't know."

"*Why* did he go?" I tried.

"I don't know."

A good thing we hadn't sat down to dinner yet. I might have thrown a platter or two.

"And Gordon doesn't know Marius is gone," I surmised.

"No. Gordon doesn't know where Marius is or what he's doing," Roux clarified.

I made a face. "That makes two of us."

Roux's eyes hit the floor, and I studied him closely.

"You really don't know?"

He shook his head. "I don't. And Gordon can't find out Marius is gone."

"Because it will get him in hot water with Gordon?"

"Because it will get *all* of us in hot water with Gordon," Roux growled.

"That was part of the deal," Bene explained. "We work for Gordon for six months, and our records are cleared. But we're all responsible for each other. If anyone causes trouble, we all pay."

Damn, did my sweet godfather/shady business magnate drive a hard deal.

"That hardly seems fair," I said.

Bene shrugged. "Those are the rules."

I shook my head. Men were truly unique creatures, accepting some rules as gospel while flaunting others — especially the ones I made, dammit.

"Maybe those are your rules," I said. "But not mine. Why should I lie to my godfather to protect someone who doesn't even bother telling me where he is?"

Tigers didn't plead, and neither did military men, but Roux looked close. "You'll be protecting us all."

Too bad I wasn't feeling my most charitable that day.

"Oh, I see. I should lie to protect you, even though you won't tell me shit. Sure, Roux. Just give me a second to turn off my intelligence and do whatever the hell you want, no questions asked." I let a beat pass, then growled, "On second thought, forget that. I won't. But if you explain…"

He grimaced. "Trust me on this one, Mina. I can't."

"Trust works both ways, and communication helps." I pointed out.

Roux grimaced, then shook his head. "Just don't tell Gordon. Please."

I didn't intend to, because frankly, I needed the rent money if I was ever going to fix the roof or the dozen other things in desperate need of repair.

As I weighed up the consequences, Madame Picard swept into the room with two platters.

"*Et voilà!* Dinner is served."

She stopped, picking up on the mood of the room, then thrust a platter toward Roux.

"Now what have you gotten up to?"

He stuck up his hands, while Bene cut in with a winning smile.

"Madame Picard, that smells delicious, as always. May I help you with those?"

He scurried to take the platters, trying to placate her through sheer momentum and that Hollywood smile.

Her glare had *Young man, do you really expect me to fall for that?* written all over it. Then she shot me a look that said, *I told you no good would come of this bunch,* and stalked back to the kitchen.

Bene bravely followed her, then returned alone with two more platters and a sullen, "She's holding dessert hostage."

The words were aimed at Roux, who stuck up his hands. "How is this my fault?"

"It's always your fault," Bene and Henrik said in unison.

Roux grabbed a plate and slapped meat, potatoes, and vegetables onto it hard enough to make me wince. Then he grumbled and headed for the door.

"I think I'll eat in my room tonight. Good night."

My mouth hung open as Henrik and Bene followed suit.

"Seriously?" I huffed.

Breakfasts, lunches, and dinners had been lonely affairs before the men had moved in. Since then, mealtimes might have had their exasperating moments, but they'd always been lively and even downright enjoyable sometimes.

Now, footsteps echoed down the hall, leaving me alone between four silent walls.

Bene paused on the threshold with a guilty look, and I pounced.

"What's going on?" I demanded.

He looked at his plate, then down the hallway. "Um, nothing?"

I stomped over. "Come on, Bene. What's going on?"

He studied his roast pork. "I'm not supposed to say."

I snorted, because *supposed to* was obviously not a guiding principle in this lion shifter's life.

"Dammit, Bene. I thought we were friends," I hissed.

I sounded like an angry third grader, but I meant it. Bene was the only one of my guests I could halfway trust. Well, apart from Marius.

"I can't tell you more. I'm really sorry." He genuinely looked it, but that didn't help me.

"Please," I tried.

He scratched his ear, then whispered, "All I know is—"

"Bene!" Roux barked from down the hall.

Bene winced and stuck his tail between his legs. Well, figuratively speaking, but it was easy to picture him slinking away in lion form.

"Sorry," he murmured on the way out.

I stood there, shocked and hurt — the new theme of my life, it seemed — long after the sounds of their footsteps and the aroma of their meals faded away. Then I filled my own plate and headed to my room. Halfway up the stairs, I backtracked to the kitchen in a truly vindictive mood.

"Aha. There you are," I murmured, sliding a tray from the refrigerator. On it were five bowls of crème brûlée.

I made space for my plate on that tray, then carried the entire stash to my room, picturing Bene sneaking back later to find dessert gone.

Mean? Childish? Vengeful?

Absolutely. But I didn't have *classy* in me just then.

I sat on my little balcony, scanning the sky for wayward dragons and drowning my sorrows in crème brûlée. It didn't help, and Marius didn't appear, leaving me with my thoughts and roiling emotions for company.

He was AWOL, and that threatened his contract with Gordon — a contract that would set him free of obligations to Gordon. Free, for example, to choose me...

...if that was what he wanted. But it sure didn't seem that way.

Later, I lay alone in bed, gazing at the paintings on the wall. Several were by my father, and a few stemmed from my grandparents' collection. Another was a recent addition — Van Gogh's *The Painter on the Road from Tarascon.*

Propped up on my dresser near that was a painting I'd recently finished. It showed the south face of the château on a misty dawn. A lion prowled across the lawn, and a tiger stalked through the bushes, both blending in so well, they were nearly invisible. The same went for the bat weaving through the west wing chimneys, and for the two figures in the windows of my suite, one tall, the other a little smaller.

I gazed at it for a long time, then pulled the covers over my head and closed my eyes.

Chapter Four

MINA

The next day, everyone went about their usual routine, but nothing felt normal. Bene didn't crack any jokes. Roux didn't bluster. Henrik didn't snicker or let out bored yawns. They had breakfast as usual, then walked to the far edge of the lawn, speaking in low tones.

Did I pique my ears and make the most of my super-sharp sense of hearing? Of course I did. But they quickly moved out of range, and I didn't catch a word.

Roux said something to Henrik, who glanced back at the house and leaned even closer to the others to reply.

Then it hit me. I could shadow-walk over and listen in.

It also struck me that I shouldn't, but I was so desperate for information, I shoved my reservations to the very bottom of the regret bin and went ahead anyway.

Grabbing Madame Picard's week-old newspaper, I sat with my back to them in a chair on the rear patio. I settled in for a moment, noting every detail, from the slight slouch of my shoulders to the height and angle of the newspaper. Then I conjured up an identical image directly on top of myself, took a deep breath, and slid away.

My hands shook as I tiptoed a few steps and glanced back. The illusion was perfect. Which wasn't too hard since it was just the back view, and the newspaper would explain why I didn't move.

But move I did — the real me, at least — feeling grateful for an overcast day that freed me from having to erase my shadow. I slunk across the lawn the way Roux did in tiger form... Okay, okay — nothing like Roux, whose movements were smooth and graceful. For me, *silent* and *invisible* would do.

On and on I crept, with no one noticing a thing. I stayed upwind, not ready to attempt to mask my scent too.

Then Henrik glanced at the illusionary me, and I froze. He looked away, then looked again, tilting his head.

My heart hammered. Summoning all my concentration, I made the corner of the illusionary newspaper wobble in the breeze. Then I went all out and made fake me turn the page.

Henrik watched for another few seconds, then turned back to Bene and Roux.

So, whew. I snuck closer. And closer...

"...if we don't hear from him in another two days..." I caught Roux saying.

I took another step, then stopped as my moral compass went from spinning aimlessly to true north. This felt wrong. Very wrong.

On the other hand, they were keeping information from me and generally being mean. Didn't that give me license to do the same?

No, it didn't, I scolded myself while creeping away. Friends didn't spy on friends. I didn't spy, period. I had principles to uphold.

Principles that were sorely tested, but they held on, if barely. I retreated to illusionary me, adjusted the real newspaper to the exact position of the imaginary one, then let the magic go.

And, *poof!* The air pressure dropped slightly, and I exhaled, then hastily turned another page. A page that remained as blank to me as the conversation taking place just out of earshot, but oh well.

My head throbbed, and I closed my eyes, hating that I had enough of a criminal mind to consider eavesdropping on my friends but not the guts to follow through. On the plus side, I'd taken the next step as far as shadow-walking was concerned. So I decided to call it a win.

A minute later, I headed inside, gobbled down a thick square of Madame Picard's baking chocolate — just to stave off another headache, I swear! — then resumed work in the upper floor of the west wing.

Two hours later, I awarded myself a five-minute break on the back step. I closed my eyes and tilted my face toward the sky, where the sun had finally peeked out through the clouds. The men had long since ended their powwow and were out of sight, though definitely not out of mind.

Footsteps sounded across the lawn, and a shadow fell across my face.

"Got a second?" Bene asked.

I cracked an eye open, raised a hand against the sun, then dropped it again.

"No."

I closed my eyes, wishing him away while simultaneously hoping he would stay.

He sat beside me and nudged me with his elbow. "I brought you a gift."

Paper rustled as he pressed something into my hands.

I'd been doing my best to stay bitchy and aloof, but I just didn't have it in me.

"A gift?" I asked, ninety percent excited, ten percent suspicious.

"Yep, a gift. Go ahead. Open it."

The "wrapping" was just a paper bag, but hey. It was the thought that counted. I pulled out a small, round object and broke into a smile.

"A snow globe!" I shook it, making fake flakes stir around a line of historic buildings. Then I read the letters beneath. "Brussels."

"Brussels." Bene nodded.

I looked at him, and he dipped his chin, confirming that was where they'd been.

My mind filed away that clue to Marius's whereabouts. Now, if only I could find a snow globe that revealed a dragon's location in real time.

I shook it again, then closed my eyes and sighed.

Bene cocked his head. "What?"

I considered the wisdom of sharing my emotions, then went ahead, consequences be damned.

"I'm just bemoaning my taste in men. I could have a guy who brings me good humor and gifts instead of one who disappears without a word."

Bene waggled his eyebrows. "Not too late, you know."

I laughed. Ah, but it *was* too late. Marius had thoroughly conquered my heart. Too bad I hadn't conquered his.

"Seriously, what's stopping us?" Bene persisted.

"Sorry, Bene. Not interested. Sleeping with you would be like sleeping with a brother. It would feel all wrong."

He leaned in with a lusty, "Believe me, I could make it feel just right."

I couldn't tell if he was joking or not. I prayed he was, because otherwise… ick. Making the moves on me after only one day without Marius? It just wasn't right.

I shook my head firmly. "You should have slept with Claudette while you had the chance."

"I did," he said bluntly.

My mouth fell open, though really, I shouldn't have been surprised. The local woman I'd hired to help with meals was a bit of a wild child.

He shrugged at my expression. "What can I say? She offered."

"I bet she did," I muttered.

"Besides, hard-to-get is much more fun," he declared.

Again, I wondered. Joke or pure flirt?

I stood to go. "Then prepare to have fun for a long, long time. Oh, and thanks for the snow globe." I shook it as I opened the back door, making flakes swirl around Brussels Town Hall.

He heaved a tragic sigh. "You're welcome."

The doorbell rang, and a moment later, Henrik called through the house.

"A visitor for you, Mina." Then he added in a disapproving hiss, "That police officer friend of yours."

My stomach sank. Clement? Here? Now?

A police officer was the last person I wanted around a house full of supernaturals with checkered pasts.

"Speaking of men you could sleep with..." Bene murmured.

"Bene!" I admonished.

"Seriously, Mina. Why hold out for a guy who takes off without a word?"

He was right, dammit.

"And lucky you for having a range of choices," Bene went on. "Most women would envy you."

"Ha. Would they also envy my leaky roof, busted plumbing, and renovation bills?"

Bene grinned. "If anyone can do it, it's you."

Deciding he meant restoring the château and not carrying on with three men at one time, I hurried to the entry hall.

"Clem," I said, trying to summon enthusiasm.

"Mina." He doffed his hat and lit up, making me feel guiltier than ever.

We traded three kisses, then stepped back. Well, I stepped back. Clem barely moved, gazing at me dreamily.

I could have beaten my head against a wall. I had two stunningly attractive men practically throwing themselves at me here at the château, but the only man I really wanted was AWOL.

"So, what brings you here?" I prompted.

Clement snapped out of whatever impossible fantasy he'd been entertaining and held up a pastry box.

"Madame Martin sends her regards."

I sighed. "Still trying to set us up, huh?"

He nodded. "Her and everyone else in town."

"Except Jacques," I muttered. The portly, fifty-plus farmer hit on me every chance he could.

Clement's eyes took on a dangerous sheen, and I waved my hands. "Don't worry about Jacques."

He jutted his jaw in a way that suggested, *Fine. I'll just worry about that dragon shifter of yours.*

I peeked in the box and practically drooled.

"Chocolate *religieuse*. Yum." The round, cream-puff-like pastry was my favorite, and Madame Martin knew it.

There were two, of course, making it impossible to turn Clement away.

"Can I invite you in? We could make tea," I offered, praying he would say no.

"Sure." He beamed.

I wrestled my grimace into a stiff smile. Didn't he have more pressing matters, like patrolling for crimes?

Of course not, because this was Auberre, where the greatest transgressions were fashion crimes like sandals worn with socks…and it was autumn, so not really the season for that. Plus, I doubted the French *Code Pénal* listed such offenses.

"This isn't just a pleasure call." Clement's voice dropped ominously. "I have a few questions for you."

My gut flipped. Henrik froze in the midst of ascending the stairs. The floorboards in the dining room creaked as Bene leaned in to eavesdrop.

"Sure," I said as brightly as I could, though my heart was pounding.

Would this visit start with pastries and end with handcuffs? Was the game up for me and my mercenaries? Was this part of a nationwide raid, with Gordon getting busted as we spoke?

Then I caught myself. Those men were not *my* mercenaries. All I was doing was renting a few rooms, right?

But, no. I'd long since followed them down a deep, dark rabbit hole, which made me just as culpable.

I led Clement to the kitchen, where I brewed tea and transferred the pastries to my grandmother's fine china. If this was a bust, I would go down in style.

But, shit. Was *accessory to illegal dealings* a felony charge? Would my criminal record transfer to North America and ruin my teaching career too?

God, I was so screwed.

Balancing tea, cups, and the pastries on a tray, I headed for the back door, which Clement opened for me.

"Over here?" He gestured to the patio table just outside the door.

I shook my head. "Over there."

Way, way over there, to a cluster of tree stumps that served as a table and chairs.

"For privacy," I murmured at his puzzled expression.

He looked around. "Privacy?"

"Privacy." I nodded firmly. We could be seen but not heard, and no one could sneak up to listen to us. "Besides, it reminds me of when we were kids."

His lips curled into a tiny smile. "Playing in the woods, then coming here to play cards..."

"My grandmother bringing us tea and treating us like grown-ups." I smiled. "Gen, Dora, and I had entire tea parties out here when we were kids."

The original tree stumps had long since rotted, but my cousin had insisted on rolling replacements to the exact same spot.

I held up the teapot before we got too lost in the good old days. I would have plenty of time to mull over those from behind bars. For now, I might as well enjoy my last moments as a free woman.

God, what would my mother say?

"Tea?" I offered.

"Please."

"Sugar? Milk?"

"I'll help myself."

Storks wading in knee-deep water would have been less stilted than this conversation.

I stirred my tea nervously and considered my pastry. Would it taste better now or after Clem read me my rights?

"So, your questions...?" I prompted.

His face fell, and his nostrils flared as he glanced back at the house.

Oh, I was definitely in deep shit.

"I saw the vampire, and I could smell the felines. Is that dragon shifter still around?"

"No. He's...out," I said in a major understatement. "Are they relevant to this conversation?"

Clement snorted. "They're trouble, Mina. You know that, right?"

Boy, did I. And I would bet the ranch — or the château — that I knew more than Clem did. At least, I hoped so. If not, we were all headed for the slammer.

I pictured Bene running through the house as Clem and I spoke, collecting his things. Roux burning documents. Henrik gathering his favorite books. Then they would pile into their van and roar down the driveway. The longer Clem and I sat out here, the farther they could flee.

I could imagine it easily, and part of me wailed. They wouldn't abandon me as their fall guy, would they?

I snorted, considering recent events. Of course they would.

"Like I said, they're just renting a few rooms," I repeated the lie I'd told myself a hundred times. "Just for a few weeks."

Clem shook his head. "They've already been here too long."

Not long enough, when it came to Marius. But I kept that to myself.

"People are talking in town..." he continued.

I huffed. "People will always talk."

"About you letting four men stay in your home?" Clement's voice took on a canine growl as his inner wolf paced closer to the surface.

I'd only let one man into my bedroom, but I doubted that would halt the rumors. Another thought I kept to myself.

"Do you want me to get a chaperone?" I crossed my arms. Clement meant well, but I wasn't in the market for a knight in shining armor to save me.

But I sure wouldn't mind a dragon shifter swooping in, to be frank.

"I want you to get yourself out of whatever it is you've gotten mixed up in," Clement half pleaded, half growled.

Saying *I want me to get out of this mess too* would be a little too incriminating, so all I said was, "I appreciate your concern, Clem. I really do. But they work for my godfather, and he needed a place for them to stay."

The truth, but not the whole truth, so help me God. And boy, could I use His help around now.

"Right. Your godfather," Clement said flatly.

I cocked my head. "What about my godfather?"

Clement shrugged. "You tell me."

I was totally at a loss. "You've met him. You know what he's done for me and my family."

Clement stared right at me, telling me to do the kind of deep thinking that had never occurred to me before Marius, Roux, Bene, and Henrik had spilled the beans. Was he onto Gordon too?

I'd long since concluded that I had to confront Gordon myself...soon. Now, I vowed to make that my priority...if Clem didn't arrest me first.

He sure didn't look too cheery — a bad sign. But that was par for the course with Clem, except in his moments of gazing yearningly into a shared future I had no interest in.

Briefly, it occurred to me that I could — maybe even should — reconsider. I could evict my guests and pretend I'd never met Marius. I could take up with Clem and live a quiet, normal life in Auberre. Well, normal apart from the wolf-shifter thing.

All rather appealing, I had to admit. He and I could wander the countryside at night and howl love ballads at the moon. We could have beautiful children and live happily ever after with our own little pack/family.

That that was a handy way to make my legal woes disappear also occurred to me, I was ashamed to realize. But as quickly as the thought came to me, I shoved it away and prepared to tell Clem the truth.

I gulped, gathering my nerves, then spoke.

"More tea?" I said, copping out with *distraction* instead of the plain truth.

He gave me a pointed look, then held out his cup.

"You are something, Mina Durant. You're really something."

"And you, Officer Dulaire, had a question for me," I reminded him.

He shifted uncomfortably in his seat, and my nerves jittered. This was it.

He opened his mouth… and promptly closed it again. But my ancestors' powers reached out of the past and channeled into me at exactly that moment, and I read his mind as clearly as a bell.

What do you see in that dragon shifter anyway? he thought, more hurt than angry. *What can he offer you that I can't?*

My heart bled. Unrequited love was a bitch, which made me… Well, the bitch. No matter how nice I tried to be, I would forever inflict pain on this man. A good man. Far better than me.

I gulped and touched his hand. "My grandmother always used to say, *Everything works out for the best.*"

Clement grimaced. "But it doesn't, Mina. Not in my world."

I stilled, picturing the cases he'd had to investigate. Murders. Rapes. Horrible injuries and terrible injustices. Crimes he must have witnessed every week, if not in Auberre, then in his previous post in Marseille.

But another image formed amid those heartbreaking scenes. A peaceful, countryside scene where a happy couple stood, wearing crowns of flowers. Other people cheered and threw more flowers. A wedding, I surmised. In a place very much like Auberrre…

I closed my eyes, grasping for more details, but the more I chased, the more they eluded me, until they were gone for good.

I stared into my teacup. Had I just glimpsed the future — Clem's future? — or the past? And who was that woman? Not me, I felt sure. Who, then?

"Some things *do* work out for the best," I whispered.

Clem pinched his lips. "I want them to. Believe me. I just don't think hoping will get me there."

"Neither do I. But the best we can do is do what's right. For each of us, I mean."

He looked sadder than ever. I gestured to the pastries.

"Time for these?"

A corner of his mouth quirked, and I saw a sprinkle of hope in his dark, canine eyes. "Good idea."

I raised my teacup in a toast, eager to lighten the mood. "To Madame Martin."

He chuckled and touched his cup to mine. "To hopeless romantics."

Did he mean her, himself, or me?

When I took a bite, chocolate cream burst into my mouth, along with flakes of soft, airy dough.

"Oh my God. So good," I moaned.

Clem shifted in his seat, and for once, I was glad no magical skills brushed over me just then to reveal his train of thought.

"Delicious." He wiped a napkin over his lips, hiding his expression.

Bite by bite, that marvel of French baking disappeared.

"So good," I sighed mournfully, scraping my plate.

He chuckled. "Next time, I'll bring more."

I froze at the *next time* part, then patted my belly. "One is my limit, thanks." Then I pursed my lips and got back to business. "You never asked your question."

His smile faded, and I braced myself for *You have the right to remain silent.*

But he stalled, clearing his throat. "Some of the guys back at QG were talking..."

QG was short for *quartier général*, the regional police headquarters. God, was I way, way up shit creek.

"The Pelletier farm flooded, so the regional police championships need a different location," he continued.

I frowned. If he was going to arrest me, could he at least have the decency to get to the point?

But that was it. He just looked at me.

"The regional police championships?" I squeaked, wondering if that was code for *Take cover, because I have agents surrounding the building, and we're about to launch our raid?*

He nodded. "Just three events. Cross-country running, mountain biking, and table tennis."

"Table tennis?" Now I was really confused. Was I busted or wasn't I?

He shot me a wry smile. "Yes, table tennis. Whoever wins goes on to the national championships, then the European police championships in November. They're in Thessaloniki this year." He brightened at the prospect, then gestured around. "It occurred to me that you have a lot of space here..."

I gaped. That was it? No bust, no arrest?

"You want me to host the police table tennis championships here?" I sagged in relief.

"And cross-country and mountain biking. On the third weekend of October. Unfortunately, there's no budget to pay for facilities, but you did say you wanted to raise the profile of Château Nocturne..."

I had, but busing in dozens of police officers wasn't high on my list — not while my houseguests were around.

On the other hand, it never hurt to have the local police indebted to you.

I was ashamed to even think such a thought, but tempted too.

Besides, I had bills to pay and loans in the works for things like new roofing. The château had to start earning its keep, and free publicity wouldn't hurt.

"You wouldn't have to do much, because the organizing committee has everything set to go. They just need a site that can host those three events."

My life was in turmoil, and it would take more than a few weeks for things to settle down — if they ever would. But I was still euphoric at not being arrested. (Yet.) Shouldn't I grab the chance to build good karma while I could?

"They'll need to visit once to measure the cross-country and mountain bike courses. They'll set up the previous day and take everything away right after the awards ceremony. So, that's only three days on-site. Not too much of an imposition?" Clem asked hopefully.

No, except for my houseguests. But, hell. Maybe I could get Gordon to send them to Naples. That was where crime gangs operated, right?

And, oops. I really was internalizing this mercenary thing now.

"Everything okay?" Clem tilted his head.

I stuck on a smile. "Fine. Yes, that would be great. I'd be happy to help."

He grinned. "And who knows? Maybe someone who attends will like it so much, they'll come back to get married here."

I forced a chuckle, thinking of the vision I'd had. "Yeah. Who knows?"

A cuckoo called from the forest. Clem checked his watch, gulped the rest of his tea, and stood. "Gotta go."

He insisted on carrying the tray into the house, while I insisted on seeing him to the door before a vampire or a tiger intercepted him and set off a deadly fight.

I held the door open, and we traded three kisses. His sage-and-lavender scent wafted over me each time, making me question my life choices. Bene was right. I did have options.

But instead of temptation, all I felt was determination. I would find Marius and fight for a place in his life — or at least get closure on an ill-fated affair.

Clem's scent wafted over again, assuring me he would be ready and waiting if — when? — that day arrived.

"Be good," Clem said. Then he flicked his eyes upstairs. "Be careful. And please. Keep an open mind."

Something told me he didn't mean the police championships.

I nodded. "Thanks for coming. And thank Madame Martin."

He flashed a grin that would make half the country swoon and stepped toward his car, calling, "*À bientôt.*" *See you soon.*

I steeled myself, because he would. Him, along with most of the regional police force. Was this really a good idea?

"*À bientôt,*" I murmured, forcing myself to wave.

Chapter Five

MINA

To call what I'd done all night "sleeping" would be a gross overstatement. By morning, I was tired, flustered, and seriously sex-deprived. Just a few weeks with Marius and I already craved him like a drug.

Was he awakening somewhere now, aching for me the way I ached for him? Or was he simply rising and going casually on his way?

Another thought hit me, and I felt sick. What if he was waking up with someone else?

I buried my face in my pillow, then groaned and rolled out of bed. It had been a shitty night, I was in a shitty mood, and it was going to be a shitty day. But the sooner I started it, the sooner it would be over, right?

I was just finishing that cheery thought when I reached the bathroom and caught a glimpse of myself in the mirror. The same old me, but tired, bitter, and getting older every day.

Maybe Bene was right. I could have a fling with him, a studly lion shifter. How bad could that be? I could eventually move on to a long-term relationship with Clem or some other man. I was single. I was capable. I was free. The world was my oyster!

But I didn't want oysters, dammit. I wanted Marius. Did he want me, though?

I ordered myself to take a cold shower, pull myself together, and forge some kind of plan.

First, I made instant oatmeal, avoiding the main kitchen and the others. Then I took out my laptop, tempted to hunt down Marius and reach some kind of closure. But where exactly would I start? Brussels?

Maybe Paris would be better. Because as many questions as Marius had raised, Gordon opened a hundred more.

My nerves jittered just thinking about it, though.

Then it hit me. I didn't have to race off on a wild-goose chase. I could start much closer to home. In my own home, actually.

Henrik owed me a favor, and it was time to call it in.

I pulled on a dark sweatshirt for a tough, ballsy look, checked my hair, and slammed the door to my apartment on my way out. Down the hall I went, down the stairs, and into the dining room. Then up to the drawing room, the card room, the music room, and into the west wing. Dammit. Where was Henrik? And why the hell had I ever decided to live in a forty-room château?

Outside the library, I screeched to a stop, spotting a tall, pale figure standing by the windows with a book.

I stomped in, gnashing my teeth.

"The library is off-limits," I snipped.

"Is it?"

Yes, it was, as Henrik knew perfectly well. I glared.

"What a pity," he said in his usual half yawn, half sigh.

He closed the book slowly, and I felt a corner of my mind prickle. The bastard was trying to thrall me into changing the rules for him, wasn't he?

I gritted my teeth and threw a thousand expletives over the wall in my mind.

He grimaced and stuck the book back on the shelf.

"Not very ladylike."

No, I supposed saying *Fuck off, Henrik* wasn't. At least, not in the era he'd been born in, centuries ago. But this was the twenty-first century, dammit, and this was my château.

"Don't break the rules, and you're more likely to see the proper lady in me," I snipped.

He shot me a sour, *I doubt it* look, which was probably justified.

Then his eyes wandered to my neck and sparkled, making me shiver — and not in a good way. I made a mental note to ask Madame Picard to double the amount of red meat she served with meals. Anything to help a vampire stave off his craving for blood.

Henrik yanked his eyes away and turned to the door, grumbling, "I'll be going, then."

The top row of windows in the library was stained-glass, and he looked paler than ever stepping through the red and yellow shafts of light.

"Don't," I said a little too sharply. Then I cleared my throat. "I mean, please stay. I have a question for you."

He smirked. "Ah, but I may not have an answer."

Vampires. Always such jerks.

"Remember that favor you promised me in Mallorca? I'm calling it in."

He frowned, and his fingers curled. Not a happy vampire, but hell. I wasn't all that cheerful today either.

He shrugged. "Go ahead."

"I need you to answer a few questions."

He shook his head. "One favor, one question."

"Five questions," I estimated. "Small ones."

He snorted. "Three at most."

I held my ground. "Five."

"Four."

"Five," I hissed. "I nearly died getting that stupid box for you."

That was back in Mallorca, in a black-market art gallery, where I'd joined the men in extracting — okay, *stealing* — a long-lost Van Gogh. We'd nearly been foiled, but I'd succeeded with Henrik's help, in exchange for a small box that had caught his eye. I had no clue what it contained, only that it meant a lot to him. Securing it had put him in my debt.

So many things about that caper made me blanch — even without the *colluding with vampires* part. How had my life come to this?

But I was hip-deep in the slime of a different world now. I might as well forge ahead.

Henrik gave his watch a pointed look. "Fine. Five small questions. Begin."

"What happened in Brussels?" I blurted, then caught myself. "Wait. It really was Brussels, right?"

"Gordon briefed us in Paris, but yes. The mission was in Brussels."

And, yikes. The casual way he spilled top secret information unsettled me. I made a mental note to never, ever trust a vampire with my secrets.

Then I stuck up a hand. "Wait. That doesn't count as one of the five questions."

"Of course it does."

"No, it doesn't!"

"Yes, it does."

"Dammit, Henrik!"

He gave me an insufferable look. "Continue."

"What happened while you were away?"

He considered, weighing up what to include and what to omit.

"Gordon briefed us in Paris," he finally said. "And he issued a warning."

I held my breath, waiting.

"He warned us that you were not to learn anything of our activities, and that none of us should even think about getting involved with his dear, virginal goddaughter." He chuckled dryly. "A warning that came a little too late."

Virginal, my ass, I nearly muttered.

"Then, when we'd completed our mission, Marius left," Henrik went on.

"Why?"

"I don't know, but he seemed upset about something. Of course, he is a dragon." Henrik sniffed, like blood-sucking vampires were so much more reliable.

"Upset at what?"

"I don't know."

"He's not working a job for Gordon, is he?"

The way his eyes flickered told me I was right. "Is that a question or a statement?"

"A statement," I said quickly, then forced myself to utter the question that might prompt an answer I couldn't stomach. "Does his absence have anything to do with Celeste?"

Henrik snickered, like I was so pathetic, which I absolutely was.

"No." Then he tapped his fingers, counting, and announced, "Last question."

I went through the long list crowding my mind, topped by one that had weighed on me for weeks. Did I dare ask that one?

I gulped, then went for it. "Do you love Delphine?"

I'd met his lover/blood donor/favorite prostitute in Mallorca and liked her immediately, despite her taste in men.

A storm brewed in Henrik's eyes.

"Don't go there. I warn you."

A warning I should have heeded, as it turned out, but I was too frustrated.

"Do you know she loves you?" I blurted. "Do you realize how she hangs on every word you utter and every move you make? Even if you don't love her, you owe it to her to at least—"

His eyes flashed, and his teeth extended as he hissed, "I don't owe her anything. I owe no one, especially not you."

His fingernails lengthened, and his eyes turned to red points. I backed away, too shocked to speak. The bored, arrogant man of noble birth was gone, and a predator stood in his place.

I stepped toward the door, but he slammed a hand against it, blocking my escape.

"Afraid?" His eyes glittered with a hint of madness.

"Of you? No." I stuck up my chin.

Bad idea, because his eyes went to my neck.

He'd moved into a clear beam of light, and yikes. It hadn't been the stained glass making him appear pale. He really was extra pale — and gaunt.

My heart hammered as I moved toward the far door of the library.

Wham! The next thing I knew, Henrik had me shoved hard against the bookcase. The smell of leather and dry ink hit me as he wrapped a hand around my throat and squeezed.

I batted at him, but he pinned my arms against my chest with his free hand.

His lips curled into a spooky grin. "Give me your blood, and I'll tell you anything you want to know."

"Stop! Let me go!" I choked out, struggling.

"Just a little," he murmured, leaning closer to sniff. So close, the tip of his nose brushed my neck.

And, shit. His eyes glazed over, and his voice took on a dreamy quality.

"Ah, so promising. So unique..."

I blanched, because that was probably true. My mixed supernatural ancestry would make me *the* exotic taste of the day to a vampire.

His eyes narrowed to pinpricks as he fell deeper into hunting mode.

I kicked and flailed, fighting for breath. "Henrik!"

"It would be so easy, you know," he murmured, more to himself than me.

I twisted and jerked. "I will despise you forever if you do this."

He chuckled. "Forever might not be too long."

His skin was so pale, his veins showed, but no pulse beat.

I tried another tack, choking out, "You'll despise yourself forever."

He huffed. "I already do."

I wouldn't have thought I had it in me to feel for him at a time like that, but somehow, I did. So, yay me. I could go to my death knowing my morals hadn't sunk as low as I'd feared.

But I didn't want to die. I wanted to find Marius and live happily ever after with him, as I discovered in that moment of terrifying clarity. And if he rejected me, then someone else, maybe. (My moral fiber wasn't all that upright, as it turned out.)

He cocked his head and leaned closer, focused on my neck.

"No!" I screamed.

Well, I tried, but all that came out was a squeak.

The far door crashed open, and someone snarled, "Henrik!"

I couldn't turn my head, so I swiveled my eyes left.

Bene! I nearly cheered.

The lion shifter advanced slowly, holding up one hand. "Let her go, Henrik. Now."

Henrik didn't speak. He hissed — literally *hissed*, like a snake, sprinkling spittle over my face.

"Henrik." Bene locked eyes with the vampire, but his voice shook. So, shit. He was scared too. For me? For himself?

The closer Bene came, the more tightly Henrik squeezed my throat.

"Leave us. Now," Henrik barked at Bene. His fangs had fully extended by then, slurring his words.

Oh God, oh God, oh God. . .

"You don't want to do this," Bene warned.

Henrik licked his lips. "Oh yes, I do."

I lifted my right foot, calculating the distance to his groin. I went for his shin instead, slamming with all my might. But Henrik was so far gone, he barely grunted.

"How are you going to explain this to Gordon?" Bene tried next.

"To hell with Gordon!" Henrik roared.

Bene shook his head, desperate for some next angle to try. Then he gritted his teeth and murmured, "What would Katarina say?"

Whoever Katarina was, I loved her, because her name made Henrik go perfectly still. He kept on squeezing my throat, but the red of his eyes went from intense points to wider, fainter pools.

"Katarina has nothing to do with this."

"Katarina would say let her go," Bene whispered.

Henrik's throat bobbed, and his grip loosened enough for me to suck in a breath. He stared at me, then at his own hand — the one choking me. With a grimace, he pushed me away, and I tumbled into Bene.

The lion shifter shoved me back, stepping between Henrik and me. I banged my knee and shoulder in the process, but I'd never appreciated him more.

Roux burst in as I crumpled to my knees, gasping for breath.

"What's going on?"

Bene shot Henrik a dark look. "Someone has gone too long between feedings."

"Dammit, Henrik," Roux cursed.

To his credit, he glanced at me, but only for a split second. Apparently, alive and gasping tallied up to *perfectly fine* in his book. The look he shot me said, *Get up — and toughen up.*

He probably expected me to jump up and yell, *Yes, sir!* too, but it was all I could do to rise shakily to my feet.

Henrik bared his teeth at Roux, but his fangs receded to half length. Still half too long for my taste, though. A moment later, he straightened his white button-down shirt — the one that would have been splattered with my blood if Bene hadn't come along — and strode out the door.

I stared, then gaped at the others. "Where is he going?"

Bene traded weary looks with Roux. "Heading out to find what he needs."

"What?" I shrieked, putting two and two together. "Where?"

A door slammed downstairs, and Bene shrugged. "Not Auberre. Somewhere with some nightlife, I guess."

My eyes bugged out. "And you're just going to let him go?"

Uh, yes, their blank looks replied.

"And kill an innocent person somewhere?" I protested.

"Probably not kill. Well, hopefully," Bene tried.

"Ideally, he'll go to Delphine," Roux sighed.

I blanched. *Ideal* in whose world?

A car revved, then peeled out of the driveway.

I fumbled for my phone, shocked and mortified. "I have to warn her..."

Roux closed a big, warm hand over mine in a firm but surprisingly gentle move.

"Delphine will be all right."

I stared. All right — with a thirsty vampire speeding toward her door?

I thought of the hours Henrik would drive to reach her. The "rest stops" he might take along the way. Then I stared at Bene and Roux, who had no such qualms. They'd come to my rescue, and I was grateful, but I was disgusted too.

I thought of the cold shoulder they'd given me. The secrecy. The ugly deeds in their pasts.

And just like that, I'd had it.

"You know what?" I barked. "That's it. You're out of here."

Bene put up his hands, much as he had with Henrik. "Now, Mina. . ."

I shook my head. This was the straw that broke the camel's back, and that camel was me.

"I want you out of here — all of you. Now."

"Now?" Roux protested.

My mind raced, and a stray thought clicked in out of nowhere. "Henrik is out starting now. You two have until the third weekend in October."

Bene tilted his head, once again proving more astute than I thought. "What's happening in the third weekend in October?"

I stamped a foot. "You're moving out and never coming back."

Right in time for the police championships I'd just decided to host, dammit, though I didn't say that.

Bene looked hurt. Roux, alarmed.

"You know what this means for us?" the tiger shifter asked in a husky voice.

I stiffened. Yes, I knew. Any one of them screwing up reflected on the entire group, and the precarious deal they'd struck with Gordon — the deal securing them second chances and a fresh start in life — was under threat.

Well, I stood to lose too. I'd found a contractor to start work on the roof soon, and to pay for it, I needed the money

Gordon paid to board his team here. Still, wasn't my life worth more than the roof?

I cleared my throat, but damn. My voice was still all husky. "I'll put in a good word for you two with Gordon. But I'll also explain why I don't want you here. Any of you."

My soul wept, because that meant Marius too. But what choice did I have? Bit by bit, these men had nudged me over to the dark side, and I needed to claw my way back to the light.

My heart bled as their eyes pleaded with me. But I had to hold firm. They weren't fifth graders, but the principle was the same. If I caved in now, all discipline would be lost — and in this case, discipline could mean my life.

"Sure," Roux scoffed. "Put in a good word with Gordon." He gestured to my phone, daring me.

I huffed. "I will. But in person, not with a call."

Roux snorted. "What, the next time you're in Paris?"

I practically bared my teeth at him. "Today. I'm leaving now."

Roux's eyes went wide, and even Bene did a double take.

"You're going to Paris? Now?"

I nodded firmly. My second spontaneous decision in five minutes, but yes.

"Yes, I am," I said, summoning the resolve to walk out the door.

It was time to take control of my life, I told myself. But at that moment, it felt more like I was tearing it apart.

Chapter Six

MINA

The train had barely left the station, but second thoughts already clouded my mind. What the hell was I doing? Had I just thrown the baby out with the bathwater? And, yikes — hosting the police championships?

But it was too late now, because I'd already called Clem to confirm the event, driven to nearby Auxerre and hopped on the train to Paris. For once, no one was on strike and the train wasn't delayed, so I had less than two hours to figure out what to do when I arrived.

Mostly, though, I stared out the window and wondered what I would someday feel, looking back on what was sure to be a pivotal (low) point in my life. The moment I'd turned my back on a group of sketchy but lovable supernaturals. A group I also counted on as a work force and as boarders whose rent offset renovation costs.

Then I remembered how close one of those supernaturals had come to killing me. Clearly, it was time for a change in the company I'd been keeping.

Even if it cost me friendships? Or worse — the château?

My emotions swung back and forth, back and forth.

Plan, dammit. Need a plan, I ordered myself.

The school I'd worked in taught students to break projects into phases: setting goals, planning, taking action, and reflecting.

I nearly started with reflecting, though. How had my life brought me to this point anyway?

But that wasn't too helpful, so I focused on goals. What were mine here?

Recalibrating my moral compass placed high on the list. Next came visiting my godfather to confirm whether he really ran a crime syndicate on the side or whether this had all been one big misunderstanding.

The train screeched around a corner as if to say, *Fat chance, sweetheart.*

Goal number three was to find Marius and do what he hadn't had the balls to do: face him and declare eternal love... or say goodbye forever.

My lips wobbled as I gazed out the window.

The regional train followed the curves of the Yonne River, and I watched as we rattled past boats, locks, and vineyards, wishing I could trade my life for that of a cargo ship captain, lockkeeper, or winegrower. I even found myself wondering how their workloads compared to renovating a crumbling château.

Gradually, the open, undulating terrain of Burgundy gave way to more densely populated areas, and soon, we were rushing through the outskirts of Paris.

So, goals — check. Now, I had to figure out a plan and execute it.

But boy, was that the hard part.

All too soon, the train pulled into Gare de Lyon, and passengers spilled out onto the platforms, then the street. I joined them, carried by a human wave. Outside, I zipped my jacket against the fall chill. The Métro could whisk me to Gordon's place in a few stops, but I procrastinated by walking.

On the sidewalk, couples embraced and businesspeople hurried to meetings.

"Taxi?" a driver asked.

I turned him down, but a couple of luggage-laden tourists accepted happily.

Cars beeped, and shop windows lured with eye-catching displays. A fashion shop here, a bakery there, plus the ubiquitous bookshops. I could have been blindfolded and had my ears plugged, and I would still have known this was Paris. The city's unique vibe pulsed all around me, making me feel more like a country mouse than ever.

The feeling grew until I found myself standing across from Gordon's building, where I steeled myself to walk over.

The door to a nearby café burst open, and I turned.

Every cell in my body tingled, first in joy, then in warning. *Marius!* I nearly cried as he stormed out.

The air around him crackled with menacing energy. His strides pounded the pavement, and his fists were tightly balled.

I frowned. Wait. Roux said Marius had gone off on his own agenda, risking Gordon's wrath and the future of the entire unit. So what was Marius doing so close to Gordon's home?

My poor, hopeful heart almost beat itself into bursting, and only the lump in my throat kept me from calling out.

A good thing, too, because the door opened a second time, and Celeste emerged.

Yes, Celeste, the scheming succubus who'd once seduced Marius, as he'd admitted in a gut-wrenching heart-to-heart we'd had after returning from Mallorca. I hated the idea of the two of them together, but I could hardly feel betrayed since Marius hadn't known me back then. Also, I'd witnessed the aftermath of her seductive powers on Henrik. The vampire and Marius were just two of countless men whose lives and emotions Celeste had taken a wrecking ball to just for the fun of it.

Worse, Celeste worked for Gordon — by choice, unlike Marius, Roux, Henrik, and Bene.

"Marius!" she called.

He spun, a tornado hovering over one spot, ready to obliterate everything.

I ducked behind a tree and peeked out.

Celeste walked toward Marius, swaying her curvy hips with every step. Marius folded his arms over his chest, his face a mask of fury.

I couldn't hear what she said, but Marius barked a few words, then stalked away. Celeste's mocking laugh followed him, but her pinched expression said things hadn't gone her way. Her sheer black dress and dark hair rippled in the breeze, and a passing deliveryman stared at her long enough to make his moped swerve. She turned, flashing him a wide, lusty smile. Then she strutted up the stairs and disappeared into Gordon's building.

My mind spun as I stood rooted to the ground. Now what?

I'd planned to drop in on Gordon unannounced, but I sure as hell wasn't going near Celeste. Besides, I knew how to find my godfather. Marius, on the other hand...

I darted from one tree to the next, following him. A good thing I ran most mornings, because Marius's long strides carried him to the end of the block in no time. The light changed just as I got there, and I sprinted across as drivers beeped and gesticulated.

I gestured back. I had a dragon to catch, dammit!

Marius strode on, a tsunami looking for a shore to decimate. Nearly a block later, I caught up and tapped on his shoulder.

Bad idea, because catching a tightly wound dragon off guard was downright terrifying. Fire blazed in his eyes, and he drew back a fist, ready to punch.

"Hello, Marius," I said, forcing the jitter out of my voice.

His lips parted in shock, and I had to battle the overwhelming urge to kiss him.

"Mina," he whispered.

His eyes bored into mine, going warm and fluid. Then he jolted a little, grabbed my shoulder, and hustled me into a side alley.

"What are y—" I started.

He stuck up a hand, and his eyes darted around, checking the area for... Celeste? Gordon? A gunman itching to spray the neighborhood with bullets?

He scrutinized our surroundings before gritting his teeth and looking at me.

And, oh.

Time slowed, and my heart beat so hard, I was sure he could hear it. His eyes continued to blaze, but the furious hue turned into something warm and yearning. I rolled onto my toes, fixated on his lips, and—

Everything that had happened in the past few days rushed into the forefront of my mind, and I raised my fist, then hesitated.

"Go ahead," he said gruffly. "I deserve it."

Did he? And was this really the best way to communicate?

"No, you don't." I lowered my hand and looked up at him.

I must have caught us both off guard, because I found myself staring deep into his unguarded soul — and into a pool of hope, joy, and yearning.

Marius loved me. He wanted me. He wanted forever. But a jungle of long, creeping vines surrounded that pool, locking it in a tangle of danger and complications.

Then he blinked — or maybe I did — and his inner shutters came crashing down again.

I swayed on my feet, as I often did after one of those brushed-by-moonlight moments when the magic of one of my ancestors welled up in me — in this case, the ability to secretly peer into a person's soul.

"Dammit, Mina..." He checked the area again, searched for words, then gave up, and went for a totally unexpected alternative.

A hug. A fierce, powerful dragon hug that nearly cut off my circulation. I ended up pressed hard against his chest, seeing, smelling, sensing nothing but him.

It was heaven.

I worked my arms around his broad torso, feeling like I'd found a treasure trove along with absolute, total certainly that everything would be all right as long as I stayed put. No one could bother us, and the future would be bountiful and glorious.

He was mine, and I was his. It was that simple.

Except it wasn't, and I knew it. Something stood between us — something as big and looming as the Eiffel Tower.

Slowly, I pulled back, gently stroking his cheek. Marius closed his eyes and leaned in, just as he had all those mornings we'd spent in bed together. Then his throat bobbed, and he took a deep breath, looking around.

"God, Mina. What are you doing here?"

I wove my fingers through his. "Looking for you."

He sighed as if I'd said, *Looking for trouble.* Then he shook his head. "You can't be here."

"And yet, here I am."

Another shake of the head. "It's too dangerous."

It wasn't Paris. *It* was something else. But what exactly?

I stuck a finger at his chest. "You might be ready to give up on us, but I'm not."

He gritted his teeth. "I'm not giving up. I'm just trying to keep you safe."

"By not telling me anything?"

He glanced behind me, and I leaned out to look. Was he worried about someone after me or after him?

More furtive looks around the alley. "I can't explain. Not here. Not now."

Not ever? I wondered.

He dragged his hands through his hair, warring with himself, then spoke.

"Meet me tonight. At the Jaurès metro station — line 2, above ground. You know it?"

I gulped but nodded.

"Wait for me on the Porte Dauphine side of the platform. Don't bring your phone, and make sure you're not being followed," he continued.

My stomach flipped. Things were that bad, huh?

"Nine thirty. Don't come early," he grunted.

Ha. The man knew me too well.

When he looked at me expectantly, I echoed his instructions. "Jaurès metro station, line 2, Porte Dauphine side." Then I tapped his chest. "Swear to me you'll come. Swear it."

"I'll be there."

His eyes didn't quite meet mine, though, so I wrapped my hands around his face, forcing them to. "Do not let me down. You got that?"

He flashed a little smile. Apparently *fierce Mina* was his favorite version.

"I'll be there," he swore, then cocked his head. "Where will you go in the meantime?"

I pointed in the direction we'd come from. "I have to visit Gordon."

His eyes flashed. "Why?"

I made a face. "He asked Gen for a favor, but she's been delayed—"

"Again?" he cut in.

I sighed. "Again."

"What's the favor?"

"To meet someone."

His eyes narrowed. "Who?"

"I don't know. That's why I have to see him. That way, we can communicate. You know, *communicate*?"

"What people say and what they want or mean can be two different things," he warned.

Oh yes. I'd definitely gotten a crash course in that in recent weeks.

"Well, the best way to recognize the difference is observing them in person," I retorted. Then I softened. "Believe me, I don't plan to do anything dangerous. But I need to see Gordon."

He scowled, then checked his watch. "Wait an hour. I could only risk coming close to his place because he was out. Celeste was the only one there, and she should be leaving soon."

"Ah, yes. Celeste," I said dryly. "I'd like to know about that too."

"Know what?"

"Know why you're talking to her and not me."

"It's not like that, Mina. I swear." He looked around, then shook his head. "I'll explain later."

"Gonna be a long meeting," I muttered.

He ignored that in favor of a final warning. "Whatever you do, don't tell Gordon anything."

I rolled my eyes. Like I need a reminder.

"I mean it," Marius emphasized. "Including the fact that you saw me."

Grabbing my hand, he stalked toward the corner of the main road, towing me along before raising a fist to signal *stop* the way commandos did in movies.

Boy, had I fallen in love with the wrong person.

The right person, a voice in the back of my mind insisted.

"All right." He gestured. "Cross the street. I'll follow at a distance. Take the next metro three stops, then backtrack. Watch for anyone who looks suspicious."

At this rate, that meant everyone in Paris. I was that on edge.

"Keep a low profile all evening, and don't come to the meeting point directly," he said.

Then he squeezed my hand, popped a kiss on my cheek, and gave me a little nudge toward the street. A good thing, too. Otherwise, I might never have pried myself away from him.

"Be careful," he finished ominously.

"And you be there," I insisted. "At our meeting point, I mean."

He nodded, then gestured me onward.

Every step I took felt like I was wading deeper and deeper into mud, but I forced myself to go. When I reached the metro stop a few blocks later, I glanced back, but there was no sign of him. No sign that he'd ever been with me either, except for the tingling spot on my cheek.

Chapter Seven

MINA

I did as Marius said, riding the Métro a few stops before back-tracking to Gare du Lyon, where I seriously considered catching the next train home.

But, no. I had a mission to fulfill, and a date with a dragon shifter afterward.

I walked to Gordon's along the Canal Saint-Martin, stopping for a fortifying éclair and tea along the way. That also helped while away the ninety minutes Marius had recommended before visiting Gordon.

His neighborhood was a strangely mixed one, with seedy bars sitting cheek by jowl with discreetly spruced-up mansions. Gordon owned several of the latter, but he lived on the top two floors of a nondescript, 1970s building that was somewhere in between. It was nice enough to have a doorman and had for as long as I remembered. But today was the first day I wondered what role Fabian filled. Was he just a doorman, or also a spy, bodyguard, or part-time hit man?

"*Bonjour*, Fabian," I said upon entering.

"*Bonjour, mademoiselle.*" The fiftysomething bear shifter's easy smile made me feel guilty for being suspicious... but I kept my guard up just in case. "Monsieur Clervaud didn't tell me he was expecting you."

"I...uh...I came to Paris a little spontaneously." The understatement of the year, though not an outright lie. "But if he's too busy for a visit..." I trailed off, half hoping Gordon would be too busy to see me.

But, yikes. Busy plotting criminal activities, maybe?

Luckily — or unluckily — Gordon was home and had time to see me. I rode the elevator up nervously.

"Sweetheart! What a surprise! So good to see you!" Gordon met me with his usual hearty hug.

He was only about my height, but his warlock aura was so powerful, the space around him tingled with magic. Otherwise, he looked like any other well-to-do Parisian businessman — medium build, high-end leather shoes, self-satisfied expression. My grandmother had always claimed he reminded her of 1960s heartthrob Alain Delon, but I'd never seen the resemblance.

"How is everything?" he asked. "I want to hear all about the château."

I wanted to hear all about why he'd asked my sister for a favor rather than me, but I forced myself to play casual and update him on everything from removing wallpaper to clearing the north stable block. I was tempted to mention the police regional championships too, but I decided to leave that out for the moment.

It struck me that that might also be how Gordon operated — not lying outright so much as selectively sharing information.

"I heard from Dora recently. It sounds like her studies are progressing nicely," he said.

I made a noncommittal sound. Not nicely enough for my cousin to finally come help me with the estate we'd inherited together with my sister.

"So I hear," I said diplomatically, then moved on to my sister. "Gen sends her greetings."

Okay, that was an embellishment, but she would have sent her greetings if I had reminded her to, right?

"Wonderful, wonderful. When does her flight arrive?"

"Unfortunately, she's been delayed."

He practically went bug-eyed. "Again?"

I sighed. "Again."

A shocked, *Now what will I do?* expression flashed over his face. A blink-and-you'll-miss-it reaction, but I had made damn sure not to blink.

A knock sounded at the door, and Gordon called out, "Come in."

The door opened slowly. A split second before the visitor came into sight, the scent of perfume hit me. Carolina Herrera "Good Girl," if I remembered correctly.

Catnip for men, my friend Delphine had called it disparagingly.

Strong words, especially coming from a prostitute.

"Ah, Celeste," Gordon greeted the woman.

I stared at the curvy, dark-haired beauty. Shit. Wasn't she supposed to have been long gone by now?

"Oh, *pardon.* I didn't mean to interrupt," she purred, though her eyes said the opposite.

"My goddaughter just dropped in," Gordon explained. "Celeste, this is my goddaughter, Mina. Mina, Celeste is my private secretary. I don't think you've met."

Ah, but we had, and in the worst possible circumstances — circumstances that demanded we both keep that secret from Gordon.

"Ah, the lovely Mina," Celeste clucked through big, pouty lips. "I've heard so much about you. The one with the château, correct?" Her voice had a long-suffering note in it.

I gritted my teeth. Yes, I'd inherited a huge building and property. Yes, I felt lucky and grateful. I just wished people understood how much work, stress, and responsibility that came with. The roof leaked, and the outbuildings were crumbling. I'd already sunk my modest life savings into the place, yet it was still closer to bankrupting me than generating any income.

"Nice to meet you," I lied. It wasn't nice, and this wasn't our first meeting.

"I just wanted to check on the arrangements for Brussels," Celeste told Gordon.

Alarms whooped in my mind. Marius, Roux, Bene, and Henrik had just been there. Was Gordon about to send them back?

My godfather made a dismissive gesture. "Just message me. I'll check later."

"Well, there's one pressing point," she said, flashing me a *sorry/not sorry* look.

Sweat broke out on the back of my neck. Celeste could reveal to Gordon that I'd been to Mallorca. That I was sleeping with Marius. She could get me in so, so much trouble.

Then again, I could tell Gordon that her interference had nearly foiled the mission in Mallorca and that she'd met Marius earlier today. So, we were at a stalemate.

Her eyes taunted me with unspoken messages like, *I slept with Marius first. I met Bene, Roux, and Henrik first. I am more beautiful, more cunning, and more successful than you'll ever be.*

The worst part was that none of those would be lies — depending on how one defined successful.

"I'll just pop out to the washroom." I scurried out, feeling very much like a country mouse again.

In the bathroom, I splashed water on my face and gave myself a stern lecture. Then I flushed the toilet, waited a few seconds, and marched back into Gordon's office with my head held high.

"Almost finished?" I asked.

Gordon and Celeste looked up from a document on his desk, and only then did it occur to me that I could have snuck over to eavesdrop and peek at the documents. Heck, I could even have shadow-walked over.

Clearly, I wasn't cut out for secret spy work.

"Well—" Celeste started.

"We're finished," Gordon told her firmly. "Thank you for your time. That will be all."

"But—" Celeste protested.

"My goddaughter and I have much to discuss. Good evening." He pointed to the door.

Celeste forced a smile, but her eyes shot daggers at me. Then she glanced at Gordon, one hand on her hip to draw attention to her generous figure. Her succubus charm didn't seem to work on him, though, and no wonder. As a powerful warlock, he was immune to all kinds of magic. A good reason not to try shadow-walking around him, I realized.

Her heels clicked over the parquet floor, and she paused at the door. "*Bon soir.*"

"*Bon soir,*" I murmured.

Gordon waved without looking, making her even angrier.

She glared at his back, and *wham!* Magic coursed through me, opening a window into her mind. There, I saw a massive, multiscreen array worthy of NASA, but where every screen flashed images of her. Celeste, Celeste, Celeste — as far as one could see, in hundreds of different scenarios and calculations that created one monstrous, narcissistic display.

All that was packed into her mind. It was exhausting. Nauseating. Terrifying.

Reeling, I grabbed for the back of an armchair.

Gordon, I nearly whispered. *Can't you see that? Who she really is and what she's planning?*

Not that I could see exactly what she was planning, but I knew it was no good and that Gordon ought to be worried.

But he didn't seem to notice, and I yanked my gaze to the windows before Celeste turned her glare toward me.

Then, whew. The door shut, and she was gone.

"Sorry for the interruption," Gordon said. "Now, where were we?"

Personally, I was ready to go vomit into the toilet. Celeste's inner machinations were that disturbing.

Instead, I grabbed a pitcher of water.

"A glass for you?" I offered.

He shook his head, and when he turned away, I guzzled down a glassful. My mind spun. Why had Celeste secretly met with Marius? How was she involved in whatever was going on? Worse, was she still involved with Marius? Had he been playing me all along?

One thing was for sure. This day was turning out to be a hell of a roller coaster, and I sensed several more loops looming. Where the hell was the exit?

"What will your next project be?" Gordon asked, more out of politeness than interest.

Celeste had thrown me off so badly, I spent the next ten minutes blabbering about paint, leaks, and faulty plumbing just to return to an even keel. Then I gradually steered the conversation back to what I'd really come for.

"Gen mentioned that you needed a favor," I said as casually as I could. "Maybe I could help you with it since she's delayed."

"How sweet of you." Gordon's light tone was a little forced, like the tight smile I replied with.

"We're always happy to help. It's the least we can do after all you've done for us."

He nodded sadly. "I know your father would have done the same for me if things had been different."

Things would have had to have been *way* different, since Gordon didn't have children. He wasn't the one who'd died young in a tragic accident either, but I appreciated his sentiment.

Then I caught myself. Just how genuine was that sentiment? Given what I'd recently learned about his business interests... Well, I found myself questioning everything.

But no. Gordon was my father's dearest friend, and he'd always been incredibly generous to Gen, Dora, and me. He might be involved in shady business dealings, but I had no grounds to suspect his affection.

"Well, I'm happy to help," I said. "And knowing Gen, well... You might have been better off asking me in the first place."

Gordon flashed an indulgent smile that said, *Oh, that Gen. Such a firecracker! Someday, she'll get her life together.*

I shared his hope, if not his optimism.

"I would have asked, but I know how busy you've been," he said.

He also knew I was the responsible one — and the one who practically lived on his doorstep.

"I'd be happy to help. And truthfully, I could use a little break," I said.

From working on the château *and* from my guests, but I left that part out.

"I can imagine," he said, pasting on a smile.

I waited. And waited. "So... the favor?"

He began pacing. Back and forth, back and forth through shadows cast by the spaces between each of the floor-to-ceiling windows.

Uh-oh. The last time I'd seen Gordon pace this much had been when he'd considered the idea of sending a group of "bodyguards" to live and "train" at the château — a plan peppered with lies and deceit, as I'd come to discover.

"To be honest, I hesitated to ask Gen in the first place," he admitted.

Hesitated because he knew Gen would mess up, or hesitated because it was dangerous and illegal?

"Particularly since it's a task with potential for certain. . . complications," he continued.

My mind filled in the blanks with arms dealers, mercenaries, and million-dollar masterpieces.

"Maybe it's just as well she can't do it," I said.

He moved his head in a yes-but-no motion. "Perhaps, though it could also be a unique opportunity." He looked at me, and I could sense the gears of his mind turning.

"Opportunity? How so?" I asked nervously.

The housekeeper entered with tea, an interruption welcomed — and possibly engineered — by Gordon. After she left, he stirred his tea for a long time, thinking.

"So, you were saying. . ." I asked against my better judgment.

Gordon studied his tea before responding.

"Complications. . . opportunities. . ." I cued.

Gordon inhaled so ponderously, his nose hairs produced a whistling sound.

"I was recently contacted by the widow of a longtime associate," he finally said. "She asked for help evaluating a potentially valuable artwork."

"You don't say," I murmured over the alarms clanging in my mind.

"Yes. And I thought. . ." He trailed off, shaking his head.

"What did you think?"

I felt like a character in a horror movie, reaching for a door-knob in a dark mansion despite an audience screaming in warning. But I couldn't help myself.

"You know as well as I how rarely such cases turn out to involve genuine artworks," Gordon said. "So I thought it prudent to conduct an informal check before calling in an expert to authenticate the painting and identifying potential buyers."

I bit back the urge to ask, *Why the hell are you getting involved in trading artworks off the open market?*

"And my mind went to Gen, of course, since she has a good eye..." he continued.

Ha. More like Gen, who was too gullible to ask any questions.

"...and I know how much she loves London," he went on, watching me.

My heart leaped. I loved London — and unlike Gen, I'd been toiling away in the boonies for weeks with a bunch of infuriating shifters. Including one *especially* infuriating shifter, but I would deal with him later.

"But since Gen is unavailable..." Gordon looked at me over his teacup.

And since I'm the one who worked at an auction house and I have experience authenticating artworks... I nearly chimed in.

But, wait. Wasn't I supposed to avoid getting sucked into another one of Gordon's sketchy missions?

On the other hand, this didn't sound anything like Mallorca, which had been downright dangerous. All it involved was looking at a painting in London. No "procurement," no "infiltration." The painting wasn't likely to be anything important, but it could still be an interesting trip.

"Who's the artist?" I couldn't help asking.

Gordon held his palms toward the ceiling. "She refuses to say. Not over the phone, nor email. Only in person. The poor woman sees conspiracies everywhere."

A little like me. But I'd been attacked by a vampire, abandoned by my dragon lover, and drawn into the dark underbelly of the supernatural world by my godfather. What was her excuse?

"All she will say is 'an early twentieth-century artist of great repute,'" Gordon said.

My mind hopped from Kandinsky to Matisse and Klimt. Or maybe Gabriele Münter?

"Honestly, this is more of a courtesy call than anything else," Gordon explained. "But I feel I owe it to her." He leaned forward. "I really didn't want to bother you, but perhaps you would enjoy a short trip to London. All expenses covered, of course."

The alarms that had filled my mind earlier were strangely muted, replaced by images of double-decker buses, cozy tea rooms, and bridges over the Thames.

Try as I might, I just couldn't see a downside. I'd been toiling at home for weeks and really needed to get out more. Preferably for things that didn't involve criminal activities, so this would be perfect.

"You know, I would enjoy that," I admitted.

Not that I would be mentioning any such thing to Marius. Otherwise, I risked a touchy dragon shifter torching half of London in a misplaced effort to protect me against imaginary dangers.

Gordon beamed. "So, you'll do it?"

I thought it over a few seconds more, then nodded. An overnight trip to London was just what I needed after the week I'd had.

"I would love to."

Chapter Eight

MARIUS

My heart hammered as I stood in the shadows at the top of the metro stairs, watching the platform on the opposite side of the tracks. A glance at my watch said nine twenty-five. I'd warned Mina not to come early, but that was like telling Henrik not to drink blood. It went against her nature.

She must have sensed the gravity of the situation, though, because so far, she'd actually done as instructed. Or, crap. Had she decided not to come at all?

She'll come, my dragon side assured me.

I half hoped she wouldn't, because this was all about parting ways.

A wisp of smoke escaped my nostrils as my dragon rumbled, *Never.*

A fiftysomething lady wrinkled her nose as she passed me, muttering something about no smoking on the platforms, even up here on the elevated tracks.

Not smoking, lady, my dragon growled inside. *Just pining for my mate.*

I'd spent weeks denying that obvious fact, then made the mistake of embracing it for a while. Eventually, reality had come along and smacked me in the head, forcing me to Plan C. I could love my mate as much as I wanted, but for her own safety, I had to stay away. Far away. Forever.

More rumbling, more wisps of smoke, more dirty looks from the lady. Luckily, the train came along and took her on her way. It chugged out of the station at nine twenty-seven, its lights blending with those of nighttime Paris. A beautiful autumn night with mostly clear skies, as a glance through the antique glass awnings revealed. Then I looked back across the tracks and—

My breath caught, and my dragon roared in glee. *Mate!*

Mina paused at the top of the stairs opposite me, looked both ways along the platform, and checked her watch. Then she fiddled with the zip on her jacket and checked her watch again. She checked the display over the platform too, which helped make her look like just another young, single Parisian late for a date rather than a woman involved in anything sketchy.

Then she whirled and looked right at me from across the tracks.

She senses us, my dragon rumbled proudly.

I'd hoped a few days apart would weaken the bond that had developed between us, but it seemed to have had the opposite effect.

I took a deep breath, reminding myself that danger lurked.

Walk to the far end of the platform, then walk back. I threw my voice into her mind and tilted my head right.

Mind-speaking with Mina was hit or miss, because we weren't actually mated—

Yet, my dragon growled.

—and she tended to block me out when she was mad. But she usually got the gist of my message, if not the details.

She blinked, then looked down the length of the platform and back to me.

Exactly, I said. *Walk down to the end, then back so I can see if you're being followed.*

But Mina was Mina, so following orders was a problem.

She threw up her hands, signaling, *Why the hell should I walk around at a time like this?*

I nearly put my face in my hands. So much for not being noticed by anyone following her.

Just walk to the end and back. Please, I shouted into her mind.

She rolled her eyes and stomped off, huffing. *Dragons!*

My inner beast practically swooned. The woman was at her best when riled up, all bold, confident, and no-nonsense.

I dragged my gaze away to check the stairs she'd taken. No one followed her, but I kept my guard up. Mina walked three-quarters of the way down the platform, whirled, and stalked back, shooting me an impatient look.

Happy?

I grimaced. No, because the entire situation was fucked. But at least it didn't look like she'd been followed.

I pointed down, then held up my hand in a stop sign.

She held up her validated ticket and mouthed an obscenity at me.

Typical Mina. Not one to waste a cent, even though she owned a château.

My dragon snorted. *A crumbling château.*

I repeated my hand signals and waited for her to — finally — obey. Then I checked the platforms one more time and descended on my side.

I found her by the ticket machines on ground level, her arms crossed, her foot tapping impatiently.

"Is this really nec—"

"Yes." I grabbed her by the elbow and hustled her out to the street.

And, *zing!* Just that little amount of contact sent electricity through my veins.

I checked our surroundings and hurried her over a bridge to the far side of the Canal Saint-Martin.

"Nice to see you too," she muttered.

"Nice to see you," I echoed, and it really was, though that wasn't the point of this meeting.

A point that grew harder and harder to remember the more I inhaled her rose-and-lilac scent.

"Oh, no one will notice us like this," she grumbled, like *she* was the expert in covert operations.

"Like what?"

"We're racing along like we don't want to be followed. It's obvious."

Well, yes, because we were out in the open, and dragons didn't slink through the shadows the way lowly felines did. (Roux came to mind, as did Bene. Two totally random examples, of course.) But Mina was a potential target, and it was only prudent to avoid being caught out.

"Got a better idea?" I grumbled.

"Yes." She settled into a leisurely stroll, wrapping her elbow around mine. "Like this. Much less obvious."

"Much slower," I grumbled, but she had a point.

Nice, my dragon sighed dreamily as she pressed into my side.

"Slower but less obvious," she whispered. "We're just two happy lovers out for an evening stroll."

I wished we were, but—

No buts! My dragon roared so fiercely, I stumbled over my next step.

"Enjoying our time together, looking at the stars..." Mina went on in that singsong voice that was guaranteed to calm my soul, every fucking time.

My breaths grew slower and deeper, my shoulders a little less tense.

Mina had once confided to me that she'd inherited such a mix of magic, she didn't know what it — or she — was capable of. But somewhere in her supernatural ancestry, there had to be a siren who lured sailors into cliffs — or away from them, if she took pity on the poor soul.

Like me?

Not magic, my dragon said with conviction. *Destiny.*

Either way, I found myself looking over my shoulder less frequently and glancing at her face instead.

"See? Much nicer," Mina murmured, pressing closer.

Very nice, my dragon agreed.

She stopped under a tree and faced me, whispering, "We can even do this."

And she kissed me. Soft. Long. Deep.

My eyes slid to half-mast, and that surveillance system I found so hard to switch off instantly shut down.

Mate, my dragon murmured dreamily.

And, shit. Even my human side agreed.

Then a moped zoomed by, and we broke apart.

Mina sighed, watching it go. Then she blushed and stuck a finger at me.

"I'm still mad at you, you know."

"Obviously."

We stared at each other for another few seconds, then fell into another deep, hungry kiss. A full minute later, I caught myself and broke away again.

"Stop. We can't."

Mina shook her head, refusing to release my hands. "We can. We did. What's changed?"

I opened my mouth, then closed it again. How could I ever explain?

Mina huffed in frustration. "I don't understand. None of this. It's like you switched off. Don't you want me any more? Don't you want *us*?"

I fumbled for words. "I want, but I can't. We can't. Not any more."

"You're saying you can't touch me?" she murmured, nestling closer.

I shook my head miserably.

"Can't kiss me?" she whispered.

My lips quirked, and I gulped hard.

"Not here... or here... or here?" She pressed kisses to my cheek, jaw, and neck.

Every muscle in my body strained as I tried not to respond.

"No more stripping each other naked and sliding into bed..." she continued, smoothing her hands over my chest. "Never?"

I went hard all over. Yes, *all* over, in the best — er, most inappropriate — way.

"Mina..." I murmured, trying to muster the strength to say no.

"No more sex?" she whispered.

Heat tore through my cheeks as memories flooded my mind. Not the memory of one particular time, but *every* time, all at once.

"Stop it," I begged, working up the strength to gently push her away. "Stop teasing."

She clamped on to my hands. "I'm not teasing. I'm trying to understand why you don't want me any more."

"I never said I don't want you," I growled. "I do. More than anything. Every day. Every night. Every fucking minute."

Oops. So much for building a compelling case.

Her mouth fell open, and she searched my eyes. "And yet, you left me."

"It's not that I don't want you. It's that I *can't*," I said over the sandpaper in my throat.

"Because. . . ?" Persistent as hell. That was Mina. One of many reasons I loved her.

Then her expression turned fierce. "Wait. Did Gordon say something? I swear, if he did. . ."

"No, not Gordon." I looked around. We were still out in the open. Time to move.

"Then who? What?" she demanded.

"I'll explain. I swear I will," I conceded, pulling her onward. "But not here."

We were nearly at the Bassin de la Villette — the wider basin where barges could turn or moor up — and we needed to move to a more private location. I led her over another bridge to the Quai de la Loire side.

"This again?" she protested.

"Just for the view," I lied, checking for anyone tailing us. I steered her past a restaurant and several benches until I reached—

"A construction site?" Mina dug in her heels.

I pulled her forward. "Trust me."

A big ask after everything I'd put her through, but Mina slowly fell into step with me.

My clenched gut slowly relaxed, and I swallowed hard. I'd never trusted — or been trusted by — anyone as much as Mina. I'd never wanted that either. But now. . .

Trust is a treasure, my dragon whispered. *A precious one, like love.*

When the beast had become such a poet, I had no idea, but every word rang true. How would I ever let her go?

You don't, moron, my dragon grumbled, sounding a hell of a lot like Roux.

I tapped the top of the chest-high barrier we reached. "Want a leg up?"

Oh please, her affronted expression said.

She stuck a foot in the lip of a trash can and hoisted herself over the fence. I vaulted it to land beside her, then motioned her onward.

"Nothing as romantic as breaking and entering," she said dryly, pointing to a sign that listed all the offenses we could be prosecuted for.

Could be, but wouldn't. I'd checked for cameras earlier, and no one was following us.

"You and me, baby," I tried a lame joke. "Like... Who were they? Bonnie and Clyde?"

Mina grimaced. "Things didn't end well for them."

"Er, I mean, nothing like Bonnie and Clyde."

Romeo and Juliet came to mind next, but they hadn't celebrated a happy end either. Dammit, was every great love story doomed? Were we?

Mina squeezed my hand, and a little hope crept back into my heart. Dangerously so, but that was the thing with hope. It was a persistent little bugger that was hard to shake, especially around Mina.

"Ah, yes. Incredibly romantic," she muttered as I led her around giant spools of wire.

No, it wasn't, but that wasn't the priority right now. Not with her safety at stake.

I made a beeline for the container that housed the construction office, all closed up for the night, and took the stairs that led to the roof.

"Shh..." I warned, making sure my boots didn't ring against the metal.

Mina followed, quiet as a mouse, then looked around. "Back there was a zero on the scale of romantic locations. Now, you're up to about a three."

I checked the perimeter, then sat facing the boat basin with my back to a higher container set behind the first.

"At least a four," I tried.

I expected Mina to sit beside me, but she nestled into the space between my legs and leaned against my chest.

Ten out of ten, my dragon sighed.

She must have done it on autopilot, because she tensed a moment later. Then she turned and held a finger in my face. "I meant it about being mad at you, you know."

I stuck up my hands. "I promise to keep my hands off."

"Don't you dare," she muttered, tugging my arms until they were crossed around her.

So, lots of mixed messages, but I was just as guilty of that as she was.

The next few minutes passed in blissful silence, and I nearly forgot the mission I'd tasked myself with.

"As nice as this is, I guess we're not here to snuggle," Mina sighed, reading my mind.

Ha. Snuggle. Not a word that applied to too many instances in my life. Only a few rare ones, and only ever with Mina.

"No, we're here because it's an elevated position where I can keep a lookout," I said, reminding myself to do that instead of enjoying her scent.

"Keeping a lookout for. . . ?" she asked.

I clenched my jaw. That was the hard part. "I'm not sure."

Mina thumped her head back against my chest in exasperation. Then she drew a long, *I shall be calm now* breath and grunted, "Explain."

I leaned to one side to pull my phone from my pocket.

"Hey, you said no phones," she protested.

Once a teacher, always a teacher. They loved sticking to the rules. She was like Roux that way.

"I said, don't bring *your* phone," I pointed out, though the *Roux* thing occupied most of my mind.

My dragon rumbled unhappily at the thought of a potential competitor, but I just snorted. Mina and Roux? As if.

Mina and that ass of a police officer who kept sniffing around the château, on the other hand...

My hackles rose. If I was forced to leave Mina, Clement would make his move fast, and he would probably earn pole position ahead of Bene, Henrik, and Roux.

"Boy, what is it with you?" Mina complained, waving a hand to clear the air of whiffs of acrid smoke.

I pulled out my phone, scrolled to a picture, and held it in front of her. She tensed, staring at the photo on the screen.

Chapter Nine

MARIUS

Mina traced the photo on the screen of my phone with one finger. "Oh. That's. . . cute."

Cute? Another word that made any self-respecting dragon shifter look long and hard at his life choices.

Which I did, but there was no contest — I chose Mina every time. The problem was the threat I posed to her, just by being me.

She tilted her head. "Where was that taken?"

"Mallorca, I think. See?" I zoomed in on the masts in the background.

"Oh," Mina murmured, reliving that moment, perhaps, as I did.

Having somehow survived a mission in which everything that could have gone wrong did, we had celebrated by taking a quiet moment together while waiting for the private jet back to France. The moon had been full, the sea breeze balmy, and Mina had never felt more perfect in my arms.

"Wait. Who took this?" she asked, slowly catching on.

"Whoever sent *this*." I showed her the accompanying message.

Her shoulders tensed as she read aloud. "*Those who love, lose.* What the hell?"

My sentiments exactly.

"Anonymous?" she read from the sender's avatar. "Have you traced this?"

"I've tried, but the source is buried too deep."

She mulled that over, then asked, "Why would someone send this?"

I waited, because it was pretty obvious, and even a mind as free of evil as Mina's could figure it out.

She gaped. "Someone is threatening you?"

I tightened my arms around her. "They're threatening me *and* you."

Any other woman would have screeched and run away, but Mina wove her fingers around mine. "Who?"

"Someone who hates me." I sighed. "It's a fairly long list."

"So, list," she growled.

I shook my head. "The more you know, the more danger you're in."

She huffed and wiggled out of my arms. "Ignorance doesn't diminish danger. And ignorance by choice is plain old stupidity — a choice you don't get to make for me."

"It's not a choice, Mina. It's a necessity."

She shook her head vehemently. "Not for you to decide. Now, tell me who you suspect."

And boy, could she do *commanding* when she wanted to.

I thought it over a moment longer, then caved. Mina was right. I just hoped it wouldn't come back to bite me — or kill her.

"Etienne is my top suspect."

"Etienne?"

I nodded, cursing the day I'd gotten involved with him. All I'd wanted was to make a quick buck, and going head-to-head against other shifters in his clandestine, gladiator-style pits had fit the bill. Or so I'd thought at the time.

"Remember that charge of attempted murder?" I asked.

"Kind of hard to forget."

I winced, praying she remembered the rest.

She did, fortunately. "You mean the fight ring/sex-trafficking guy, right? Do you think he's out for revenge?"

"It's possible."

"Let me get this straight," she said, more to herself than me. "You nearly killed him — out of principle..."

I shrugged, trying to make light of it. "He owed me money too."

She snorted, telling me she didn't buy that, then continued puzzling it out.

"You didn't succeed, but trying was enough to land you in hot water, and that's what brought you to your plea-bargain thing with Gordon."

I waited for her to figure out the rest, which she promptly did.

"Etienne got in trouble too, I guess?"

"Yes. His businesses were shut down, and he was forced into a deal similar to mine, though I don't know the details."

"A deal with Gordon?" she yelped.

It said a lot about Mina that for all the dirt she'd learned about her godfather, she still clung to her misplaced faith in him.

I gulped hard. The same way she had faith in me?

I shook my head. "No. A different warlock dealt with Etienne. An associate of Gordon's."

She grimaced but didn't say a word.

"Etienne would love to get back at me, and hurting you would be the best way to do that."

She looked up at me, whispering, "Is it?"

I tightened my arms around her. "It is."

Hurting Mina was the worst possible punishment I could imagine. No form of torture would come close, and no other person stood in that category. Only Mina.

As chilling as the thought was, we were back to cute and snuggly. What was it with me?

Mina cupped my face, whispering, "Did I ever tell you I love you?"

I shook my head slowly. No, actually. Neither of us had ever dared utter that four-letter word.

"Well, I do. I love you. Desperately, even though I tried not to."

I bit my lip, then admitted, "I tried that too."

Her eyes lit up. "You did?"

I nodded. "Didn't work, though. Miserable failure."

She poked my ribs. "Miserable?"

"I mean that in a good way." I cleared my throat, working up the nerve to say, "I love you too." It came out as a mumble, so I gave it a second try. "I love you, Mina. I miss you. I hated leaving."

She wrapped her arms around mine and nodded softly. "I miss you too."

Another crack formed in my heart, but the fact that she didn't slap me and retreat kept the pieces from falling apart completely.

The next minute passed in weighty silence. At some point, Mina let out a long breath and nestled closer. Close enough to make my mind go blank of everything but the feeling of her in my arms. Her scent. The rightness of it all.

Destiny, my dragon murmured.

Yes, but where would it all lead?

Mina kissed me softly. As our lips moved, my senses dimmed, losing track of everything but her. Our bodies pressed closer, and the heat between us began to flare, melting away my plan to keep away from her forever.

"Mm," Mina murmured as our kiss grew deeper.

I stroked her curves, losing myself in a sensual haze.

Not supposed to, a warning sounded in the back of my mind. *Must resist...*

But it was hard to remember why. Hard to think of anything but how perfect we were together.

Forever, my dragon hummed.

I dragged my cheek along hers, marking her with my scent. I trailed kisses down her neck, so hot and hard that she arched and moaned. I snuck a hand up from her ribs at the same time, barely aware of what I was doing. Barely aware of the clouds parting, allowing the moonlight through.

Magic swirled around me. I could feel it. Irresistible, insistent magic, and Mina was just as caught up in it.

Claim, the moon chanted quietly. *Claim your mate.*

Did Mina hear that too?

"So good," she breathed, pulling me closer.

My groin ached, and I wished we were somewhere else. Somewhere with a bed.

Claim, my dragon hummed.

Her breath hitched when I swiped a thumb over her breast, and she let her hands wander over my body.

Need you... Want you... Her thoughts registered in my hazy mind.

It was crazy, how quickly we'd gone from *normal* to *inferno* and how insistently my beast chanted, *Claim, claim, claim.*

There was more at work here than just her and me, a blurry corner of my mind realized. Something like destiny.

"Oh..." she breathed, melting in my arms as I kissed, rubbed, and nipped her skin.

Claim, my dragon demanded.

Moonlight bathed our bodies, casting blueish light over our tangled limbs.

No time to waste, the moon urged. *Claim her before you lose her. Make her yours forever.*

Mine... Forever... my inner beast agreed.

And hell. Even my human side agreed. I loved her, and she loved me. So why not claim her with a mating bite?

My gums ached as my dragon fought to emerge. *Claim her. Now. No one can take her from us, then.*

I sensed a fault in that logic but was too lost in the moment to care. Intoxicated by her scent, I nipped her neck and rubbed my chin over her soft skin. Scrubbing it, almost.

She leaned closer, begging for more. More I was happy to give.

Beeeep! A car careened around the closest corner, then raced away.

We broke apart, panting. Then we exhaled. False alarm.

For a full minute, we sat there, our chests heaving. Then Mina ran a hand over her neck, mumbling, "Wow, that was good. Is a neck orgasm a thing?"

I grinned, though an unsettled thought poked at the edge of my mind. But the past week had been hell, and the present felt so, so good. Why not bask in this feeling for a while?

"I mean it. That was incredible," she said, still touching her neck.

My groin ached as if she'd rubbed there too, and moonlight shimmered over her skin. I froze, staring. In the heat of the moment, I'd come close to a mating bite. Things hadn't gone that far, but I'd nuzzled her hard. Too hard?

I snapped back to my senses, suddenly afraid. It was one thing for a shifter to mark their lover with their scent. But there was another type of mark an overzealous shifter could leave when circumstances were just right. One in which destiny intervened to propel two lovers closer to a *forever* bond.

Marked by moonlight, I'd heard it called. Something much deeper and longer-lasting than the usual, faint remnant of a lover's scent. A moonlight mark glowed, announcing a shifter's intention to mate to his rivals.

"Mm," Mina murmured, nuzzling my chin.

I glanced at her neck. Had I slipped up and allowed my inner beast close enough to the surface to mark Mina with its leathery hide?

A cloud drifted over the moon, and the shimmer faded. Or had I imagined it?

My heart pounded. On the one hand, I loved the idea. But if I'd inadvertently given Mina a moonlight mark, there would be no hiding my love for her, and she would be in that much more danger.

And, fuck. I had plenty of supernatural enemies waiting to exploit my slightest vulnerability. Until now, that hadn't been an issue, because I didn't do *vulnerable.* But loving Mina exposed me in a whole new way — and exposed her to all kinds of dangers too. In which case, I couldn't stay away from her. I had to make sure she was safe.

I craned my neck, studying hers. But there was nothing now. No way to tell for sure.

"Wow. That was intense." She chuckled. "I was ready to screw you right here. Maybe it was a good thing that car came along."

Yes, but had it come a moment too late?

I gulped hard, murmuring, "Yeah. Good thing."

Mina cocked her head. "Something wrong?"

"No. I mean, yes. I'm just worried about that picture I was sent," I bluffed.

She grimaced. "Right. What do we do about that?"

Easy answer, for a change. "You go home, stay safe, and leave it to me."

She snorted. "Don't even start. If I wanted *overprotective*, I would be with Clem."

My gut churned at the thought of her with the police officer. Still, he would protect her until I could get back there myself, and that was what counted, right?

"I mean it, Mina. You're safest at the château until I figure out who sent that photo."

Until I wipe that ass off the face of the earth was more like it, but Mina didn't need to hear the blunt version.

Still, what then? The rest of my enemies wouldn't need a photo to know Mina meant everything to me. Inadvertently marking her would make that just as obvious.

Simple. We protect her to the end of our days, my dragon vowed.

Mina sighed. "Too bad asking Gordon to help trace that picture isn't an option."

No, it wasn't. But that did bring us to why she'd traveled to Paris.

"What did Gordon want?" I asked.

"Nothing sketchy. It's totally innocent. Maybe even fun."

My dragon paced and swished its tail. *Innocent? Gordon? Not a chance.*

She must have picked up on that, because she raised that commanding finger again. "Oh no. Do not even think of interfering."

"Wouldn't dream of it," I lied.

"I mean it, Marius. Don't ruin this for me."

"Ruin what?"

She crossed her arms firmly. "Need-to-know basis."

Ouch.

"The question is, what did Celeste want? I saw you with her outside Gordon's," she demanded.

I cursed the succubus for the hundredth time.

"She called me, claiming to have information about Etienne," I explained.

"Lucky her to have your number." Mina's voice dripped with sarcasm. Then she frowned. "Wait. Why would Celeste know about Etienne?"

I grimaced. "Because Celeste keeps tabs on anyone who might prove useful to her someday."

"Useful. . . how?"

I ran a hand through my hair. Where would I begin?

Then I looked around. We were still out in the open. Time to move.

I stood and held out my hand. Mina took it and rose. "Meeting adjourned?"

I nodded and led her back to ground level. "Where are you staying?"

"Gordon's guest apartment, around the corner from his place."

We hopped the fence and hurried across the street to the darker sidewalk. Minutes later, we reached the corner closest to her destination.

"Do you want to come in?" she asked.

I shook my head. "Too risky. Gordon has the place wired with cameras."

"Cameras?" she hissed. "Like, in the bedroom?"

I doubted it, but I shrugged. "Maybe there too."

She thought it over, then flashed me a saucy look. "Then I guess I shouldn't touch myself and cry out your name, huh?"

My mouth hung open.

She snorted. "What do you think I've been doing all week?"

I knew what *I* had been doing all week, and I wasn't proud of it. But, hell. Women did that too? Even nice girls like Mina?

She rolled her eyes, catching the gist of my thoughts. "Like men have a monopoly on dirty fantasies."

I did my best not to indulge in any as I hugged her again. Her arms closed around me just as fiercely, and her lips brushed my ear.

"I don't want to go."

Neither did I, dammit.

"I'll get in touch. Soon," I promised.

Yes, it was a jerk move not to offer her my number, but it was for her own safety, and I could get in touch with her through Roux.

Nodding slowly, she eased away and stepped toward the apartment. I studied her neck for any sign of a mark. But with the moon behind a cloud, it was impossible to tell.

I raised a hand in farewell. "Be careful. I mean it."

She didn't roll her eyes, which told me she knew how serious this was. Which was good, but totally fucked up at the same time.

Her eyes locked on mine as she whispered, "You be careful too."

Chapter Ten

MINA

That night in bed, I lay awake, yearning for Marius and clarity. My train of thought was very PG until I touched my neck where he'd nuzzled me.

And just like that, my mind ran off with wild fantasies. So wild, I touched myself and cried out, imagining Marius driving me to the very heights of ecstasy — cameras be damned, if there were any.

I lay panting for a long time afterward, wondering about dragons, forever, and destiny.

I woke before dawn and headed to Gare du Nord for my six-thirty train to London. Premier class, no less.

I practically kissed my ticket and cried, *Thank you, Gordon!*

Ten minutes before departure, I settled into my seat and stared out the window, twirling my hair absently. I brushed my neck in the process, and boy, was my skin warm and tingly. Pleasantly so. The dirty kind of pleasant, I realized, yanking my hand away.

The older woman in the seat facing mine gave me an odd look, and I lectured myself. This was not the time for daydreams about my irresistible — er, infuriating — dragon shifter. It was time to focus.

I knotted my hands in my lap. *Focus, focus, focus.*

But Gordon hadn't given me enough to focus on, so I ended up thinking about the previous evening. The anonymous photo troubled me — deeply — but I was pleased about one aspect. If getting involved with me was the worst thing Marius could be threatened over, that was pretty encouraging, considering his past. A past I'd never asked the details of and probably never would.

I sighed. Like last night, when I'd resolved to drag every mystery out of him, only to melt in his arms. I couldn't think straight around the man, let alone maintain any resolve. So maybe a little time-out was a good thing.

The train slowly pulled out of the station, and passengers settled in for the ride. There were two seats on my side of the aisle, and two sets of two facing each other across from us, occupied by several businessmen. Their cologne hung in the air, and my super-sensitive nose — a hand-me-down from the shifters in my mixed ancestry — picked the scents apart. Two of the men wore sea-breeze colognes. A third had gone a little over the top with an overpowering sandalwood fragrance, while the fourth used a sporty deodorant.

My nose twitched and backed up to Mr. Sandalwood. The scent was pleasant enough, but something didn't fit there. What?

Then it hit me. Every other man's cologne mixed with his natural scent, but Sandalwood Guy had no underlying odor.

My eyes popped open, and my gut twisted. Vampire?

The moment my eyes met his, his thin lips curled.

I yanked my gaze away and gulped. Shit. A vampire. On the train. With me. What were the chances?

Slim — unless, of course, I happened to be involved in something sketchy. Say, something set up by my godfather.

I did my best to keep my heart from hammering, which would only excite the vampire.

My mind spun. Surely Gordon wouldn't do anything to endanger me. Maybe the vampire was some kind of undercover protection?

I dismissed the idea immediately. Sandalwood was definitely not one of the good guys.

Okay, okay — *good guys*, I'd learned, was relative. For me, it meant supernaturals who weren't inclined to kill me. Guys I'd gotten to know, like Marius, Bene, Roux, and H—

I halted the thought and crossed Henrik off that list forever.

"Tickets, please," the conductor said.

Everyone had shown theirs at the station turnstile, so he must have been checking Premier Class for freeloaders with standard class tickets.

Sandalwood held up his phone agreeably enough, but I was tempted to ask the conductor, *Could you check for fangs along with his ticket? I think he's a vampire.*

But what would the poor man do? Die defending me?

I clutched my phone, tempted to call Gordon. But I couldn't exactly voice my suspicions, not with the vampire so close, along with so many other passengers.

I could picture it now — dozens of heads turning as I waited for Gordon's reply to *Just checking if you happened to send a vampire to tail me to London. No? Never mind, then.*

Sandalwood held up a newspaper, but his eyes didn't sweep across lines of print. They focused on one point while he observed his surroundings with his peripheral vision.

Scratch that — not his surroundings. He observed *me.*

I gazed studiously out the window. Could I text Roux or Bene?

Being followed by a vampire. Dark hair, dark eyes. Appears about fifty years old, but who the hell knows. Any chance you know the guy?

Then it hit me. Weeks ago, I'd been stalked in the château gardens. Roux, Bene, Henrik, and Marius had chased away the intruder without getting a firm ID, but their prime suspect was a vampire named Szabo.

I swallowed hard. Was this Szabo? Was he stalking me?

I considered snapping a covert picture and sending it to Roux, but Szabo — if that really was him — would definitely catch me at that. Also, would a vampire even appear in a photograph? I wasn't sure.

The lady opposite me dropped her bookmark, and Szabo leaned over to retrieve it.

"Oh, *merci,*" she gushed.

He bent into a slight bow, and that clinched it. With manners that were at least a century out of date, the guy was definitely a vampire. Not a good-guy vampire or even a tolerable, not-too-horrible vampire. I could sense it.

I turned my phone on just as the train shot into a tunnel. My ears popped, and I turned it off again. Zero reception, and there was no way anyone a phone call away could help me now.

The train blasted back into the open, and sunlight bathed Sandalwood's side of the train. He winced, further backing my conclusion. The older a vampire got, the better he — or she — could tolerate direct sunlight, though they preferred to avoid it.

I gritted my teeth, thinking desperately for some means of getting away from him. Pronto.

Shadow-walking came to mind, but I scratched the thought immediately. It worked best at a distance, where folks couldn't make out the details. Also, I had no confidence in my ability to maintain an illusion in a moving train. My illusionary double would probably start drifting across space, and the rapid changes in light and shadow would be impossible to keep up with.

So I went back to basics with the oldest trick in any woman's book: fleeing to the toilet.

I stood, grabbed my bag as casually as possible, and walked toward the toilet. It was occupied, giving me the excuse to walk to the end of the next compartment.

I glanced at the reflection in the compartment door and, shit. Sandalwood — Szabo? — was following me.

I locked myself in the next toilet and stood there, thinking as the train rocketed along. Did the vampire know I was onto him? Did he care? What exactly did he want with me?

The slowest minute of my life ticked by, followed by another, and another.

Someone hammered on the door.

"Everything all right in there?" a woman called impatiently.

I flushed the toilet, splashed my face with water, drew in a deep breath, and exited. And, crap. Szabo stood two steps away with his arms crossed and a smug expression on his face that said, *Where are you going to go now, sweetheart?*

Somewhere. Anywhere. I turned to hurry through the dining car, and Szabo followed.

A steward came by, and I considered asking for help. But that would endanger an innocent person...or land me in a psych ward.

I continued to the next wagon and the next, desperate to hatch an escape plan. The train went directly to London, with no intermediate stops and no unsecured doors to jump out from. Besides, we were whipping along at about 300 kilometers per hour and would soon travel under the English Channel.

One more car, I decided. I would walk through one more car, then turn around and confront the bastard. He wouldn't attack in public, would he?

The doors before me slid open. I passed the first four rows of seats, then halted in my tracks, staring at a man napping a few rows ahead.

"Marius?"

It was barely a whisper, but his eyes popped open.

My heart warmed, because his first expression was shy joy. Next, his brow creased into a *Damn, I'm busted* expression.

Wait. What the hell was he doing on *my* train?

The compartment door slid open behind me, and a wave of cold, ominous air heralded Szabo's arrival.

Marius's expression changed instantly. His eyes spelled murder as he jumped to his feet and stalked past me with a gruff, "Stay here."

I usually made a point of *not* following his orders, but my inner wimp declared this a worthy exception.

Szabo's loathing expression mirrored Marius's, but step by step, he backed away. The doors slid open behind him, and he continued into the next car. Marius disappeared after him.

My heart rate dropped slightly, only to spike again. Yikes. Would those two battle it out to the death in the dining compartment?

I waited helplessly for a minute. Then I remembered I didn't do helpless and hurried after them.

Halfway through the next wagon, I caught up with Marius and grabbed his shoulder.

"Wait."

He shook his head. "He'll get away."

"He has nowhere to go."

Marius grimaced. "That's almost as bad."

Good point. What would Szabo do if cornered?

A man looked up from his meal, giving us dirty looks. A long minute of hushed pleading later, Marius followed me back to his seat. The young metrosexual guy in the seat beside his looked annoyed until I flashed him my Premier Class reservation.

"Would you like to swap? I just bumped into my friend here, and we'd like to ride together."

He jumped up like the Energizer Bunny, snapped a picture of my reservation, and headed off. . .hopefully not to his doom.

"Don't worry," Marius said, reading my mind. "Szabo won't be interested in him."

I slid into the window seat and whispered back. "So, that was Szabo, huh?"

Marius nodded and sat beside me. We both faced the carriage door, so Szabo couldn't approach without our noticing. I caught a peek of him watching us through the glass before he retreated out of sight.

"Now what?" I murmured.

Marius pulled out his phone and dialed. "I'll call Roux."

Marius tapped his fingers impatiently. I put my hand over his, worried his dragon claws might emerge. When Roux picked up, Marius got right to the point.

"What the fuck is Szabo doing following Mina to London?" he hissed quietly.

I leaned closer, catching Roux demand, "Szabo is where? How do you know?"

"I'm on the same train."

"What the fuck are *you* doing, following Mina to London?" Roux exploded.

Marius ignored him. "I need you to get everything you can on Szabo. Now."

"But—" Roux protested.

"Just do it." Marius grunted, then hung up.

I gave him a pointed look. "Great communication."

He shrugged. "Roux's always been that way."

Not what I meant, but I let that slide. I owed Marius for this, big-time.

"So, now what?" I asked a few minutes later.

He crossed his arms, making every muscle bulge. "We wait until we arrive in London."

"Then what?"

He studied my face, then dropped his eyes to my neck. Heat flashed through my veins, and my cheeks flushed.

He looked away — quickly — and murmured, "Then we'll see."

Not encouraging, because *we'll see* could translate to any number of things in dragon-talk. Things like, *I'll rip his head off* or *I'll roast him alive, along with most of St Pancras station.*

A glance at my watch told me I had over an hour to convince Marius of a better plan.

Minutes ticked by as I wondered what that might be.

"What are you doing, going to London anyway?" he growled.

"What are *you* doing, following me?"

"Would you prefer I hadn't?"

"It's the principle of the thing."

"You want principles, or you want to live to see the sunset?"

Okay, he had a point there. I took a few deep breaths and gently nudged his ribs. Well, I was going for his ribs, but they were cushioned by a wall of muscle.

"Thank you," I whispered.

"*De rien,*" he grumbled, not at all pleased. Then he tore his eyes away from the door long enough to shoot me a dark look.

"Seriously. What are you doing, going to London? I told you, you were in danger."

"In London?" I protested.

"Everywhere."

I crossed my arms, annoyed. "You expect me to go home and hide?"

"Yes," he muttered. Then he sighed and shook his head. "I just want you safe."

I ticked a list off my fingers. "I want me safe, you safe, and no Szabo. But I also want communication. Trust. Honesty. Does that make me greedy?"

A lock of hair fell over his eyes, making his expression even more menacing. "Am I allowed to say yes?"

"No."

He snorted, then wrapped his big, callused hand around mine. "Okay. Communication. Trust. Honesty. You start. What are you doing, going to London?"

I gave him a look. "Not what I meant." But since I owed him my life, I relented. "Gordon wanted me to visit an old acquaintance—"

He groaned and lowered his face to his hands. "You fell for that?"

"I was suspicious at first, but it's fine."

"How is *that* fine?" He pointed toward the door of our compartment, where Szabo still lurked, out of sight but still too close for comfort.

Okay. Another point for the dragon.

"Is there any chance Gordon sent Szabo to protect me?" I tried, then slumped at Marius's expression. "No, I thought not. But I'm sure — totally sure — Gordon didn't expect any trouble. It's just some old lady who—"

"It's never *just* anything with Gordon."

"That may be, but I can't believe Gordon would send Szabo to harm me."

"He wouldn't," Marius conceded. "But someone else would." He frowned, pointing toward Premier Class. "Did you tell Gordon what train you were taking?"

"*He* told *me*. He made the reservation."

Marius snorted. "Gordon makes deals, not reservations. That's what his minions are for."

I froze. "Like Celeste?"

Marius nodded slowly. "Possibly."

Definitely, I decided. But why would she sic Szabo on me?

"There's no limit to what that woman is capable of," Marius muttered.

"Including working with Szabo?"

He nodded. "Celeste was the one who sent Szabo to check on us at the château. Remember that night in the garden?"

I made a face. How could I forget?

"Are you saying she's keeping her finger on the pulse of Gordon's operations?"

He huffed. "There's keeping a finger on the pulse, and there's sinking your teeth in like a fucking vampire."

I grimaced in the direction Szabo had disappeared. "Why would Celeste undermine Gordon if he's her boss?"

"Not sure she sees it that way."

I shouldn't have been surprised after the machinations I'd glimpsed in her mind. But, yikes. Were some people really *that* devious?

Then I slumped, because the answer was yes — and worse, I was that gullible. Celeste probably saw herself as the boss — if not now, then in the near future.

My mind spun. Should I warn Gordon? And, dammit, as devious as he was, did he not recognize the danger Celeste posed?

I closed my eyes and leaned my head against the seat in front of me.

"So, back to what you're doing in London. Tell me everything," Marius said.

Dragons. So darn persistent.

I rocked my head from side to side. One thing was for sure. The long, carefree walk I'd planned from Regent's Park to Kensington Gardens was definitely off the agenda.

Chapter Eleven

MARIUS

That two-plus-hour train ride was the longest of my life, what with the woman I loved at my side and a vampire in the neighboring wagon. I counted every fucking second and doubly cursed each extra that came with our ten-minute delay into London.

Otherwise, I spent the time watching the door, with just the occasional glance at Mina. But I kept those to a minimum because I had to remain vigilant, and because I might kiss — or kill — her otherwise. Mina was smart as anything, so how the hell had she decided going to London was a good idea? Hadn't she realized she couldn't trust Gordon?

"Wait. How did you know I was on this train?" she asked out of the blue.

I shrugged. "I just sensed it."

She stared at me. "Seriously?"

I kept my eyes on the door. "I also staked out Gordon's guest apartment."

She rolled her eyes. "You had me for a minute there."

The train rushed along through another kilometer of tracks before I whispered, "I *can* sense where you are. Not the precise location, but whether you're near or far."

She clasped my hand. "Same with me. I can even tell how you feel sometimes."

Now we were in truly scary territory — on par with blood-thirsty vampires or Gordon's criminal schemes.

I tipped my head closer to hers, and my dragon made me whisper, "Destiny."

She nodded slowly, then leaned in. "So why fight it?"

"Because destiny doesn't always have your best interests at heart. Sometimes, it just toys with you."

Like the previous night, when it had made my mind go blank long enough to mark her, or so I feared. It was still too hard to tell for certain, however.

"I think it's more that destiny *tests* us," Mina said. "To check if you've earned what it has in mind for you, I mean."

"Feels like a hell of a lot of testing. Like school, only worse."

She chuckled. "Not all of school. Like art class — not a lot of testing there."

I kissed her hand. Somehow, she always found a way to put a positive spin on things.

Still, I gave sheer luck the credit for bringing me to Mina's side, rather than destiny. I'd staked out Gordon's guest apartment, figuring she would go for her usual morning run. She'd headed to the train station instead, and I'd barely had time to buy a ticket. It was also sheer luck that I had my travel documents with me, and that was only because I'd been couch-surfing from friend to friend over the last few days in Paris.

Fucking Brexit, my dragon sighed. *Used to be so much easier.*

"What were you doing in Brussels?" Mina asked out of the blue.

I shook my head. "Unrelated."

"The way I thought London was unrelated to Gordon's other business dealings?"

She had a point there, so I amended my answer to, "That's confidential. Sorry."

I wished I could tell her how harmless that job truly had been, at least compared to Gordon's sketchier assignments. Ironically, the one mission Mina had joined us on was the most dangerous job we'd done for Gordon. Brussels and the mission previous to that had been walks in the park in comparison. But Mina only had Mallorca to go on, so I couldn't blame her for assuming everything we did was wildly illegal and hazardous.

She crossed her arms and sat in stony silence for the next forty minutes. Only when we exited the Channel Tunnel and emerged back into daylight did she reveal her plan — what little there was — for the day ahead. Walk a bit, visit an old lady, enjoy London. All perfectly innocent, but I knew better. If Gordon was involved, there was sure to be trouble.

"Now what?" Mina asked as the train pulled into St Pancras station.

I looked out the window. "We wait and watch."

Passengers exited, flooding the platform, making it hard to spot Szabo. On the plus side, that would also make it hard for him to spot us, so after a quick look around, we joined the crowd, then started on a long series of meanders designed to reveal anyone tailing us.

I didn't often miss Roux, Bene, and Henrik, but I would have loved to have had them around now.

Mina and I continued the game on the Underground, hopping from station to station until finally making our way to Hyde Park Corner. By then, it was noon, with only an hour until Mina's appointment.

She led the way across the park to the address while I obsessively checked our surroundings.

"That's it." She pointed.

I looked up and whistled. "Nice place."

We were just off Palace Gate, only a few blocks from Kensington Palace, a neighborhood dotted with embassies and high-end townhouses — the type where people decorated with genuine masterpieces, not cheap prints of Monet's water lilies.

The building before us was divided into four units. Mina scanned the options, then rang a bell marked *A. Petrova*.

"Yes?" A voice came through the intercom.

"Hello. I'm Wilhelmina Durand, calling on behalf of Gordon Clervaud."

"Third floor," the woman replied, buzzing us in.

Mina craned her neck as we climbed the central stairway — a grand but squeaky stairway, like the one in Mina's château. I doubted these residents did their own home repairs, though.

We climbed to the third-floor landing, where an apartment door opened — just a tiny sliver, though. It was secured by a laughably thin chain that wouldn't hold up to a preschooler, let alone a dragon shifter. I could have kicked through it in an instant.

I didn't, of course. Not after Mina had nagged me about good manners the whole way over.

An older woman studied us through that gap, though all I saw of her was one pale blue eye, a halo of white hair, and a few beads of her pearl necklace.

She eyed me suspiciously. "Gordon only mentioned his god-daughter."

"This is... um..." Mina waved at me.

"Security detail, ma'am," I said quickly.

The lady shut the door, and I couldn't tell if I'd convinced her or blown the whole deal.

Then, whew. The woman fumbled with the chain, opened the door, and greeted Mina. "Anastasia Petrova — but please, call me Ana. Do come in."

Her English was flawless but layered with a light Slavic accent. My mind put the clues together — old associate of Gordon's, rich, plus the accent — and decided *widow of a Russian oligarch* was most likely. That also fit the icons on display in the entryway and the floor-to-ceiling bookshelves packed with Cyrillic titles.

Our shoes clicked over intricate parquet floors, then padded over thick Persian rugs. My eyes roved, taking in molded ceilings and walls covered with paintings. *Nice place* was an understatement. It was huge and vaguely regal, as if its owners hobnobbed with the residents of Kensington Palace.

But it was all a little aged and dusty, like the help hadn't been by in a long time — and not too many visitors either. There were gaps on the walls too, where artwork had been recently removed or sold.

I glanced at our hostess. Had her funds dried up when her husband died (or been bumped off), leaving her struggling to maintain her old lifestyle?

Anastasia led us to a living room with a plush but faded sofa and armchairs.

"Please make yourself comfortable. I'll fetch the tea."

Her words were aimed at Mina, not me, so while she settled onto the sofa, I headed for a corner where I could keep an eye on Mina, the door, and the windows.

I hissed quietly, then jerked my head to the right.

Mina frowned, then scooched along the couch, watching me.

I made a *stop* motion, then nodded.

She rolled her eyes and spoke into my mind. *Is this really necessary?*

Moving her out of the clearest line of sight from the front aspect of the building? Yes.

Standard procedure, I growled back.

When Anastasia returned, she served sandwich slices and bite-sized cakes from a three-tiered platter that screamed *teatime in Britain.* The tea was served Russian-style, however, in glasses set in silver holders, and the hot water came from a samovar in the adjoining room.

"Oh, one more thing..."

When Anastasia toddled off again, Mina held up her glass and tapped the design on the holder.

I squinted at the rocket and letters engraved into the silver. I knew enough of the Cyrillic alphabet to slowly spell out *Sputnik* — the first satellite launched into space, way back in the 1950s. A truly vintage, old-school piece. Like its owner, I surmised.

"There." Anastasia added a plate of lemon wedges to the coffee table and took a seat. "Now, tell me about yourself, dear."

Mina considered, then started haltingly.

"Well, Gordon and my father were close friends. My mother is French, my father American..."

Understandably, she left out the *supernatural* part and the part about her château.

"I majored in art and art history, and I worked as a middle school art teacher..." Her eyes lit up as she summarized that aspect of her résumé. "I also worked at an auction house, so I'm familiar with the process of authenticating paintings."

Anastasia asked about siblings, places Mina had lived, and politics, studying her like a hawk the whole time. This wasn't chitchat. This was judging whether Mina could be trusted.

With your life, and definitely with precious artwork, I burned to say. *She even risked her life for a lousy Van Gogh.*

My dragon grumbled at the memory, and Mina coughed into her hand.

Watch it, she warned.

Then Anastasia drilled Mina on art. What were her favorite styles, painters, and artworks? What was most important in Impressionism — the light, the moment, or what a painting left unsaid? What about post-Impressionism? If Mina could have brought another guest to tea with Anastasia—

I shuffled, trying not to take that personally.

—would she pick Kandinsky, Toulouse-Lautrec, or Modigliani?

Mina giggled. "Oh, definitely Modigliani."

I made a mental note to look up the guy.

Clearly, that was an A-plus answer in Anastasia's book. Before long, they were laughing and chattering like old friends. I quickly lost the plot as they discussed artists, movements, and paintings the way some people talked about sports teams, players, and incredible plays.

"If you could commission any artist from any era to paint any subject, what would it be?" Anastasia asked next.

Mina laughed. "Well, seven-year-old me would ask Franz Marc to paint a unicorn or a pegasus."

Anastasia flashed an indulgent smile. "What would you ask for today?"

Mina thought it over, gazing out the window. "Does it have to be a famous artist?"

Our hostess shook her head.

Mina cleared her throat, but her voice was still a little husky when she spoke.

"I would ask my father to paint a family picnic at my grandmother's house. And I would like to stand beside him and talk while he worked."

Anastasia sat quietly, picking up on Mina's bittersweet tone. A lump formed in my throat, because she'd brought me to that picnic spot not too long ago and shared the memories that made it so special.

Your grandmother's house, *huh?* I threw the tease into Mina's mind to lighten the moment.

Should I have said château? she shot back while sipping her tea.

No one would think you snobby, I pointed out. *Not in this neighborhood.*

"Your father was an artist?" Anastasia asked.

"He was an art historian, but he painted in his spare time." Mina flashed a sentimental smile, then turned the question back on Ana. "What painting would you commission, and by which artist?"

Ana smiled slyly. "I wouldn't have to. I already have the painting I would wish for."

Mina bit her lip, then quietly ventured, "I would love to see it."

She hit exactly the right tone, not too pushy or eager. Just another passionate art lover, like Anastasia.

Anastasia waved to the cakes and sandwiches. "Please, help yourself first."

Was that a yes or a no to seeing the painting?

Mina might have been burning with the same question, but neither of us had eaten for hours, and she tore into a triangular cucumber sandwich, then devoured a second one. Tuna.

Saliva pooled in my mouth, but neither Anastasia nor Mina took mercy. I sighed.

Eventually, Anastasia folded her napkin daintily and got down to business.

"Lovely chatting with you. Truly. But I did ask Gordon for an expert to help me with my painting."

I winced. It would kill Mina if this fell apart before she could see the mystery painting. Even if it didn't prove to be anything much, her curiosity was definitely piqued. It was like leaving a dragon to stare at a locked treasure chest. Torture, in a word.

Mina nodded. "I understand. But since you were, er...careful about sharing the details of your painting..."

I held back a snort. That was putting it mildly.

"...Gordon didn't know which expert to contact," Mina continued. "So he asked me to make a preliminary assessment. That will allow him to be equally discreet when it comes to engaging a respected expert to authenticate your piece."

"Oh, it's authentic. I guarantee it. But my late husband taught me to always ask myself, how do I know whether a person is trustworthy?"

Mina flashed a tight smile. "I ask myself that all the time."

I tensed. Did that mean me?

Then Mina added, "But even more important is whether I can trust my own judgment, I think."

Anastasia shrugged. "Two sides of the same coin. So, tell me. How do you decide about someone?"

Mina thought it over. "I think of a person's deeds instead of their words. I think of the little things..."

My mind sped away, desperately trying to catalogue everything I'd ever said or done around Mina.

Her sky-blue eyes slipped to mine, then jerked back to her hostess. "I tell myself not to trust my heart, but sometimes, I can't help it."

My soul warmed, and Mina flushed a little. And, damn. Her skin took on a glimmer, especially around the neck. Was that the sign of a moonlight mark, as I feared?

Anastasia refilled her teacup. "Are you saying I should trust you?"

Mina shook her head. "I'm saying you should make your own decision."

Anastasia stirred her tea for a while, then turned to me. "And what about you?"

I blinked. "Me?"

She nodded. "What do you think? Can I trust this woman?"

Ha. Easy answer.

I nodded. "Her only fault is her honesty."

Anastasia chuckled. "And you? Any faults?"

I shuffled a little. "Too many to list, ma'am."

She laughed outright. "I like him." She turned back to Mina. "And I like you." With that, she stood. "Come. Let me show you my painting."

"How is honesty a fault?" Mina muttered as Anastasia led us to the upper story of her maisonette.

I munched down the sandwiches I'd snagged off the tray before following her, using that as an excuse not to answer.

"It's here, in my study." Anastasia led the way into one of three rooms at the front of the building.

I wondered, not for the first time, what rich people studied.

Light poured in from two large windows, while a third window, between them, remained curtained. Paintings hung frame-to-frame on the side walls, though a couple of gaps showed. Anastasia had recently sold some of her artwork. I was sure of it. And now, she'd contacted Gordon about selling her greatest masterpiece?

I wondered what it was. How much it was worth. Why she wasn't selling the rest first if this was her favorite.

"Have a seat. It's best viewed from here." Anastasia sat on the sofa that faced the windows and patted the space beside her. Mina joined her.

"Will you do the honors?" Anastasia asked me, gesturing to the curtain over the middle window.

I stepped over, looking for the drawstring that would open the curtains. They stirred, and I caught a glimpse of blue paint on canvas. So, that wasn't a window behind there, but a painting. A big one, with portrait, not landscape orientation.

Taking hold of the drawstring, I looked at Anastasia. When she nodded, I pulled, revealing the painting.

Mina's eyes went wide, and she covered her mouth in shock.

I glanced at the painting, then back at her. What?

A tear slipped out of her eye. Then another and another.

I cocked my head at the painting. Was it that bad or that good?

Anastasia patted her hand. "It really is something, isn't it?"

Mina nodded, speechless.

I frowned. The painting was bold. Colorful. But truthfully, a little basic. A couple of horses, some mountains, and a rainbow. I wouldn't cry over that. Hell, I wouldn't even sniffle.

But Mina stared at the painting with tears running down both cheeks.

Chapter Twelve

MINA

Anastasia handed me a tissue, and I did my best to pull myself together. But, heck. It was like glimpsing the ghost of a loved one you thought you would never, ever see again. My heart fluttered, and my skin prickled with goose bumps.

Marius tilted his head at me, then at the painting, confused.

"Franz Marc. *The Tower of Blue Horses*," I murmured.

Recognition dawned on his face. "Like the horses on your mug?"

I smiled. "A lot like that."

The mug was my father's, actually, and the only one I refused to share.

The horses stood one behind the other as if on an incline, giving the painting its name — *The Tower of Blue Horses*. Filling the right side of the long canvas with energy, curves, and sharp lines, they gazed left over a stylized mountain landscape.

Marius put a hand on my shoulder, letting me cry, while signaling he was there for me. The man was definitely a keeper.

Crying felt silly, but I couldn't help it. Why? Because of the sheer beauty of that artwork. Because of my father, who would have given an arm to find this masterpiece. Because of Franz Marc and everyone killed in senseless wars — people with great talent and potential, snuffed out at a tragically young age.

I reached up to touch Marius's hand. He might not understand why that painting meant so much, but he respected that it was important to me, and I loved him for that.

Well, I loved him for a lot of things.

"This painting has been lost for decades," I explained, then caught myself. "If it's the real thing."

Anastasia snorted. "Not lost. Carefully guarded. And as for genuine, have a look for yourself."

I stood to inspect it. But it was very much like the Van Gogh I'd come across in Mallorca — I already knew it was real. I could sense it. A true masterpiece had an aura to it, as if marked by the artist's passion and genius.

Was that one of my magical abilities, or did I simply have a practiced eye? I wasn't sure which, but boy, did that painting look like the real thing.

I leaned closer, checking the canvas...the brush-strokes...the kaleidoscopic effect on the horses' bodies...

My eyes stopped at a line that didn't fit in — then another, and another.

"Sadly, there was some damage," Anastasia explained, seeing my reaction. "My father had it repaired, but a keen eye can spot it."

Her father, huh? I tucked that tidbit away for later.

"We call it the painting's war wound," she chuckled. "Something only healed after its long journey home."

My mind conjured images of war-torn landscapes, weary soldiers, and officers snapping up booty under the guise of reparations.

Franz Marc had painted *The Tower of Blue Horses* in 1913, not long before joining the German army to fight in World War I. He'd died at the Battle of Verdun, along with hundreds of thousands of other soldiers. The painting had ended up in the private collection of a top-ranking Nazi before disappearing in the last, chaotic days of World War II. So, Anastasia's story fit.

Most art historians agreed the artwork had been carted off by the Soviet Army, while others believed it to be locked in a Swiss vault. But here it was today, in London. Right in front of me.

I wanted to pinch myself. To grab my phone and call my mom, sister, and cousin. Better yet, to shout to heaven. *Big news, Dad! The Tower of Blue Horses has surfaced — in London!*

He would have had so many questions, as did I. But I had to be sure it was the real thing in a way I could explain to Gordon.

I leaned in, studying every detail, like the crescent moon and stars painted into the curves of the horses' bodies. Then I touched the frame and turned to Anastasia.

"May I?"

When she nodded, I eased the painting away from the wall to peek at the back. Marius held it while I flashed my phone light. I saw traces of a stamped inscription as well as slanting script, though I couldn't make out the details. Those could probably be traced to a museum or art dealer to establish the painting's authenticity.

Would that convince an expert? I was sure it would, and anyway, this was definitely worth Gordon's time to follow up on.

"Incredible," I said, returning to the couch to stare at it.

Anastasia smiled. "It is, isn't it?"

Marius shuffled behind me, bringing my mind back to business.

"Gordon said you wanted to have someone evaluate it," I murmured. "Does that mean you hope to sell it?"

She nodded sadly. "I'm an old woman, and it's time to put my affairs in order."

I followed her gaze to the cracks in the plaster walls and dust on the chandelier. And those were just the superficial jobs needed in one room of many.

Boy, could I relate. Would I find myself in Anastasia's position someday, selling my most prized possession to finance my living expenses? Worse, would possessions be all I had to show for my life, rather than years of health, love, and happy memories?

I gulped and made a mental note to myself. *Check own priorities.*

"I hate to part with it," Anastasia said, "But selling it now allows me to ensure it goes into the right hands."

My heart thumped as I asked the million-dollar question —
or rather, the multimillion-dollar question, given the painting's
value.

"By the right hands, you mean. . ."

"Someone who will love, cherish, and protect it the way I
have."

My heart sank, because that sounded a lot like *hidden in a
private collection.*

Still, I played dumb. "You mean, like a museum?"

She scoffed, clearly disappointed in me. "Oh, my dear.
Don't you know? Museums are fine in theory, but they're run
by political appointees and mediocrities."

I had a few negative opinions of my own, but none quite as
cutting.

"So, not a museum," I said flatly.

In my imagination, the horses in the painting stamped and
snorted, equally unhappy with such an outcome.

Anastasia shook her head vehemently. "I refuse to let it
go to a museum, a capitalist, or an egoist." Her face twisted
with anger, and her hands cut the air as she spoke. "They're
criminals, all of them. And I can't let it back into Russia. . ."

"Would you prefer it remain in England, then?" I tried.

She snorted. "Royalists make up a third of this country,
and the other two-thirds are provincials who read the *Daily
Mail.*"

I blinked. For a little old lady, she could get pretty damn
vicious.

"It must go to someone who knows art. Who appreciates
it," she continued. "Someone like you, dear, though I doubt
you can afford it." She patted my hand agreeably.

I winced. She was right, but it would have been nice to put
that a little more delicately.

"Pity," I murmured.

"But I'm sure the next guardian of this remarkable masterpiece can be located," Anastasia went on in a slightly happier
tone. "That's why I contacted Gordon."

In my imagination, the horse at the top of the tower whin-
nied in alarm.

Marius tapped me on the shoulder. "Don't forget about your next appointment."

There was no other appointment. He was pulling the plug on this, and I couldn't blame him. But I never wanted to leave. I gazed at the painting, trying to imprint it in my memory forever.

"We still have that cake downstairs," Anastasia suggested.

Normally, my sweet tooth would make me jump at such an offer, but I'd lost my appetite. The painting was destined to disappear for another generation, only to be seen by a few elites. An elite I didn't belong to, along with most of the world's art lovers.

"No thank you," I said.

Silence fell over the room, and Anastasia looked at me intently.

"Yes?" I asked as politely as I could.

"Aren't you going to ask to take a photo?"

Ha. If Gen were here, she would be snapping selfies with the painting. But that didn't feel right somehow.

"No photo can capture what I feel when I look at it," I said.

That must have been a test of sorts, because Anastasia smiled. "Good girl. However, I insist that you take a photo — although only of one corner, in order to convince Gordon's expert of its authenticity."

I considered briefly, then snapped a shot of the lower right corner, showing part of one horse's legs and chest against a red background. Then I went back to soaking it all in.

It was one of those all-too-fleeting moments I wanted to capture forever, because I might never experience the magic of it again. Like an especially spectacular Maine sunset I'd watched with my father, many years ago, or the first time Marius had truly smiled at me.

He cleared his throat, signaling it was time to go.

"So, I'll hear from you soon?" Anastasia moved toward the door.

I didn't follow. I couldn't. Just another few seconds...

"Yes, but it's likely to take a few weeks to make the arrangements," I replied.

"Weeks? How many?" Worry clanged loud and clear in Anastasia's voice.

Apparently, she was in a rush. Why?

I shrugged. "It's hard to say, but I can't imagine it will be less than four weeks. More like six, I suspect."

"Six weeks?" she cried. "No. It must be sooner."

Her voice went shrill, revealing a woman accustomed to getting what she wanted, when she wanted.

"I'll be sure to pass that on to Gordon," I said.

Another shake of the head, because that wasn't good enough. "I need it sold by October 28 at the very latest."

A suspiciously exact deadline. Suspicious enough for me to heed Marius's insistent gesture to get moving.

I looked at the painting one last time, counting down the seconds on my self-imposed deadline. A huge lump formed in my throat as a thousand emotions rose up, trying to escape.

Anastasia kissed me on both cheeks, urging me to act quickly. Then I turned and marched out the door, leaving that painting — that dream come true — behind me forever.

∞∞∞∞

Neither Marius nor I spoke until we were several blocks away. He was back in bodyguard mode, studying our surroundings for potential threats, while my mind remained on Franz Marc's horses.

"Don't even think of getting involved in this," he finally grumbled.

I scoffed. "Because a little old lady and her painting can be so dangerous?"

"A little old lady and a valuable painting," he countered. "Or am I wrong?"

I shook my head. "Very, very valuable."

"How valuable?"

I thought it over. "Another Franz Marc painting — *The Foxes* — sold a few years ago for fifty-six million dollars."

He stopped in his tracks. "Fifty-six million?"

I nodded, waving back in the direction we'd come from. "But that painting would be worth much, much more. It would be the find of the century, if it came into the public eye."

Marius's skeptical look told me what he put those odds at.

"Fifty-six million reasons for you to stay away from it," he warned.

I scowled, but he was right.

He touched my cheek, then showed me the red smudge on his finger.

"Anastasia went a little heavy on the lipstick," he explained.

That made me smile, but a block later, I found myself pouting a little.

"Well, I've done what Gordon asked, so I won't be involved any more."

I ought to have consoled myself with having seen the painting in person, but my mind was too busy releasing those horses into an open, rugged landscape, as their creator intended. A painting like that shouldn't be hidden away for only a few to see. It should be out in the world and celebrated.

"Gordon is going to have a hell of a time finding a buyer that fits Anastasia's specifications," I added. "I don't think his network includes any art aficionados who aren't capitalists, crooks, or... what was it?"

"Mediocrities," Marius grumbled. "Another reason you don't want to get involved."

I tilted my head in question.

"A class act like you mixing with the rabble?" He shook his head at the notion.

Ha. Me, a class act? My fingernails were chipped and caked with flecks of old paint from all that scraping I'd been doing.

Marius pulled me along for another few blocks, making a beeline for the nearest Tube station. The sights and shops of Kensington High Street were a blur to me, though. All I saw were those horses, prancing impatiently in place on the wall in Anastasia's lovely but fading apartment.

Chapter Thirteen

MINA

I thought about the painting and its fate throughout my trip back to Paris. A vampire-free trip, thanks to Marius, but one still fraught with fears and anxieties.

"Repeat after me," Marius insisted before I left him to report back to my godfather. "I will not get involved in any of Gordon's deals."

"I will not get involved in any of Gordon's deals," I echoed sullenly.

"I will not do any favors for him, no matter how innocent they seem," Marius went on.

I echoed that too, partly through gritted teeth.

Marius was right, but I hated the situation. *Really* hated it to the point that it consumed me. I wanted to find a buyer for *The Tower of Blue Horses* — someone who would do the right thing. I wanted to trust my godfather again. I wanted to live my life without worrying about criminals, vampires, and unseen enemies.

On the plus side, seeing the painting made me feel closer to my father. We'd always been close, but he hadn't lived long enough for us to talk as adults. Now, an entire conversation played out in my soul. A dialogue about art, ownership, and sharing, as well as principles, risk, and responsibility.

My father, I knew, would urge me to act on principle and make sure that painting found its way into good hands.

My mother would tell me principles didn't pay bills and that I could find plenty of responsibility closer to home — like at the château.

Mom and Marius won out. I reported to Gordon and hopped on a train to Burgundy the very next morning. The same familiar landscape blurred by, and many of the same thoughts occupied my mind.

Marius escorted me all the way home, but he turned around and headed back to Paris after a short, private powwow with Roux and Bene. He was hell-bent on hunting down Szabo and Etienne, or whoever had sent the threatening message with the photo. His plans for returning to the château were vague, though. So vague, I worried he might never return.

He didn't even accept a ride to the nearest train station. Not from me, at least. Roux drove him.

"Seriously?" I gaped, seeing him off at the front steps.

"It's better this way," Marius said, a little hoarsely.

Better in what way? I wanted to scream.

I thought he might leave without a further word, but he cupped my face and kissed me, soft as a whisper, hinting at deep — and deeply hidden — emotions.

When Roux revved the van in a none-too-subtle hint, it took everything I had not to cling to Marius. But a meek little groupie, I was not. I could be strong when I wanted.

I just chose not to at that particular moment.

Please don't go, I nearly begged, though I managed to croak, "See you soon?" instead.

The hesitation before his nod killed me.

"As soon as possible," was all he said, making me *really* want to cling to him.

When he drew away, I closed my eyes, listening to his shoes scuff over the stairs, then the van door shutting. I listened for a long time after the sound of wheels over gravel faded. Then I stepped inside without risking so much as a glance down the driveway. If I did, I might be tempted to run after him, and there was no dignity in that.

"Coffee?" Bene offered quietly.

I sighed and looked around the vast entrance hallway. The carpet runner up the center of the stairs was torn and faded. The massive chandelier was made up of hundreds of crystals, and each desperately needed cleaning. The ceiling molding was just as dingy, and that was thirty feet up.

I started calculating the price of scaffolding, cleaning, and new carpeting, but just thinking about it made me despair.

"Coffee *and* cake?" Bene tried, doing his best to cheer me.

My heart wasn't in it, but hey. Cake was good for the soul, and my soul definitely needed it.

∞∞∞∞

"So, how was Paris?" Bene asked, taking the seat opposite mine in the drawing room.

I took in the peaceful, leafy view out the huge rear windows, so different from any scene in London or Paris.

"Fine." I sipped my coffee. "Gordon sends his regards."

Bene snorted. "He did not."

No, but it seemed like the polite thing to say.

I looked around. "Where's Henrik?"

He shrugged. "No sign of him since... er... "

"Since he attacked me?" I filled in, then grunted, not all politely, "Good."

Bene smiled, but his eyes didn't sparkle with humor the way they usually did. We spent the next few minutes in silence — silence so profound, it practically echoed through the empty rooms of the château.

Minutes later, I sighed and spoke my mind. "I liked it better when you were all here."

He nodded quietly. "I liked it better too."

As we lapsed back into silence, I rued the decisions I'd made. Did I really want to kick Bene, Roux, and Marius out of the château? Or should I accept reality, host the police championships, and move on with my life?

I found myself clenching my fists, telling myself to fight like hell for the man I loved — and for my friends. They'd always come through for me when it really counted, but they had a way of letting me down when it came to countless smaller things.

My mood changed gears. Clem, in contrast, brought me cake, tore up parking tickets, and generally treated me like a goddess. Wasn't friendship a better foundation for a strong relationship than raw passion?

I sighed again. Maybe if I focused on renovations for a few days, things would fall into place. I just hoped they wouldn't plunge into an abyss.

"More coffee?" Bene offered.

"Please." I set my mug in front of him.

The morning had been chilly, so I'd started with my hoodie zipped tight. As the coffee warmed me up, I unzipped the hoodie a few inches.

Bene glanced up briefly, then did a double take, splattering coffee over the table as he stared at my neck.

Crap. Had Marius given me a hickey that night we'd gotten all hot and heavy in Paris?

"Dammit," he muttered, grabbing a napkin to blot the spill, though he peeked at me several more times.

I zipped my sweatshirt high and hid behind my coffee cup.

Bene gulped down his own refill, then stood abruptly. "Gotta go, sorry. Work calls."

I watched him go, unsettled. Bene only ever rushed to meals. What had gotten into him?

I touched my neck, then shook my head and finished my own coffee. I had a château to fix, and progress wouldn't be made sitting around feeling sorry for myself.

∞∞∞∞∞

I walked around the house, reviewing where I'd left off on various tasks. I started in the ballroom, where I was sure I'd only scraped paint from two of the floor-to-ceiling windows and stripped wallpaper from one corner. But I found all five windows scraped, sanded, and primed, along with two walls free of wallpaper.

I continued upstairs, where I'd tested how time-consuming it would be to remove hopelessly outdated bathroom tiles. And, oh. The walls were bare. Two big boxes stood in a corner, one with rubble, another with carefully stacked tiles and remnants.

Wow. Roux and Bene hadn't been lazing around while I'd been away.

Next, I wandered through the dining room, where I'd fought an ongoing battle to keep the area free of half-filled mugs, dirty plates, and used silverware. Now, it was spotless.

I swallowed hard, looking around.

Madame Picard had left a dinner of *coq au vin*, and Roux, Bene, and I shared it that evening in silence. They kept peeking at my neck, and I kept cursing the hickey Marius had given me. I hadn't been able to spot it in a mirror, but I could feel the warmth emanating from it.

We sat in the dining room, a vast, empty space that crowded in from every direction, all the more so when I pictured eating alone once everyone moved out. Was that really what I wanted?

"Thank you," I murmured at some point. "For the ballroom. For the bathroom tiles. For everything."

Roux kept his eyes on his plate. Bene shrugged. "Must have been the house elves."

Ha. Lion- and tiger-size house elves, no doubt.

"Well, the elves accomplished a lot, and I'm grateful."

Bene looked at Roux, who nodded.

"The elves were wondering what to do next — more wallpaper or the other bathrooms?" Bene asked.

Guilt washed over me. Did I really want to terminate our contact early and get them in trouble?

My voice was a little shaky when I replied. "Either would be great. Thank you."

Roux nodded silently, then motioned to Bene. "Pass the pepper."

Bene huffed. "I'll tell Madame Picard."

Roux's eyes took on an offended glow. "Pass the goddamn pepper." He snatched it from Bene's hand, then muttered, "If you tell Madame Picard, I'll kill you."

I didn't know whether to laugh or groan. A girl ought to watch what she wished for.

A week passed without a word from Marius — and not a lot of words from Bene or Roux either. Leaving the ballroom to them, I took measurements for new fixtures in the upstairs bathrooms. Sunlight streamed through the windows in the adjoining room — Marius's room, technically — drawing me toward it. I gazed out, catching a glimpse of a tiger moving smoothly across the lawn before blending into the shadows of the forest.

I looked the other way, spotting a lion sunning himself on the patio. With a faint smile, I looked into the sky, half expecting to see a dragon.

Then I frowned, and my heart ached, because Marius was gone.

I stood there for a long time, thinking about him. Us. *The Tower of Blue Horses.* Wishing I could take action — any action — on any of those things.

Then I looked around, despairing at all the work awaiting me. This was just one room in a huge château. How would I ever get it all done?

My eyes caught on the wall beside one window — a big, blank space perfect for a painting. Like *The Tower of Blue Horses*, for example. But who was I kidding?

A fit of anger took over me, followed by a sudden inspiration, and I rushed to the stash of paint cans we'd salvaged during a recent clean-out of the stables. Picking out the colors I needed, I schlepped the cans to Marius's bedroom. A second trip secured me brushes and a roller, and in no time, I'd coated the corner wall in off-white paint. Then I cleaned my hands and dashed to the library for one of my father's art books.

"Lunchtime," Bene called from downstairs.

I wasn't hungry, but the paint needed to dry, so I opened every window and joined Bene and Roux for a sandwich. Afterward, I hurried back upstairs with a pencil. I studied the art book for a while, then began to outline on the wall. Four lumps to the right and a row of inverted V shapes on the left. I blocked out areas for each of the key figures, then double- and triple-checked that everything balanced.

"Dinner," Bene hollered, though I could have sworn no more than an hour had passed.

But, oh. It was a growing dark outside, and hmm. Was that my stomach rumbling?

"Mina," Bene called impatiently. He even rang the service bell only Madame Picard was allowed to use.

"Go ahead without me," I called.

That became a familiar refrain over the next few days. I sweated over renovations all day, then awarded myself an hour to work on my painting before dinner. Sometimes, I worked straight through dinner. I was that driven to complete the one thing in my control.

Bene and Roux started bringing meals up to me. During lunch on the fourth day, they pulled out a couple of chairs and sat facing the wall as if it were a wide-screen TV.

"What are you doing?" I asked.

"Watching." Roux balanced a plate piled with food on his lap.

"This is about as interesting as watching paint dry," I said. "Literally."

Bene spoke through a mouthful of food. "Sadly, that's still more interesting than anything else going on here." He looked on for another minute, then murmured, "It's kind of like watching a really, really slow movie. One of those French ones that makes no sense."

Roux shook his head. "It's beautiful."

Was it? I stepped off the ladder I'd used to reach the top section for a better look.

And, wow. It *was* beautiful, now that I was close to finishing.

Four blue horses stood in a tight stack, swishing their tails. They all gazed left over a row of mountains and to the real view outside the window.

"What is it?" Bene asked.

To my surprise, Roux beat me to it. "Franz Marc. *The Tower of Blue Horses.*"

Wow. Either he knew his art, or he'd been talking to Marius. I certainly hadn't mentioned it.

Bene shook his head. "Nah. This one's by Mina." He peeked at the original in my father's art book, then nodded firmly. "And it's way better than that one."

Not by a long shot, but I appreciated the sentiment.

Bene set his plate aside and leafed through a few pages of the book, then tilted it toward Roux. "Oh, look. A tiger." Then he continued through the pages, murmuring as he went. "Horse...horse...mule...monkey... Boy, this guy really liked animals."

Roux held out the plate he'd brought for me, and I grabbed a sandwich.

"More horses..." Bene continued. "A dog...a deer..." He reached the end of the book and looked up in disappointment. "Not a single lion?"

I shook my head. "I don't think he painted any."

Bene shook his head in disbelief. "The man paints every animal on Noah's Ark but skips the king of the jungle?"

I decided not to comment.

He continued looking through the book, then tapped on a photo. "Most of these paintings are upbeat, but this one is a little scary."

I looked at *The Wolves*. "Franz Marc painted it on the eve of World War I."

Roux's eyes took on a distant look, and I wondered what combat zone — or zones — he'd served in before leaving the military.

"Well, I like yours better." Bene thumped the book down.

"Me too," Roux murmured.

"Oh! You could do the whole room." Bene lit up, delighted with his own idea. "Monkey over there. Deer over there. And a big lion, right there." He gestured to the most prominent wall in the room.

"What about a tiger?" Roux protested.

Bene shrugged. "Maybe over by the closet."

I hid a laugh, then sobered, wondering how to paint a dragon in the style of Franz Marc, and whether I had the heart to try it.

"Seriously. You want to rent these rooms out, right?" Bene continued. "And since boring old châteaux are a dime a dozen—"

I nearly choked on my sandwich. Boring?

"—you need to stand out." Bene waved around. "With an art theme, for instance."

"Not a bad idea," Roux admitted.

"It's a *great* idea," Bene declared. "We could have a Frank Marc room..."

"Franz," I corrected.

"Whatever." Bene breezed on. "A water lily room by what-shisname..."

"Monet," I murmured.

"A Van Gogh room," Roux chimed in. "Didn't he paint his bedroom in Arles? You could decorate in the same style."

Wow. He really did know his art. And, double wow. What a cool idea.

"We could fix up the bathrooms the same way..." Bene continued.

"We'd have to decorate the entrance too," Roux mused.

"And clean up the garden. Oh, and the hedge maze." Bene's eyes lit up. "Can we clean up the maze?"

I laughed, because he'd been fixated on that maze from day one.

"That's phase four of the project," I said, trying to slow him down.

"We should move it to phase one," he declared.

Roux shook his head. "Plumbing and wiring come first."

Bene snorted. "Do you know anything about wiring, man?"

Roux made a face. "How hard can it be?"

That spun off into a whole new argument. I followed with amusement until it hit me. There would be no *we*. Soon, it would just be *me*.

And just in case my heart hadn't crashed low enough yet, Roux's phone rang.

He frowned and answered. "*Allô?*" His frown deepened, and his amber eyes cautiously met mine. "Oh. Hello, Gordon."

Bene and I froze.

Roux winced. "You want us in Paris? Tomorrow?"

My stupid hopes crumbled, because *us* meant *them*, not me, and one more mission meant one more rift dividing our little community. Worse, one more chasm between Marius and me.

Roux's eyebrows popped up at whatever Gordon said next, and he stared at me. "You'd like Mina to come too?"

My heart thudded. Was it about Marius? The painting?

"Yes, I'll check with her." Roux looked at me.

The guys didn't *check* orders from Gordon. They were supposed to follow them to the letter, no questions asked.

But check Roux did, giving me an out if I needed.

I found myself asking why I had ever considered evicting him or Bene.

Slowly, I nodded.

Roux waited a long time, willing me to rethink that.

I nodded again, more firmly.

He didn't look happy, but he relayed the message to Gordon. "Yes, sir. She says she's available."

More like at his beck and call. But if it meant seeing Marius — or getting another look at the painting — I was in.

Roux listened briefly, then nodded. "Yes, sir. Noon tomorrow, at your office. We'll be there."

Chapter Fourteen

MARIUS

"Marius." Roux greeted me with a nod.

It was a cool, wet day in Paris. The wind rushed up the Canal Saint-Martin, making Roux's jacket flutter.

Bene was right behind him, and Mina behind him. It took everything I had not to rush over and hug her.

"Hello, Marius," she said casually.

A bluff, but one she pulled off better than I did.

"*Bonjour,*" I managed on my second attempt. The first got caught in my throat.

The next gust of wind teased her hair — and my heart. During the nights we'd spent together, I'd often stayed awake just to marvel at her. Her soft, trusting touch. Her light, peaceful smile. Her silky hair, splayed over the pillow...

Mina sucked in a sharp breath and jerked her eyes away.

Damn. Even after a week apart, our connection was stronger than ever.

A lifetime won't change that, my dragon growled.

Her scarf fluttered, catching my eye. One I'd never seen before. In fact, I'd never seen her wear a scarf at all.

My heart pounded. All week, I'd been wondering whether I'd marked her or not. What did the scarf mean?

Mina must have noticed my sharp look, because she fingered the scarf as we moved toward Gordon's front door and hissed, "It's hiding that hickey you gave me."

A hickey was the least of our problems, judging by the faint glow radiating from the edges. Damn. I really had given her a moonlight mark that night.

123

And the problem is...? my dragon rumbled proudly.

Big problem, though Mina seemed not to have noticed. Bene's knowing look said he had, however. Roux too. Had the scarf been their idea?

You're welcome, the tiger shifter grumbled into my mind.

I did my best to maintain my dignity by growling, *Hickey?*

Bene shrugged. *We thought we'd leave the explaining to you, champ.*

Can't believe you fucking marked her, Roux added.

I couldn't either. A moonlight mark was akin to an engagement announcement. What the hell had I been thinking?

Destiny, my dragon murmured happily.

Someday, I might be ready to take that step. But not without her permission, and not at a time like this.

It took forever to talk her into the scarf, not to mention the perfume, Bene added.

So that explained why her scent was more Coco Chanel than her usual blend of rose and lilac. Not a trace of my scent on her either.

Like I said, you're welcome, Roux muttered.

I owed them, big-time. But, damn. I did not look forward to explaining any of this to Mina.

Something else seemed off, and I looked around with a frown.

"Where's Henrik?"

Roux looked at Bene, who looked at the clouds. Mina crossed her arms and glared at no one in particular.

"He said he's coming," Roux finally said in a muted tone.

Four words, not a lot of context. What was going on?

By then, we'd reached Gordon's building. Bene bounded up the stairs and held the door open.

"Ladies first."

"Safety first," Roux muttered, squeezing through to enter before Mina.

The tiger annoyed me in a hundred different ways, but damn, could the guy be counted on to fulfill his brief. When he'd called me to pass on Gordon's orders, I'd made him swear to watch over Mina.

Which made me just as guilty of *few words, no context* as him, I supposed. But I had good reasons, dammit. What were his?

The past week at been hell, and though I'd put the fear of God into a number of old enemies, I'd come no closer to tracking down the source of the threatening message I'd received. My primary suspects, Etienne and Szabo, were nowhere to be found, and now, I'd had to put my search on hold and respond to Gordon's summons.

I cursed under my breath, counting down the days until I was free of my obligation to him.

Six weeks, my dragon grumbled, picturing a happily-ever-after with Mina.

I jutted my jaw, knowing it wasn't that simple.

The doorman waved us upstairs, and minutes later, we all filed into Gordon's living room — the formal living room, not the private one on the top story of his two-level penthouse. Mina had probably been up there, but I'd never been invited up the stairs that divided Gordon's work and personal life.

My dragon grumbled inside. *Mina shouldn't be here at all.*

No, but there she was, marching in ahead of Bene and Roux to kiss Gordon on both cheeks.

"Good to see you again," she murmured.

And, whew. He didn't seem to notice her rosy glow or the perfume masking my scent.

"Always lovely to see you, sweetheart," Gordon replied.

Funny how a guy could order a dozen cold-blooded hits, yet love his goddaughter.

The thing was, the bastard used her too. Mina was starting to catch on, but obviously, old loyalties were hard to break.

Behind us, the door opened, and Henrik breezed in, along with a slice of cold air. Mina tensed.

Henrik's dark eyes met hers, then hit the floor.

I bristled, ready to grab him by the collar and shake him hard. What the hell had he done?

Bene dug an elbow into my ribs. *Not now, man. Not here,* he barked into my mind.

What did he do? I demanded.

Bene's lips quirked. *Nothing we couldn't handle.*

Now, I was really alarmed. *What happened?*

Roux sighed into my mind. *Henrik lost control, but Bene stopped him.*

My stomach lurched.

None of that would have happened if you'd stuck around, champ, Bene grumbled, brushing by me to greet Gordon.

I bit back a growl. He was right, and that killed me. No matter what I tried, I couldn't win. Mina was in as much danger at home as she was with me.

So, stick with her, my dragon roared. *Easy solution.*

"Please take a seat, gentlemen."

Clearly, Gordon was on his best behavior around Mina. If it had been just us there, he would have us lined up like a goddamn chain gang.

My dragon sighed. *Not far from the truth.*

Another reason Mina ought to keep her distance. She was a sweet, classy art teacher. I was a dragon who would never fit in with the conventional world.

But her body sang to mine, even now, in the crappiest of circumstances.

"I've called you in because of a special project I've taken on," Gordon began.

I glanced at Mina, reminding her of the vow I'd made her take.

I will not get involved in any of Gordon's deals. I will not do any more favors for him, no matter how innocent they seem...

And boy, did Gordon's expression ooze innocence. Enough to choke a kitten, or even a tiger.

Roux shot me a dirty look. *Not to mention a dragon.*

"Mina kindly visited an acquaintance of mine in London last week," Gordon started.

Funny how *acquaintance* sounded so much better than *client* or *widow of an oligarch.*

"You made quite an impression." He grinned at Mina, who flashed a tight smile. "And you'll be glad to hear that an expert has authenticated the painting."

Mina bit her lip, proud yet dismayed.

"Not that I expected any other result." Gordon continued buttering Mina up before turning to us. "I've already contacted potential clients who are eager to view the painting. That means I need a security presence in London for the painting and for Mina."

"For me?" She blinked.

Uh-oh. Bene muttered in my mind. *Here he goes again.*

A growl built in my throat. This was classic Gordon, slipping things in as if no one would notice.

Gordon smiled sweetly. "I'm afraid I need to enlist your help again, my dear. Madame Petrova insists on having a trustworthy advisor at her side, and she won't trust anyone but you."

Mina's eyes went wide, but I wasn't surprised. Mina practically radiated trustworthiness. In fact, Gordon had probably been counting on that all along. Who better to create a veil of legitimacy than a young, principled art teacher?

He smiled at her. "I know it's a lot to ask, but I hope a few days in London might entice you, not to mention the chance to view that masterpiece again."

The bastard was laying it on thick, dammit.

Mina's eyes darted to me, then away. "As much as I appreciate the offer, I really can't accept."

I nearly did a fist pump.

Gordon frowned. "Of course you can."

And that's that, his tone added.

She glanced at me, and I willed her to keep up the resistance.

"I'd love to help, but..."

Gordon's smile grew a little forced. "As I said, Madame Petrova won't trust anyone but you."

Mina put a hand over her heart. "I'm touched. Really. But I think it's better to leave this to the experts. I'm sure Anastasia will feel as comfortable with someone from Christie's or Sotheby's."

A public auction, in other words.

Gordon shook his head. "She refuses to go that route. Too much bureaucracy, not to mention the outrageous commissions they charge."

My dragon snorted. *And too many questions about how she'd come into possession of a masterpiece that went missing during World War II.*

"Well, I can suggest a few museums..." Mina tried again.

Gordon nodded eagerly. "You can suggest them to Madame Petrova."

Not what she meant, and he knew it.

"But—"

Gordon cut in, practically patting Mina on the head like a child. "Working with Madame Petrova means you can ensure the painting finds its way into good hands."

Unlikely, given the contacts in his network.

Mina studied her feet miserably.

"Your father would be so excited. So proud," Gordon murmured.

Damn the bastard for going for her soft spot.

Mina's eyes went glassy, and I sensed the same roiling emotions she'd shown in London. The painting had made her weep, and I guessed that had as much to do with her father as the canvas.

"He would be." She flashed a sad smile.

Gordon's was more of a crocodile smile, and I knew she was done for.

"It's the opportunity of a lifetime," he said, giving the screws one more twist. "An opportunity your father would tell you to jump at."

Mina's throat bobbed, and she nodded slowly. "All right. I'll do it."

I winced. Bene and Roux too. Henrik looked at his fingernails, like he couldn't care less.

Gordon practically rubbed his hands in glee. "Wonderful, wonderful. You won't regret it."

Oh, she definitely would.

"Now, on to the logistics," Gordon continued. "As mentioned, I'll need security to travel to London with Mina — not that I expect any issues, of course."

Liar, my dragon rumbled.

"Therefore, Henrik will accompany Mina to London and remain there until the deal is closed."

Mina's eyes just about popped out of her head, and Henrik jerked his chin up.

"Henrik?" She paled.

"Me?" he protested at the same time.

My dragon lashed its tail in rage.

"Yes. Is there a problem?" Gordon's voice took on a dangerous tone.

Roux gritted his teeth, and Bene pleaded with Mina with his eyes. Henrik too. But I willed her to speak the truth. Anything to keep her safe, even if it doomed us.

Mina twisted her fingers in her lap as the clock ticked. Finally, she flashed a tight smile.

"No problem. That would be fine."

Bene shot her an incredulous look. "Say what?" When Gordon shot him the evil eye, Bene stuck his hands up. "I mean, well..."

"What he means to say, sir, is that I am better suited to the task," Roux interjected.

"He is," Bene, Henrik, and I spoke in chorus.

Mina exhaled.

"In what way?" Gordon growled.

His warlock power crackled through the air, making my hair prickle in alarm. None of us had ever witnessed Gordon's legendary power on full display, and we never wanted to.

"I'm more familiar with the art, sir," Roux said. "And I worked on the Loretti case last month. The one with the private auction of... er..." He trailed off, tilting his head toward Mina.

The Loretti case was an auction of a major arms shipment seized in Montenegro. I hadn't been part of it, but Roux and Bene had, and they'd shared some of the less savory details.

Gordon shot Roux a look of warning, because God forbid his goddaughter found out where his millions had *really* been earned.

"Roux does know a lot," Mina chimed in. "About art, I mean," she added when Gordon gave her a sharp look.

"I do, sir. Henrik just isn't suited to the task," Roux continued.

Normally, that would earn him a flash of fangs, but Henrik nodded immediately. "Not at all."

"And why might that be?" Gordon demanded.

"Because...er..." Roux looked around, but we were all stuck.

"Because Henrik is better suited to vetting potential buyers," Bene finally threw in.

"*Much* better suited," Roux underscored.

Which just went to prove that even felines could be brilliant sometimes.

Gordon stroked his chin, thinking. "So, Roux on security, and Henrik to vet prospective buyers." Then he nodded to himself. "Fine. Marius and Benedict, I'll need you back in Brussels."

My nostrils burned as my dragon protested, and I nearly roared. *Not an option.*

But Bene raised his hand first. "If I may, sir..."

"What now?" Gordon grumbled.

"Mina *and* the painting both need protection. That means two on security — Roux for the painting, and Marius for Mina."

I didn't know whether to kiss or kill him. Of course, I wanted to protect Mina. But staying close to her meant resisting temptation every day — and possibly tempting my enemies.

Fuck. I was so screwed.

"Then there's the payment," Bene went on. "If the deposit is made in cash..." He paused, scratching his cheek. "Or will cryptocurrency be accepted?"

Gordon huffed. "Of course not. Cash or bank transfer."

Preferably through his account in the Cayman Islands, I guessed.

"Well, if it's cash. . ." Bene trailed off.

Cash? Mina's horrified expression said. Nothing screamed *illegal* more than cash, especially in a deal worth millions.

". . . you'll need security to follow the cash too," Bene finished.

Gordon frowned. "You're right."

Bene's smug look said, *Of course. I'm always right.* Then he counted on his fingers and summarized. "So, that makes four working this case. Roux covers the painting. Marius covers Mina. Henrik vets buyers, and I make sure payment goes smoothly."

Gordon made a face. "Four staff?"

Bene shrugged. "You want to gamble with such a valuable painting and such influential clients? You want to gamble with Mina's life?"

"Of course not," Gordon conceded. "But four is excessive. And there's Brussels to consider."

"We can reschedule Brussels," Roux assured him.

Mina looked at Gordon with innocent, saucer-sized eyes. "I would feel better knowing every eventuality was covered."

Ha. Her turn to go for a cheap blow Gordon couldn't resist.

His face took on a sourpuss expression, but what could he say to that?

"Fine. You'll all go," he finally declared.

Mina gulped, glancing at me, then Henrik.

I knew how she felt. Was this a win or a terrible mistake?

Gordon checked his watch. "If we're lucky, there will still be seats available on one of the evening trains. I'll have Celeste check."

Mina froze, and it was all I could do not to growl. My investigations over the past week hadn't revealed any recent communications between Celeste and Szabo, but I still didn't trust the woman. And as for Szabo. . . I half hoped he would turn up. That way, I could kill him.

Gordon picked up his phone, dialed, and barked, "Get me five tickets on the train to London. Yes, tonight." He frowned at whatever Celeste said, then replied. "Two in premier — my goddaughter and Monsieur Aecher. Standard will be fine for the others — Messieurs Anand, Bembridge, and Velchynsky."

I shot a smug look at Roux, Bene, and Henrik, having scored a better seat than them.

But Mina looked pained, and I could already see her offering her seat to one of the others. Probably Bene, that ass.

"We'll also need reservations for a hotel near Madame Petrova's address. Get back to me as soon as you have something." Gordon hung up on Celeste without so much as a goodbye or *merci.*

Great. Another reason for Celeste to resent us.

To us, he said, "Prepare to depart. I'll be in touch as soon as the arrangements are made." Only Mina got a warm smile. "Thank you, sweetheart. I really appreciate it." Then he pinned me with a glare. "And you, Monsieur Aecher — I mean it when I say my goddaughter's safety is not to be compromised. Don't let her out of your sight."

My whole body heated, and Mina's eyes went wide.

My best dream — and worst nightmare — had just come true.

"Yes, sir," I vowed.

Gordon shooed us to the door. "Go on, then. All of you — except you, Monsieur Anand. I need a word."

Roux looked grim as the rest of us filed out, leaving him alone with Gordon.

Bene strode down the hallway, chipper as can be. "A couple of days in London. On a harmless art case, no less!"

Henrik scoffed. "As harmless as the last one?"

Bene shook his head. "We knew that would be tricky going in. This will be easy. I promise you."

Easy to resist Mina?

Ha. Just try, my dragon growled.

Chapter Fifteen

MINA

"All right. Everyone ready? It's time to get started," Roux began bright and early the next morning.

Well, not all that bright, but very early — barely dawn in London. We'd arrived on the last train from Paris the previous evening and fallen directly into bed.

Bene let his teeth extend, then slowly retract in a massive lion yawn. "Whose idea was a six o'clock meeting? And what about breakfast?"

"Room service is on the way, so you can eat while you work. And it's already seven in France," Roux pointed out.

We were gathered in the living room area of our hotel suite. Yes, a suite — a single, unlockable space I now shared with Marius, Roux, Bene, and Henrik.

God, did I hate Celeste. Couldn't she have put Henrik on a separate floor?

At least I trusted Roux and Bene to stay in the room they shared. I also trusted Marius. I just didn't trust *myself* around him.

But I didn't trust Henrik farther than I could throw a silk-lined coffin, no matter how ruddy and sated he seemed after his recent visit to Delphine.

It pained me to imagine that. How could poor, deluded Delphine love any vampire, let alone one as unsociable as Henrik?

Then again, I could be called deluded for loving Marius. For aching for him, morning, noon, and night, and even imagining a future together. Who was I to judge Delphine?

Henrik, on the other hand, was fair game, and my judgment of him was harsh and final. I hated the vampire, and I wanted him gone.

But he wasn't gone. He was bunked out in the room adjoining mine. Both rooms opened onto the living area, where Marius had slept on the couch.

We'll see how long that lasts, Roux had sighed the previous night.

Not long, I hoped, but Marius hadn't tiptoed into my room, no matter how hard I wished for him to.

But, no — no nocturnal visit from Marius. No visit from Henrik either, but I still hadn't slept well. No one had, judging by the bleary expressions of the others.

Roux checked his watch. "Mina is scheduled to meet Madame Petrova at ten. That gives us a few hours to look through Gordon's list of potential buyers and eliminate anyone who seems fishy. We're looking for candidates the client is likely to approve of who also have sufficient funds."

I frowned. "Define *sufficient.*"

"More than anyone else," Henrik said bluntly.

"Are you saying we want a bidding war?"

Henrik shrugged. "It's in the client's interest to get the highest amount possible."

"But Anastasia said she wants to sell it to the right person," I countered.

The vampire snorted. "Money always talks in the end."

"It's also in Gordon's interest to get the highest amount possible," Marius added a little more gently.

Gently, maybe, but it pounded yet another nail into the coffin of my innocence.

Gordon was earning a commission, I realized. I shouldn't have been surprised, but I was. Surprised and disappointed in Gordon — and in myself. I would get another chance to see a rare masterpiece, but at what price?

"Let's say two bidders offer a similar sum," Bene asked. "Who would Anastasia choose in the end?"

Roux scanned a sheet of paper covered with notes. "According to Gordon's intel, Madame Petrova has her principles, but they're scrambled as hell. Her father was a Red Army officer who entered Berlin in 1945 with one of the Soviet looting divisions assigned to 'safeguard' cultural treasures." He made air quotes. "That explains how the painting came into her possession."

I took mental notes, as if I might someday pen a footnote for an art history book.

Roux continued his briefing. "Our intel shows that Anastasia has always been a committed Marxist. She married an economist who was a communist visionary like her and equally immersed in Soviet cultural circles."

Bene raised an eyebrow. "Communist visionaries who end up in Kensington?"

Henrik nodded. "Paris and London are full of Marxists with gilded tastes. Once they experience the good life, they never go back."

Roux backed that up with the next part of his report. "Anastasia's husband rose through the ranks of post-Soviet finance, put his principles aside, and got rich during the Yeltsin era. He died eight years ago, leaving everything to her." He squinted at the report. "The summary here says, *a woman who believes in art for the people but despises most of the people she's met.*"

I sighed quietly. Yes, that certainly fit.

"She said she refused to let the painting go to a museum, a capitalist, or an egoist," I recalled.

Bene snorted. "Who does that leave?"

"I don't know, but she really does love that painting," I said. "I can't see her selling it to someone who won't value it the way she does."

"What way is that?" Roux asked.

I made a face. "Selfishly. Exclusively. Passionately."

Bene sighed. "That won't make it easy to find a buyer."

"She'll sell," Marius grunted. "When we visited, she was in a hurry to move the painting."

Roux tapped a stack of files. "These are the candidates Gordon provided. We need to look through their files and come up with a short list to present to the client at ten." He checked his watch. "We'll each read a few, report to each other in ninety minutes, and then make our decision."

Bene leafed through the pile. "Seven files. Five of us."

"Those of us who can read above sixth-grade level can fight over doing two each." Roux pointed to Henrik, himself, and me.

Marius growled, but Bene just shrugged. "Less work for us, *amigo*." He grabbed the files and peeked into the first. "Sergei Levitsky. Deals in Russian oil and gas. Looks like a shady character." He handed it to Henrik. "Perfect for you."

Henrik showed his teeth but took the file.

Bene glanced into the next file, then waved it around. "Bogdan Karachanov. Bulgarian arms dealer. Going once, going twice..." He thrust it into Marius's hands. "Sold."

Marius jutted his jaw and glared at Bene, then the file.

"Wow. Sheikh somebody-or-other." Bene lit up at the next one. "I'll take that one."

I groaned. "Where did Gordon come up with these?"

Roux shrugged. "He said he put out quiet feelers among contacts he trusts to be discreet."

I put my face in my hands. What did that say about the people my godfather associated with?

Bene looked through the next few files. "Here's a Swiss foundation for the arts..."

I practically snatched it out of his hands. Maybe there was hope after all.

A knock sounded at the door. Roux, Marius, and Henrik jumped and spread out in defensive positions around the door. Bene yawned.

"Room service," someone announced.

Roux opened the door a crack, then pulled in a trolley. "Thank you. I'll take it from here."

Yikes. Either this wasn't the harmless mission Gordon had described, or old habits died hard. They even checked the trolley for wiretaps and explosives.

Then they settled down again, and Bene thrust a second file at me. "Here. Raisa somebody-or-other from Latvia."

That left two files. Roux took one and gave the other to Henrik. Everyone piled their plates with food and spread out, and the room quickly settled into the relative silence of munching, the shuffle of papers, and the tap of fingers over keyboards.

I peeked around, impressed. For all their moaning and ribbing, the guys certainly took their work seriously.

Helping myself to a yogurt, I sat on the couch and focused on the two files I'd been assigned. Well, I tried to focus, but my eyes kept drifting to Marius, while my hand drifted to my neck. Without realizing it, I caressed my skin, and all kinds of steamy images drifted through my head.

Then I caught myself, blushed what had to be beet red, judging by the heat in my cheeks, and whipped my hand away. God, what was it with me these days?

Marius shifted uncomfortably in his seat, and when he looked over, his eyes blazed with heat.

Oops. *Sorry,* I murmured into his mind.

The look he shot me in reply vacillated between *Get your mind out of the gutter* and *Come hither and let me have my evil way with you.*

Sex-starved as I was, I was all for option two. But we had a job to do, so I turned to face the windows.

Gordon's notes were thorough and terrifyingly detailed. Could he find out as much about me if he desired? And, yikes. Had he already done so?

I corroborated and supplemented his findings with some online snooping, then studied the file on the Swiss art foundation.

In the hour that passed, Bene must have changed positions a dozen times, from slouched in an armchair with his feet hooked over the side to belly-down on the floor, like he was reading on a beach — although I doubted he would devote beach time to reading. Playing volleyball and flirting was probably more like it.

Marius took a seat at the dining table, as did Henrik, while Roux paced by the windows. Not one for sitting still, that tiger. So I assumed it was him when someone came by and refilled my water glass.

"Thanks," I murmured, barely looking up from my files.

"You're welcome," Henrik murmured.

Then I looked up, because holy crap. Since when was Henrik considerate?

Either it was a peace gesture, or he was sneaking poison into my drink.

I discreetly poured it into a plant and got my own refill, just in case. The plant didn't instantly wilt, which was a plus, but I decided to withhold judgment.

Time flew, and before I knew it, Roux was calling everyone to order.

"All right. Time to compare notes. Henrik, what do you have?"

Henrik shuffled through his research material and held up a picture of a heavily jowled man with a stern expression. "Sergei Levitsky, CEO of Siberitrans."

I shook my head. "Anastasia said she doesn't want the painting to go to Russia."

Henrik pointed to a page in his file. "Well, he can keep it in his villa in Saint-Tropez. Plus, he was a friend of her husband's."

"Doesn't mean he's a friend of hers," Marius pointed out.

"Well, this one is intriguing." Henrik held up his second file. "A Scandinavian tech billionaire."

"Let me guess," Bene interjected. "Nils Øren Jensen."

I blinked. "Who?"

Bene shook his head sadly. "We really have to get you out of that château from time to time."

I sighed. He could say that again.

"Another capitalist Anastasia won't approve of," Marius decided.

"Well, he certainly has the funds," Henrik said.

Roux looked to me. "Who did you have?"

I held up the candidate I planned to push as much as I could. "The Marguerite Tobler Arts Trust. It sounds perfect."

Roux rubbed his fingers together. "Do they have the cash to compete with Nils Øren Jensen?"

I grimaced. Probably not. I leafed to the second candidate. "This one has potential. Raisa Kepke, former Cultural Minister of Latvia."

"Former?" Marius asked.

I made a face. "She was until she was implicated in a corruption scandal involving EU arts funding." I sighed. "Another friend of Gordon's, I suppose."

"Mina is finally catching on," Bene stage-whispered to Henrik.

"According to the file, she's also a raven shifter," I added.

"Makes sense. They're sneaky as hell," Bene said. "And they love shiny new things, a little like dragons."

"Nothing like dragons," Marius grumbled.

"She now runs an NGO that claims to protect European cultural heritage," I finished. "But it's a little murky, at best."

"Just like Gordon," Bene pointed out.

I snagged the last chocolate croissant from the breakfast platter, desperate to improve my mood.

Roux pointed to Marius. "Who's your guy?"

"Not *my* guy," Marius grumbled.

"He's an arms dealer, right?" Henrik asked.

Marius nodded. "Bogdan Karachanov. Bulgarian. Bear shifter."

"Wait. What about the client?" Bene asked.

Marius shook his head. "She's human. No reason to believe she knows about shifters."

Bene stroked his chin. "Well, if this Bogdan guy is an old-time Marxist, that could appeal."

"Who do you have?" I asked Roux.

Roux held up a picture of a smiling platinum blonde. "I'm not sure what to make of this one." He glanced down at his notes. "Charlotte de Mézières."

Bene did a double take. "The countess?"

Clearly, the lion shifter kept up with the society pages.

"Aristocrat slash influencer," Roux read. "A former beauty pageant contestant from America who married a Belgian aristocrat. Now she runs social media accounts under *The Philosophy of Beauty* label."

Bene nodded cheerfully. "That's the one."

"She 'curates private spiritual retreats in Provence where guests commune with select masterworks,'" Roux read.

I shook my head. "Anastasia will never go for her."

"She will if Charlotte charms her socks off," Bene countered.

"You're on a first-name basis with the countess?" Henrik smirked.

Bene huffed, a little hurt. "Everyone is. She's super friendly."

"When the camera is switched on," Marius muttered.

"What about the sheikh?" Henrik asked Bene.

"Well, he *definitely* has sufficient funds. He's sponsored high-level sporting events in the Middle East and plans to move into art and tech next."

"Art *and* tech, or art *or* tech?" I asked, trying to picture what either actually meant.

Bene shrugged. "Not sure he cares, as long as it brings publicity."

"Well, that's who we have," Roux concluded. "We need a short list of about three. Who can we eliminate?"

"**Everyone but the Swiss art foundation," I said, but everyone ignored me.

"That Russian — Levitsky," Henrik proposed. "And the sheikh."

"Agreed." Marius nodded.

"And the Swiss arts foundation," Roux said.

I shook my head. "We have to give it a try."

Roux pulled the file from me, leafed through it, and pointed to the spreadsheet detailing their net worth.

I drooped. Boy, did the world suck sometimes.

"So, no arts foundation," Roux concluded.

"Well, then you can cut the tech guy too," I said a little vindictively. "Anastasia will never go for him."

Roux shook his head. "The tech guy stays in."

"Why?" I asked.

"The tech guy stays in," he repeated firmly. "What about eliminating the countess?"

"No way!" Bene protested.

"The client wants secrecy, right? There's no way an influencer is going to keep a deal like this quiet," Roux reasoned. "Plus, I doubt she can outbid the others."

Things went on in that vein for a while, and tensions rose because the guys, as usual, couldn't agree.

"We can't cut the countess," Bene insisted.

"She's the first we should cut," Henrik retorted.

"No, that would be the tech guy," Marius grumbled.

"The tech guy remains." Roux's eyes took on the heated sheen shifters got when they were agitated.

I patted the air with my hands. "Enough. Enough already!" I shouted when they didn't respond. "We've eliminated three. I say I present the remaining four to Anastasia and let *her* decide. It's her painting," I added a little bitterly.

Roux glanced at his watch, clearly irritated that we hadn't used our time more efficiently. We were still on schedule — just not *ahead* of schedule, as he preferred.

Ping! His phone chimed with a message he read aloud.

"Apparently, the countess is unavailable to view the painting in person. She's doing a photo shoot in Bali."

"Bummer," Bene lamented.

Roux crossed her name off the list. "That leaves us with three."

"Who do you think the client will choose?" Bene asked.

I shrugged. "I find her impossible to predict."

He stood and reached into a massive feline stretch, then scratched his belly. "I wonder how long this will take, and where Gordon will send us afterward to wait for our next assignment."

"Back to Château Nocturne," Marius said, as if it were obvious.

Henrik's eyes hit the floor, while Roux and Bene glanced at each other, then at me.

"Not the château?" Marius asked, puzzled.

I bit my lip. Had I made the right decision?

"Henrik has not proven that he can follow the rules," I said in a major understatement. "I'll be letting Gordon know when we finish here in London."

"And if he's out, we're all out." Bene glared at the vampire.

Marius stared at me, and I burned to say something like, *I was kind of hoping you and I could work something out.*

But he'd barely spoken a word to me since that night in Paris. And no matter how my body burned for his — more than ever lately, for reasons I couldn't explain — that didn't exactly form a solid foundation to build a healthy relationship upon.

"Maybe you could reconsider," Bene tried.

"You mean, reconsider if I want to be alive or dead?" I snipped, glaring at Henrik.

"I apologize. A thousand times," the vampire said, sounding genuinely contrite. "If I could go back in time and change what happened, I would."

"Well, you can't go back in time. Especially once someone is dead," I snapped, cutting him no slack.

Bene scratched his head. "Maybe we can find a better solution."

I was all ears, but no one said a word. And even if they'd been bursting with ideas, there was another complication.

I swallowed hard. "That will be tricky, now that I've agreed to host the regional police championships at the château."

Everyone stared.

"The regional police championships?" Marius's voice registered hurt and betrayal.

If I could have shrunk to the size of a mouse and scurried away, I would have.

Instead, I forced my chin up and indicated Henrik. "Are you telling me I have grounds to reconsider?"

Marius's throat bobbed, and even Henrik appeared mired in a well of regret.

Roux shook his head. "No. You're right, and we have to live with that."

My heart sank. Could they, though? And could I live with myself if the consequences were as dire as they'd hinted?

I glanced at Marius, hoping to find understanding in his eyes. But his face hardened, and he turned coldly to the door. "Time to go. The client will be waiting."

Chapter Sixteen

MARIUS

The fifteen-minute walk to Anastasia's apartment took Mina, Roux, and me across the short side of Hyde Park, and I cursed Clement the entire time. Police championships? In what, stealing another man's woman?

"Regional police championships?" I couldn't help muttering.

Mina looked straight ahead.

"Let me guess," I grumbled. "That ass of a wolf shifter put you up to it."

She gave me a fierce look. "Clement is not an ass, and he didn't put me up to anything. He asked nicely."

"I bet he did," I muttered. "Did he butter you up with cake or something?"

Her step hitched. Then she continued stomping along.

"What would you have me do?" she muttered back. "You left without a word. Bene and Roux wouldn't tell me anything, and Henrik attacked me. Oh, and meanwhile, I have a business to develop."

"A business hosting police events?" I grumbled.

She ticked off one finger at a time. "It will allow me to test the logistics of hosting large groups of people. It will help spread the word that the château is available for events. And it never hurts to be on good terms with the police."

My dragon sent whiffs of smoke through my nose as I pictured police officers partying it up in the stables I'd helped clear. Mina waved a hand in front of her face.

Was I being childish? Yes, and I knew it.

I kicked the ground and uttered a sullen, "Sorry."

"Are you?" she shot back.

"Yes," I said.

Sorry about not kicking that no-good wolf shifter's ass, my dragon quietly added. *Yet.*

I sighed. It was hard to be good when bad was so much easier.

Mina is worth it, my beast decided.

True, but she'd just announced we weren't welcome at the château. Where did that leave me? Where did that leave us?

"What?" she demanded, reading my face.

I shrugged. "Just wondering where we'll go after this mission. Me and the guys, I mean."

Mina slowed, then stopped altogether. I stopped too, bracing myself for one of her outbursts.

She sucked in a deep breath, calming herself, then towed me to a spot under the trees.

"Uh, guys...?" Roux called back.

She shook her head at him. "Give us a minute."

The tiger shifter turned away, muttering to himself in French.

Mina took both my hands and looked me straight in the eye. "It's not that I don't want you at the château. I want you there. Desperately." She swallowed hard. "I want you in my life. But coming and going without a word won't cut it." Her tone went sharp, then softened. "Not even if you're trying to do the right thing."

She was right. But, crap. Doing the right thing meant telling her about the mark I'd left on her, and I hadn't done that either.

She shook my hands a little, forcing me to look up. "All I ask is that you talk to me. Please."

I opened my mouth. Crap. Where to begin?

"I love you. I mean it," I managed. "But everything is a mess right now, and I keep getting pulled away. First, Gordon... Then that threatening text... Now, this job..."

I decided to leave out the mark I'd left on her neck for the moment.

"I know what you mean," she said. "But once we get past all that..."

Getting past all that was the day I lived for, but it always seemed further and further away.

"Besides, we're in this together," she said.

I gripped her hands tighter. "There's a lot I want to be in on with you, but not when it involves predatory vampires and Gordon's sketchy business deals."

Her face hardened. "Trying to protect me is one thing. Assuming I'm stupid or helpless is another."

"You're not stupid *or* helpless. Not by a long shot. But we could be up against some really dangerous thugs here."

She snorted. "Like Anastasia?"

I shook my head. "Like Szabo. Like Gordon. Like half the buyers on his list."

She grimaced but ceded my point.

Roux motioned at his watch impatiently. "It's five minutes to ten."

"Seven to ten," Mina snipped, then turned back to me. "All I ask is that you talk to me."

"When? Here? Now?" I motioned around. "Or in a hotel room with all the other guys? When have I had the chance?"

A fair point, I thought, but Mina stuck a finger at my chest. "*Make* the chance, dammit."

I gritted my teeth. Clement had probably been making chances every opportunity he got — and he got plenty as a cop in Auberre, a town with zero crime to speak of. So I wasn't competing on a level playing field.

But that was the story of my life, and if I wanted Mina, I would have to earn that privilege, wouldn't I?

Damn right, my dragon agreed.

I sucked in a long breath, steeling myself for all the obstacles that lay ahead. Then I kissed her knuckles softly. "I will. I swear."

You'd better, her expression warned me.

"*Now* it's five to ten," Roux grumbled, tapping his watch.

Mina dropped a kiss on my cheek and turned to him. "Coming."

∞∞∞

Anastasia, as expected, wasn't enthused by the candidates Mina presented — not even the ones at the very bottom of our list. That led to a long phone call to Gordon on an old-school rotary phone that came straight out of the seventies. Anastasia ended the call with a slam and a great deal of pouting.

"Fine," she muttered after fuming for five minutes. "I'll meet them tomorrow. The Bulgarian and the Latvian."

"And the Swiss art foundation?" Mina tried.

"As if they appreciate art." Anastasia snorted and whirled out of the room.

I gripped Mina's shoulder before she followed.

"But..." she tried.

When I shook my head, Mina slumped, muttering, "God, I hate this. Everything about this."

I pointed silently to *The Tower of Blue Horses*, and she sighed.

"Okay, everything except that."

I left her there to appreciate it in silence while Roux and I finished making arrangements with our hostess. Then I tugged Mina out of the study and bid Anastasia goodbye.

The moment we exited the building, Roux was on the phone.

"Good news, Gordon. We have a go for two candidates. The client has invited the Bulgarian and the Latvian."

Maybe not such good news, because he grimaced at whatever Gordon said and went on in a measured, "Anything you say. Can you see if they're available?" He nodded a few times, then halted in his tracks.

Mina and I stopped, looking at him.

"You have? I-it is?" Roux stuttered a little, then composed himself. "Roger. We're on it."

He clicked the phone off and stared at it for a good ten seconds.

"What?" Mina asked.

His expression was pained. "I forget how quickly Gordon moves sometimes. He's already booked the suite adjacent to ours to hold meetings in, and he's had the clients on standby, so they've already confirmed for tomorrow."

Mina blinked. "How did he know which buyers Anastasia would choose?"

Roux's eyes drifted to mine, and I sighed. Yes, Mina was that naïve when it came to the way her godfather operated.

"I guess he has good instincts," Roux said tactfully.

When we were a block away from the hotel, he tapped Mina's arm.

"I forgot one thing. Can you help me order flowers and food for tomorrow?" He gestured toward Kensington High Street.

"Shouldn't we check the new suite first?" she asked.

He shook his head so vehemently, I knew something was up.

"No. It's identical to ours. Marius can have a look and let us know if any changes are necessary. But I really need your help on this."

Mina knew about as much as he did about flower arrangements and finger food. Another sign of something amiss.

I go where she goes, I growled into the tiger's mind.

He gave me a firm look. *Better that you check the new suite before Mina does. I'll keep her safe.*

In other words, safely away from that suite. What the hell was going on?

He jutted his head toward the hotel, then stuck on a fake smile for Mina. "It won't take long, I promise."

Mina followed him glumly, giving me an uncertain wave. "See you soon."

"See you," I forced myself to say, though every instinct screamed for me to remain with her.

I watched them walk to the end of the block, then bolted into the hotel and hurried to our suite, where I banged on the door.

"Coming, coming," Bene called irritably. And not just irritated with me, I realized when he opened the door. He grimaced, then tilted his head to the right. "Ah. You've heard about our new neighbor."

As if on cue, the adjacent door opened, and a curvy woman stepped into view.

"Marius. So good to see you," she purred.

My mouth fell open. Celeste?

"What the hell is she doing here?" I demanded of Bene.

Celeste chuckled. "Happy to see you too, *cherie*. Now, where is that delightful goddaughter of Gordon's? She and I have so much to discuss."

Not if I could help it, dammit.

Bene gave me a pained, *This isn't my fault* look, and for once, I didn't blame him.

"Fucking Gordon..." I muttered.

"I'd much rather fuck you," Celeste chuckled.

Bene grabbed my arm as I stormed toward her.

Her eyes sparkled. "In that much of a hurry, huh?"

To wring the life out of her? Yes.

Bene pulled me back. "Be nice, kids."

"Ah, but Marius is so much better at *bad*," Celeste hummed, giving the words layers of subtext. "Aren't you, *cherie*?"

I wrenched myself away from Bene, shoved Celeste into her suite, and slammed the door behind us.

"God, you're something when you're angry." Celeste grinned.

Sultry, succubus magic swirled through the air, trying to get a grip on me. In the past, I'd had to fight hard to resist. Now, it was easy.

"Whatever you're here for, you will leave Mina out of it. Do you hear me?" I half shouted.

"That would be difficult since we're here for the same thing. The art deal, of course."

Her sugar-sweet tone suggested otherwise.

"If you so much as touch her..." I started.

Celeste hooted. "Oh, I wouldn't dream of it, just as I'm sure you wouldn't dream of touching her. Oh, wait. You already did."

I snarled, clenching my fists before they flew at her.

"Touchy, touchy," Celeste scolded. "And all for that scrawny, spoiled snob. Really, what do you see in her?"

I barely bit back my dragon's roar. Mina wasn't spoiled. She worked her ass off, and she didn't have a hint of Celeste's entitled attitude. And as for scrawny...

"Quite the Achilles' heel, you know, caring about someone," Celeste went on.

The blood froze in my veins, and I stalked closer, hissing. "What did you say?"

Celeste's eyes didn't so much as flicker. "I said, quite the Achilles' heel. Even if you're only fooling yourself about your feelings for her — or fooling her." She cackled.

"What the hell does *that* mean?"

Celeste huffed. "Believe me, I know every trick in the book. Sooner or later, she'll realize that you're only after her money. That you'll never fit into her world. Then she'll kick your sorry ass out of that fancy château, and where will you be?"

If Celeste weren't so dangerous, I might have laughed. Peeling paint and broken plumbing hardly qualified as fancy, and Mina was broke.

But there were two kernels of truth in her words — *never fitting into her world* and having my sorry ass kicked out of the château.

I gave myself a little shake, trying to dislodge the tendrils of succubus sweet talk that had closed in around me.

"You think I don't know your tricks?" I growled.

"You know a few. But I have so many more," she hummed, slipping back into seduction mode. "Wouldn't you enjoy it if I shared them?"

I bared my teeth. "Share them with someone else. Gordon, for all I care." Then I narrowed my eyes. "Or Szabo. You like vampires, don't you?"

She dismissed the notion with a flip of her hand. "You're mixing up what I do for business and what I do for pleasure."

"I wonder what Henrik would have to say about that?" I asked, recalling what the two of them had gotten up to in Mallorca.

She bristled. "Is that a threat?"

"Absolutely."

"Henrik can hardly blame me since it was business for him too. Not that business can't be enjoyable." Her eyes sparkled. "But I'm sure you agree that genuine connections bring about the highest levels of pleasure."

As she drew out the last word, magic spun around the room, sparkling like tiny fireworks.

Fireworks that flickered and faded around me, unable to penetrate my defenses. Even a succubus couldn't trick her way around those when they were built upon love — true love for my destined mate.

"What about Szabo?" I went on, keeping the focus where I wanted it.

"Who Szabo screws is his business." Bitterness laced her voice.

Interesting. Had Szabo shacked up with one of her rivals?

"What about who he conducts business with?" I demanded.

Celeste shrugged. "Irrelevant."

To her, maybe, but not to me. Not with him stalking Mina.

Luckily, a knock sounded at the door, because I was ready to throttle Celeste.

"Yes?" she called sweetly.

Bene opened the door and indicated the phone at his ear.

"I have Gordon on the line for Marius."

Celeste smirked. "Go ahead, *cherie*. See what your master wants now."

Her words were laced with venom — and not all of it aimed at me.

I gave her my hardest, darkest look, then stalked into the adjoining suite, where I stuck my hand out for the phone. I was out of the frying pan but into the fire.

But Bene grinned and put it away. "I lied. No call from Gordon. Just me keeping you from killing that bitch." He sighed. "The big boss wouldn't like it."

I exhaled slowly. "No, he wouldn't."

Bene went back to his takeout meal on the dining table. "You owe me, man. Again, I might add."

"You're right," I murmured. "I owe you."

I leaned back against the door, calculating how to protect Mina from Celeste. Because that succubus was always up to something.

Chapter Seventeen

MINA

"And here I was, thinking things couldn't get worse..." I grumbled.

"Just keep your cool," Marius murmured, as much to himself as to me.

Because, crap. Now we had Celeste to deal with too?

It was almost ten a.m. the next morning, and we were arranging things in the new suite, where we expected Anastasia and the first of the potential bidders any minute.

Correction — Celeste was arranging things, because this was her suite.

Yes, a whole suite to herself, with me crammed into the adjoining one with four men. But they were just as adamant as I about keeping their distance from the succubus. Even Henrik.

Feel free to move in with Celeste, Gordon had phoned to say the previous evening.

Over my dead body, I'd nearly barked.

Could he really imagine us painting our nails and giggling over girl talk?

As if.

Oh, no thanks, I'd said as casually as possible. *I'm already unpacked and settled in my room. You know, with my dresses...shoes...hair products...*

I had exactly two dresses and two pairs of shoes (including my running shoes), plus a brush and a couple of scrunchies, but Gordon didn't need to know that.

"You might want to check your hair, *cherie*," Celeste said, fussing over the flower arrangement.

The flower arrangement *I'd* picked, dammit, and it was perfectly fine. Like my hair, I decided after a glance in the mirror.

"Ignore her," Marius murmured through clenched teeth.

Dealing with Celeste on her own would be bad enough. Dealing with Celeste and Marius at the same time was downright hellish. I could practically see the emotional baggage piled up in the room. Suitcase upon suitcase of it, threatening to tip over and crush us.

And while I disliked Celeste — strongly — she downright *despised* me. Truly, thoroughly, bitterly. Any chance she found to rub her past with Marius in my face, she grabbed and scrubbed violently.

"Here. Let me fix your tie," she told him, shooting a knowing sigh in my direction. "Every time we went out, I had to do this. The man can't dress himself."

Her playful tone hinted that she'd done a lot of undressing too.

Now I was the one holding Marius back and gritting *my* teeth, wishing myself back to my room and away from this nightmare.

A window opened in my mind, along with a perfectly clear vision of how I could walk through the intervening wall if I wanted, and even take Marius with me. I blinked at that *brushed-by-moonlight* moment and nearly held out a hand to test it.

Then someone banged on the door, and that window came crashing down again.

Bene called through the door. "Pizza delivery."

I held the door open while Bene and Henrik carefully maneuvered in a huge crate and carried it to the easel we'd prepared.

"Pizza?" I scolded.

Bene grinned. "The Frank Marc special."

"Franz," I grumbled.

Celeste unnecessarily oversaw them unbox and set up the painting.

"Perfect," she stood back to declare minutes later, as if all that hard work had been her doing.

"Yes, your work here is done." Henrik held the door open for her.

She put her hands on her hips. "You're not suggesting..."

"That you leave? That the client refuses to deal with anyone but Mina? Yes," Henrik snipped. "Or no. Not suggesting. Stating."

I cringed. Like Celeste needed another reason to hate me.

The vampire motioned to the door. "You may leave now. We'll be sure to inform Gordon what a fine job you've done."

"Or will it be me informing Gordon about you?" Celeste hissed, stalking to the door. On the threshold, she paused and stuck up her hand. "Key?"

No one budged.

"To *your* suite, I mean," she said irritably.

The men all looked at one another or at the floor.

Celeste gaped. "Where do you expect me to wait throughout this process?"

Marius's stormy expression answered her not at all politely.

"Unbelievable. This is *my* suite!" she raged.

"And Gordon's orders," Henrik told her, his expression stony.

In Mallorca, he hadn't shown much remorse for falling under her spell, but apparently his conscience — such as it was — had him reconsidering.

I found myself warming a little toward him. As in about one degree above freezing. Still, it was something.

With a last, lethal look at me — *me!* — Celeste whirled and stomped down the hallway. Henrik slammed the door, and everyone exhaled... slightly.

"Where do you think she'll go?" Bene asked.

Roux ran a hand through his hair. "Wherever it is, she won't be far enough."

Marius jutted his jaw in silent agreement.

We all stood mute for a full minute. Then I rearranged the flowers back to the way they'd been, just to spite Celeste. Taking several deep breaths, I turned to the painting, reminding myself to focus on the positives. I got to spend another few hours in the company of a true masterpiece, and I wasn't about to poison that time with bitterness.

Bene tapped Henrik on the shoulder. "Come on, man. Off we go to lobby duty."

Henrik followed with a sour look, but he didn't argue the point. They'd been assigned that post in order to meet each buyer and escort them to this suite. Now, I realized that also allowed them to ensure Celeste didn't interfere.

I glanced at Roux, who'd assigned everyone their roles. Had he had that much foresight?

Of course I did, his hard look told me.

I shook my head. Boy, was Marius right. I was in way over my head here.

He held up a white sheet and, at my nod, covered the painting.

Ten minutes later, a knock sounded, and Roux opened the door to Bene and Anastasia.

"Thank you," Anastasia said warmly, patting Bene's arm.

Clearly, the lion shifter had turned up the charm for her. He wasn't a succubus, but stunning good looks and polite manners could have a similar effect.

"My pleasure, ma'am."

"We'll be outside if you need anything," Roux said, stepping outside with Bene.

She kissed my cheeks in greeting, leaving lipstick prints Marius gestured for me to wipe away. Then she and I reviewed the schedule for the morning while Marius stood nearby, quiet as a mouse but menacing as a dragon. The ultimate bodyguard, as my girl parts couldn't help noticing.

I slid a hand over my neck, then whipped it away before my body heated.

Another knock sounded, and Roux showed in our first candidate.

"Ms. Kepke," he announced. Then he stepped outside, leaving just me, Marius, Anastasia, and her visitor.

"Nice to meet you." Anastasia didn't bother rising from her chair, but she did lift a hand to grip her guest's in a brief, feminine greeting. Then she waved, introducing me. "This is Wilhemina. I've asked her to sit in on my appointments today."

Subtext: *You're one of several potential buyers, and I can choose whomever I want, so you'd better impress me.*

"Pleasure to meet you," our prim, middle-aged guest replied smoothly. "And please, call me Raisa."

She and I sat on the couch facing the covered painting, while Anastasia sat in an armchair kitty-corner to us.

"Now then, tell me about yourself," she ordered.

I was impressed. Raisa was cool, calm, and professional. She laid out a stellar résumé, speaking passionately about art and knowledgeably about business. And no wonder — this was a woman accustomed to addressing national and international assemblies.

Then again, she had also been ejected from the European Parliament on corruption charges. A detail we'd mentioned to Anastasia in our briefing.

She'd barely waved a hand, muttering, "Now, there's the pot calling the kettle black."

"I've established a private investment group with the aim of protecting European cultural heritage..." Raisa explained, going on in more detail.

She made it all sound legit, but my research said the opposite.

I watched our guest closely. *Raven shifter*, Gordon's file had said. It fit. Her dark eyes never stopped roving, quietly assessing everything from the flowers to the antique Chinese vase in a corner of the suite.

She appraised Marius too, sniffing discreetly. I knew the moment she identified the dragon in him, because her eyes widened, and she glanced over under the guise of fixing her raven-black hair. If I hadn't been watching closely for any tell, though, I would have missed it.

She also appraised me, but my supernatural heritage was so mixed and my powers so weak, I came off as human. Also, I'd practically bathed in perfume. Roux had insisted, for reasons I tried not to take personally.

Raisa talked about an investment group, but most of her statements were in the first person.

"My goal is to create a mobile cultural museum..."

Yes, my research had indicated as much. Reports showed the idea going back a decade, but she still had nothing tangible to show, despite dozens of investors tossing in ten million euro apiece for their part of the action.

I'd hoped Raisa would convince me — of herself, her motives, and her investment group. But my hopes faded quickly. Too many catchy phrases, too few practical details.

"My museum will serve as the heartbeat of pan-European modernism..." she continued.

Anastasia wasn't impressed, I sensed — to the point that I wondered if she would even permit Raisa a look at the painting. But Raisa must have sensed it, because she quickly baited a bigger hook and flashed it before Anastasia.

"Your painting would be exhibited in its own wing," she promised. "A wing named in your honor. After all, we owe the painting's existence to you and your family."

I did my best not to cough at that airbrushed version of history.

Anastasia practically glowed, though. "My father nearly lost his life protecting that painting."

Before or after he'd pillaged it as war booty? I nearly blurted.

Marius shot me a look of warning.

"Of course, my museum will only cater to the most exclusive clientele," Raisa assured her.

"Of course," Anastasia agreed, as if anything less would be a deal-breaker.

Eventually, Anastasia signaled for Marius to unveil the painting. When he did, Raisa clasped her hands to her chest. Her throat bobbed, and her eyes shone. Signs of genuine interest, or plain old avarice?

"Interesting.   Very interesting," Anastasia mused after Raisa had made her final pitch — er, goodbyes — and departed at the end of her thirty-minute time slot.

Marius silently covered the painting for maximum dramatic effect on the next candidate. Gordon's idea, no doubt.

"What do you think?" Anastasia asked me.

I thought Raisa's "museum" was more of a private club — if she ever actually launched it. Until then, whatever paintings she managed to secure with her investors' money would be at her disposal.

Aloud, I was more tactful. "An interesting business model, but perhaps overly ambitious."

Marius smirked. *You got that right.*

Fifteen minutes later, Roux ushered in the next candidate.

"Mr. Bogdan Karachanov," he announced, then retreated.

I steeled myself, because this was the arms dealer.

Surprisingly, though, Bogdan turned out to be a bit of a charmer and not at all what I'd been expecting. Well, apart from the Eastern European accent and sturdy, bear shifter build.

"Madame. My pleasure." He bowed deeply to kiss Anastasia's knuckles.

At least, I figured that's what he said, because he said it in Russian.

Her eyes danced, and she motioned him to take a seat much more warmly than she'd invited Raisa.

"Anastasia Nikolaevna," she insisted, using the patronymic common to both their cultures.

His nostrils flared, and from under his thick, bushy eyebrows, his eyes darted to Marius. Clearly, his bear side had caught the scent of dragon. Then again, as an associate of Gordon's, he wouldn't question the presence of another shifter at a deal like this, especially if that shifter was a closemouthed dragon assigned to security.

Bogdan and Anastasia quickly switched to English, thank goodness, except for side remarks Bogdan threw in from time to time in Russian to keep Anastasia's happy vibes going. He did the same in English, tossing in little colloquialisms to show what a nice, down-to-earth arms dealer he was. He didn't get them right all the time, but hey — bonus points for effort in what had to be his second and third languages.

You hit the nail on the hammer, was one such comment, and *A blessing in the skies* another. The effect was unexpectedly endearing.

He and Anastasia hit it off instantly, as only a couple of aging Marxists who missed the good old days could. Bogdan's old-world manners rivaled Henrik's, which Anastasia clearly appreciated. The man could even quote Pushkin, to her delight.

"Better the illusions that exalt us than ten thousand truths," he commented in a quote I remembered my father citing.

Clearly, Bogdan was a man of the world and a bit of a silver fox — er, silver bear? — with a head of thick hair and shoulders big enough to set off his slight paunch. All in all, a man I could see laughing and sipping brandy with my godfather.

And that was exactly what made me keep my guard up. For years, Gordon had hidden his dark side from me. He was still hiding it — and worse, he didn't shy away from using me for his own purposes. Like now, when he'd set me up to lower the average age in the room and contribute occasional observations about art that gave all this a cultured, legitimate air.

I felt sicker and sicker with every passing moment.

Anastasia played with her pearls, chuckled, and blushed like a schoolgirl. She even pulled a miniature album out of her purse to show Bogdan a picture of herself at age six.

"That's me, presenting Nikita Khrushchev with a bouquet of flowers..." she narrated.

Bogdan oohed, aahed, and reminisced about happy days in Komsomol youth camps.

She had a picture of that, too, and of her father in his Red Army uniform. Even I leaned in for a peek at that one.

"Oh yes. Very handsome," I murmured, indulging her.

Marius stared off into the distance in a master class in feigning disinterest.

I smiled faintly, thinking of how he'd done the same in his first days at the château, when he, Bene, Roux, and Henrik had just moved in. But that mask had cracked, and I'd caught glimpses of the real him — and his interest in me.

My body warmed. We were a true love story.

Then I frowned, because even true love needed honesty and open lines of communication.

He must have read my mind, because his eyes caught mine and swore, *I'm working on it.*

I gulped, sympathizing for once. Our circumstances didn't exactly allow for openness and honesty. Not as long as we were submerged in Gordon's world of intrigue and shady business deals. But the moment we were free...

I flashed him a smile, but only a quick one, because again... those pesky circumstances.

Meanwhile, Bogdan continued charming Anastasia. He danced around his line of work, calling himself "an investor in post-Soviet surplus industries." (Gordon's file called it *retrofitting Cold War weapons for modern mercenary use in developing countries*, a business that had earned Bogdan billions.) He styled himself as a budding philanthropist rather than someone trying to sanitize his public image, and he was humble about his art knowledge, patiently allowing Anastasia to lecture him on that subject.

I looked at my watch, wondering if they would ever get to the painting. So far, this was more of a first date than an art deal.

"Well, I won't brush around the bush any longer," Bogdan chuckled in another of his mixed-up idioms. "May I see your painting?"

Anastasia gave Marius the go-ahead to unveil it, which he did in his usual straightforward manner. Anastasia, I guessed, would have preferred a little more flourish.

"Magnificent," Bogdan immediately proclaimed.

Anastasia looked at it like a proud parent at a high school graduation, and it occurred to me that she probably loved that painting more than she'd ever loved a person. That sad thought went right to my heart, where it resonated in warning.

Anastasia waxed on poetically about all the details of the painting, and Bogdan listened attentively, interrupting only to butter her up.

"My goodness, you do know your art. I can only hope to sound as cultured one day," he joked.

Which, I suspected, was his goal — to earn (or buy) a place in high-class society.

If Roux hadn't popped his head in to point out the time, who knew how long Anastasia and Bogdan might have kept up their flirting. She even stood to see him out the door, and afterward, she gripped his business card like a winning lottery ticket.

"A very appealing candidate, don't you think?" she murmured, stepping to the window to wave goodbye when he appeared in the street below.

I answered carefully. "I think his values align with yours."

Anastasia smiled coyly. "Yes, they do. They certainly do."

Marius's lips twitched.

Even Roux's knock on the door didn't break her dreamy reverie.

"Your last appointment is here, ma'am," he called softly.

She frowned, and I did too. "What appointment?"

"Mr. Jensen." Roux admitted a tall, thin man, then disappeared back into the hallway.

I caught a glimpse of a svelte young woman holding a tablet. The tech billionaire's personal assistant?

"Nils Øren Jensen," the man corrected, folding his arms and staring at the painting.

Marius looked at me, then at the drop cloth, but it was too late for that now.

"Who?" Anastasia crooned, clearly displeased.

"Nils Øren Jensen," he repeated, icy blue eyes still fixed on the painting.

He was in his early forties, I estimated, with thinning, unkempt hair and very pale skin. Clearly, he didn't get out much. According to Roux's files, the guy had a brain the size of London but, yeesh. Zero social skills.

Anastasia frowned at me, and I flipped through my clipboard of notes. "Um, Mr. Jensen isn't on my schedule."

He didn't seem to hear or care, creating a truly awkward moment. One I felt compelled to smooth over, though it wasn't of my making.

"I believe Mr. Jensen works in software," I said, stepping to the door.

He nodded absently. "Neuro-mapping software, but I'm moving into neuroaesthetic optimization."

Neuro-*what?* I wondered.

"Well, he's not on the schedule," Anastasia declared.

I opened the door, confronting Roux, who didn't even have the grace to look apologetic.

"Gordon added him to the schedule," he said curtly. "He believes Madame Petrova will find it worthwhile to hear out Mr. Jensen."

Anastasia crossed her arms and glared.

"I don't like him," she announced as if Jensen weren't even there.

He moved to consider the painting from a new angle, unperturbed. Either he hadn't heard, or he was accustomed to inciting that kind of reaction. People skills were definitely not part of his portfolio — a very hefty portfolio, if I remembered correctly.

Anastasia huffed. "I said—"

"Eighty-six million," Jensen cut in.

Anastasia looked stunned, then offended. "Are you suggesting money is all I'm after, young man?"

"I'm suggesting a price. Everything else is irrelevant," he said in one of those enviably unaccented Scandinavian "accents."

I shivered. What a scary world he lived in. Doubly scary, because Roux's brief had noted that Jensen's billions afforded him insider access to politicians and other influential figures.

"Eighty-six million dollars in an offshore account that no one has to know about," Jensen went on.

We all stared.

"Not even that woman suing you for her share of your late husband's estate," Jensen added, pointing his laser gaze at Anastasia. "His illegitimate daughter, correct?"

My jaw dropped. This was straight out of *Oprah*.

Anastasia stiffened. "His daughter from before our marriage."

Jensen shrugged. "Neither she nor anyone else needs to know about the painting or our transaction."

I stared. Was that a threat?

Every potential buyer had signed a nondisclosure agreement, but I had the feeling Jensen was accustomed to finding ways around such things. If there really was an illegitimate daughter suing for part of the Petrov estate, and if she discovered that it included a painting as valuable as *The Tower of Blue Horses*... Well, not optimal for Anastasia.

Her eyes blazed as she came to the same conclusion.

"Do you know anything about art?" she huffed. "Do you care?"

The man had the air of someone who would sell out his own mother, so no. I really doubted it.

He shrugged. "It's my aim to democratize high art. We're developing methods that can map every feature of a masterpiece in ways never before attempted."

"You want to digitize the painting?" Anastasia sniffed. "Well, I think *you* should be digitized."

This really had the makings of an *Oprah* moment. I could see it now: Anastasia slipping off one of her heels and brandishing it like a weapon while Jenson grabbed a chair to defend himself.

A good thing Jensen was so calm and detached, even robotic. Otherwise, they might have gone at each other.

He gazed at her wordlessly, thought a little, then upped the ante. "Eighty-seven million."

Anastasia looked scandalized... but also tempted.

Jensen glanced at the painting, then headed to the door with a casual, "Your people have my contact details."

Actually, I didn't, but I bet Gordon did.

"Let me know once you've reached your decision," he said, striding toward the elevator.

Roux stared at him, then at us with a *What the hell just happened?* expression.

I felt the same way.

"The nerve." Anastasia grabbed for her teacup and stirred violently. The motion grew slower and more thoughtful over the next few seconds, though, and she murmured without looking at me. "How much did he say?"

I swallowed hard. "Eighty-seven. Million."

Well below the market price for a painting of this caliber, but this wasn't exactly an open market.

Anastasia gazed down at the street, watching him leave, while stirring and mumbling to herself in Russian.

I couldn't be sure what she said, but I was willing to bet it was *Eighty-seven million...*

Chapter Eighteen

MARIUS

Anastasia departed shortly after Jensen, and we all gathered to review what had transpired. Well, everyone except Celeste, who was still out prowling London. And hallelujah, because that was all we needed to top this shitshow of a day.

"I had to add Jensen to the schedule. Gordon's orders," Roux explained, looking defensive.

"Fucking Gordon," I muttered.

"I can't believe he would do that." Mina shook her head.

"Believe it," Henrik told her coldly.

I growled at him, but he pointed at her mercilessly.

"You're in his world now, and this is how he operates. Either open your eyes, or get out while you can and go back to believing the world is all butterflies and rainbows." He held up a hand before I could punch him and added, "I mean that. Before she learns the hard way."

She socked him with a murderous look. "I think I already learned the hard way."

Only Roux's iron grip on my arm stopped me from throttling the vampire. The next chance I had, I would rip his undead ass to pieces.

"He's right," Bene interjected in a softer tone. "Trusting Gordon could get you killed." He raised his hands at Mina's shocked expression. "Not purposely, but anything could happen, given the people he works with."

I winced, because that included us.

Mina turned to the painting, looking sadder than I'd ever seen her.

Bene's phone beeped, and he looked at it. "Oh goody," he said in a flat tone. "Celeste is on her way back."

"What a day," Roux grumbled, looking at his watch. "And that's before I brief Gordon."

"Who do you think the client will go for?" Henrik asked.

"Jensen," Roux and I said at the same time.

Mina's expression soured. "Bogdan might have a chance."

I doubted it, but I kept that to myself.

Roux's phone rang, and he answered with a roll of his eyes. "Hello, Gordon." He paused. "Yes, everything went well."

Now Mina was the one rolling her eyes.

"Is there a clear front-runner at this point?" Roux passed Gordon's question to Mina.

I would have put the odds at nine-to-one in Jensen's favor, not that I would admit as much to Gordon. It was always good to hold back a little information, just in case.

Maybe Mina was learning, because all she said was, "Hard to say at this point."

Roux relayed that to Gordon on the way back to our suite.

"Quick, before Celeste turns up," Bene joked, following him.

Mina's face went hard. Thinking fast, I stepped inside, grabbed our jackets, and turned to Mina, who was still out in the hallway.

"Come on," I murmured, pulling her toward the stairs.

"Where are you going?" Henrik demanded.

"Out," I muttered.

"Out?" Mina asked.

I nodded firmly. "Out."

Henrik knew me too well to protest, and minutes later, Mina and I slipped outside via the hotel's back door. Yes, the back, to avoid Celeste.

It was barely noon, but I already wanted the day to be over. Hell, I wanted this whole mission to be over. I wanted to be back at the château, sitting over a good meal after an honest day's work clearing out the stables or tearing out old plumbing.

Then I caught myself. Since when had home repair and countryside living featured in my fantasies?

Since Mina, my dragon murmured dreamily.

I looped an arm over her shoulders and led her down the back alley. Mina zipped her jacket high and hunched against the wind. Clouds chased each other across the sky, barely allowing the sun to spear through before the next cloud blotted it out again. Leaves whirled across the grass of Hyde Park, and anyone wearing a hat kept one hand firmly over it. A blustery day, in other words, but a refreshing change from the stuffy suite.

"Where are we going?" Mina asked.

"Wherever you want."

She sighed. "Does home count?"

I flashed a thin smile. Apparently I wasn't the only one thinking along those lines.

A little voice reminded me the château was Mina's home, not mine. But I just didn't have it in me to listen.

"Soon," I promised, then motioned around. "For now, any-where you want in London. A gallery, maybe?"

"God, no," she groaned. "Maybe just walking."

Walking was fine with me. Anything to relieve some of the tension that stiffened every joint in my body.

We walked for hours. All the way across Hyde Park, to Buckingham Palace, St. James's Park, and eventually, on to the Thames. There, we stopped briefly at the statue of Boudica, which Mina regarded in silence.

A tribal heroine who'd led an uprising against the Roman army. No surprise Mina found something to admire there.

"Left or right?" I asked, the first either of us had spoken in the past hour.

Mina thought it over, then pointed right. "Fewer tourists this way."

Fine with me. We set off and walked another full hour. Then Mina pointed out a teahouse, and we took a break from the weather. We barely spoke there either, but our eyes met over our teacups, and for the first time, Mina flashed more than a shadow of a smile.

It was the nicest, quietest *together* time we'd had in... Well, forever, it felt like.

We had sandwiches, then cake, then more cake, because, as Mina declared, "We freaking deserve it."

Then her phone rang.

"Oh. Hello, Anastasia," she answered, looking at me.

I waited, curious.

"Of course. A very difficult decision..." Mina made soothing noises.

I snorted. What was so difficult? I would sell to the highest bidder.

Then I caught myself. If it made Mina happy, I would sell it to the lowest bidder or not sell it at all. But that wasn't my decision, was it?

"Okay. Talk to you tomorrow." Mina hung up. "She wants to sleep on it. She'll call before noon."

Frankly, I was surprised Anastasia had anything to sleep on. But I was sure the money would win in the end.

Mina gazed out the window, looking defeated. "What would you do for eighty-seven million dollars?"

I thought it over. "Not as much as I used to."

Mina flashed a smile. "Getting older and wiser?"

"Older, yes. Not so sure about wiser. Maybe it's just that you're rubbing off on me."

She chuckled. "In a good way, I hope."

I bit my lip. For that to be true, I would have to finally get a few uncomfortable truths off my chest. Starting with the fact that I'd marked her.

"Listen, Mina," I started, but it came out all raspy. "There's something I have to—"

She cut me off with a shake of her head. "I'd like to put the real world on hold for a little longer, if you don't mind."

I opened my mouth, but my dragon side forced it shut again, and all I could do was nod. "Sure."

We left the teahouse and walked another hour, then stood contemplating our choices.

Mina sighed. "I guess we should head back."

I checked my watch. She was right, though I would have preferred to keep walking — all the way back to France if necessary. Anything was better than dealing with what awaited us back at the hotel.

But like good little crime boss minions, we did head back, taking the Tube, then walking. The sun was close to setting by then, though clouds still hid any sign of it, threatening to dump rain.

When we were two blocks from our hotel, Mina squeezed my hand.

"Thank you. For saving my day. For everything," she added softly.

I raised her hand to plant a kiss on her knuckles — then froze, staring. A heartbeat later, I hustled Mina back around the corner.

"What—?"

I cut her off with a sharp motion and peered around the corner.

"What is it?" she whispered, leaning in behind me.

"Not sure." I studied a dark alcove in the alley.

Szabo, my gut screamed in warning, though I hadn't gotten a good look at him.

I led Mina back in the direction we'd come while digging out my phone.

"Szabo?" Mina's eyes went wide as she listened to me talk to Roux.

I clicked off the phone and led her down the street. "Maybe. Roux is on it."

"Where are we going?" she asked, barely keeping up with my long strides.

As far from him as possible was as deep as my thinking went at that point.

"You mentioned another trip you made to London," I said. "Where did you stay?"

"A basement Airbnb in Belgravia."

"Did that trip have anything to have to do with Gordon?" When she shook her head, I added, "Good. See if you can book it."

She looked startled as hell but pulled out her phone and started scrolling.

∞∞∞∞

An hour later, we were in a compact, white-on-white studio apartment half a story below street level. Not a dragon's top choice of locations, but we could make do. Roux had called to report no trace of Szabo, but that didn't mean much since vampires left no scent trail.

I wasn't leaving anything to chance, though.

"Keep an eye on Celeste," I told Roux after promising we would check in in the morning. "Try not to let on that we're not there."

"Oh, that will be fun," he grumbled.

Yeah, about as fun as one of those team-building exercises Gordon had made us do when he'd first thrown us together. Worse, even, since it involved Celeste.

I hung up and flopped back on the bed, staring at the ceiling.

The mattress dipped as Mina sat beside me.

"You okay?"

"Peachy," I grumbled at the ceiling.

Rain pattered the sidewalk outside, and I hoped Szabo was out there in it.

A quiet minute went by. Then Mina murmured, "Would it help if I said you were right about not getting involved in all this?"

I shook my head and did my best to look for a bright side. It took a hell of a lot of looking, though.

"At least you got to see the painting," I tried.

She dropped dejectedly back beside me. "Not sure it was worth it."

A no-brainer to me, because no painting was worth this hassle, let alone putting one's life in danger. But this wasn't just about a painting, and I knew it.

"What would your father say?" I asked quietly.

She chewed that over a long time before answering. "He would say, *Next time, listen to Marius.*"

I laughed, and she chuckled, then gripped my hand. "I mean it. Next time, I will."

I turned and cocked an eyebrow. "Can I place a very large bet on that?"

She grinned. "Counting on winning big?"

Borrowing a page from her playbook, I came up with a diplomatic answer. "I think the odds lean in my favor."

She laughed and stuck out her little finger. "Ready to pinkie promise on that bet?"

"I am."

I hooked my finger around hers, and we shook, smiling. I didn't let go afterward. I couldn't.

Mina rolled to her side, propped up on an elbow. I drew her free hand to my chest and held it there.

"What?" I asked after a few seconds passed.

"Nothing. Everything." Then she sighed. "What's that saying? Situation normal..."

"All fucked up," I filled in.

She nodded somberly. "At least we have each other." Then her throat bobbed as she caught herself. "And this nice room," she added quickly, trying to joke it off.

"I prefer the château," I whispered. "And not because it's bigger or grander."

Mina nodded. "I prefer it too."

We regarded each other quietly, and it occurred to me that this was one of those *chance to talk* moments. But where to begin?

I opened my mouth, determined to do my best to come clean. But just as I did, Mina sighed and nestled up against me.

"Finally, something nice in this crappy day."

I snapped my mouth shut. So much for talking about the difficult stuff.

"Well, walking was nice too," she continued. "And that teahouse. Not to mention that cake..."

"It is nice," I whispered, kissing her hair. Oh, and her forehead — twice — before I realized where that was bound to take us.

She looked up, and those blue eyes caught mine. Blue and sparkly, like sunlight playing over the ocean. A deep, mysterious ocean I wanted to spend the rest of my life exploring.

She raised her chin, and we kissed, on the lips this time. Closed lips, then open.

"Hmm," Mina murmured, sliding a hand over my ribs.

I rolled a little closer as my body heated.

And just like that, I was a goner. Because destiny was in the room with us, picking up the corners of the bedding to roll us even closer together. The silky strands of Mina's hair ran through my fingers, and soon, my limbs were wrapped around her. Unconsciously. Inevitably. We were a couple of marionettes doing fate's bidding.

And boy, was destiny in a hurry, because our movements grew faster and more urgent. Mina tugged my shirt upward, covering my body in kisses. Stomach. Nipples. Neck, which she reached by burrowing under the bunched-up fabric.

"Dammit..." she complained, stripping me of the shirt entirely. A process complicated by the fact that I was attempting the same with hers. We ended in a hot, sweaty tangle.

"If you go that way—" I wiggled my trapped elbow.

"No, *you* go that way," she murmured irritably, like it was my fault and not destiny's.

When we finally got both our shirts off, she practically crowed in triumph.

"See? I was right."

"So right," I mumbled.

"You should always listen to me," she decided, getting to work on my pants.

"Just in bed or everywhere?"

"Everywhere," she declared, going all bossy.

"Yes, ma'am," I murmured.

She ran with the theme, issuing commands between breathless kisses.

"Lie back," she ordered once I'd ditched the rest of my clothing.

"Yes, ma'am," I said a little breathlessly. There wasn't much left on her to remove either, and it had been far too long since we'd let our bodies play this game.

Mina braced her hands on either side of my head and leaned down for a kiss, all while straddling me. Multitasking I couldn't keep up with, so I lay back and took what she had to give. Which turned out to be everything, as I discovered. No surprise, really, but finally, a *good* one.

Very good, my dragon hummed when she lined us up and sank down, letting me fill her.

Her lips parted in a blissful *Oh,* and she tilted her head back. Then she started dancing over me. A slow dance, then a flirty cha-cha, followed by an all-out, passionate samba. I gripped her hips and followed, because she definitely had the lead here. But seconds later, when she moaned in frustration, we rolled, and—

"Oh!" she cried, wrapping her legs around me.

Soon, we were slamming together, as desperately as our very first time. Even more so, maybe, because there was more at stake now. This wasn't about one night, but about forever.

"Yes..." Mina hissed, lifting her hips and clamping her inner muscles around me.

My senses tuned out everything inconsequential and amplified the impact of everything that remained, like the soft flesh of her inner thigh. The warm welcome of her body as she rose up to meet me again and again. The faint glow around her, signaling to the world that I'd marked her.

We can do more than mark her, my dragon roared.

I clenched my teeth, holding back my dragon fangs while powering into her. Again and again, until she clamped down one last time and cried out in ecstasy.

I barely held back a roar of my own as I exploded inside her. Then we collapsed, too blissed out to care about what came next.

The next time I opened my eyes, we were limp, panting, and clutching each other like we'd just survived the apocalypse.

How did I ever think I could live without you? I nearly said.

A good thing my vocal cords, like the rest of my body, weren't all that responsive. All that came out was a croak.

"I know this is London, but I swear, we're just around the corner from heaven," Mina whispered.

I lay panting, incapable of thought or deed, other than vowing to hold on to her forever.

Eventually, we separated, but just long enough to clean up before spooning together under the sheets.

A minute later, Mina whispered fondly, "There you go again."

I frowned. "What?"

She snuggled closer, not exactly protesting. "Protecting me."

Damn right, I would. Against Gordon. Szabo. Celeste. The whole fucked-up world.

Need to protect her against yourself, a corner of my mind chided.

In that respect, I was failing miserably. But I would deal with that later. Right now...

I listened to her heart beating. To the quiet patter of rain. To the electric hum of a streetlight.

Mina snuck a hand around my side and tickled my ribs. I covered her hand gently.

"Already ready for more?"

She turned in my arms, facing me with a mischievous expression.

"Well, we do have a lot of lost time to make up for."

I faked a groan, though I was totally on board with that plan. "We have a long night ahead of us, then."

She grinned, snaking her hand down from my ribs to my waist and beyond. "I'm game if you're game."

Oh, I was game, all right.

"I call the top," I said, rolling onto her.

She wound her arms and legs around me, then pinned me with a stern look. "You mean for this round. Now that we're all warmed up and everything."

I broke into a laugh. If that was just a warm-up, I was in serious trouble. But dragons loved a challenge, and the night was still young.

"You think you can keep up?" she went on teasing.

"I'm sure I can rise to the occasion."

She groaned, and I blushed at the unintended pun.

"Looks like you already have," she murmured, touching me to prove it.

Enough talk. More action, my dragon side grumbled.

I obeyed, silencing us both in the only way that mattered.

Chapter Nineteen

MINA

That night, I slept better than I had in weeks. I woke intermittently, but always with a feeling of joy and wonder, and I always slipped right back into sleep... except the time Marius happened to wake at the same time. His soft touches led us into another round of sex — a quiet, slow round that could have been poetry, it was that rhythmic and perfect.

Afterward, we'd held each other wordlessly.

Bong... Bong... A church bell struck four times, indicating the full hour, then twice more in a lower tone.

"Two in the morning," I whispered, just because.

Marius's lips played over my bare shoulder. "So close your eyes, Sleeping Beauty."

I smiled and did as I was told, listening to his steady breaths and the tap of rain over the sidewalk. For once, my mind left me in peace, allowing me to enjoy the moment instead of worrying about the future.

The next time I woke, a garbage truck was rumbling down the street, and not long after, the church bell struck three quarters of an hour. I glanced at the clock, shocked to discover we'd managed to sleep until seven forty-five. All too soon, my mind brought me back to my natural state — namely, stressing. Marius was sound asleep, so I reached quietly for my phone and started scrolling. And scrolling...

"Let me guess," Marius grumbled sleepily sometime later. "You're researching the buyers. Again."

"Maybe I'm comparison shopping drywall prices," I bluffed.

He shook his head. "You bite your lip when you comparison shop. But you frown when you think about anything related to Gordon."

I frowned. Did I?

He gestured toward my phone. "Anything new?"

"Well, I figured out what Gordon wanted to discuss with Roux before we left Paris."

"What?"

"Making sure Jensen got pushed to the top of Anastasia's list."

Marius yawned. Clearly, that wasn't news to him. "It figures. The more a buyer is willing to pay, the higher Gordon's commission."

"How much is he charging?"

Another shrug. "No idea. What's standard?"

"Well, Sotheby's takes fifteen percent for anything valued over eight million."

Marius snorted. "Knowing Gordon, he'll charge more."

"Unless he loses the deal entirely," I hinted.

Marius's brow creased. "And how might that happen?"

I reached for my phone and shuffled around, lying on my back beside him. "Here's a recent interview with Jensen." I started to read. "*Nils Øren Jensen: the tech visionary's keys to success.*" I skimmed over the text to reach the relevant section. "*Number six: cut out the middleman. 'Whenever possible,' Jensen says, 'I cut the middleman. It's called streamlining.'*"

Marius didn't look impressed until I clicked back to my search results that listed article upon article quoting the same strategy: *cut the middleman.*

"Would Jensen be bold enough to go behind Gordon's back?" I wondered aloud.

"Not sure if that's bold or reckless," Marius muttered.

"Well, he might try it."

Marius thought it over, then shrugged. "Gordon's problem, not ours."

I wasn't so sure about that, but I snuggled back up with Marius.

That inexplicable heat that started in my neck quickly maneuvered us into a sensual clinch, and nature took its course — doggy-style this time. And blimey. A couple of happier, hornier hounds were not to be found anywhere in the kingdom. We lay in bliss afterward, then took a shower — and headed straight back to bed, where Marius laid me out like a feast, went down on me, and...well, feasted.

A good thing the walls of this basement apartment were thick, because the sounds I produced made me blush afterward. But all I could think was, *Heaven, heaven, heaven.*

I, of course, felt obliged to reciprocate, and soon, it was Marius's turn to moan and grip the sheets in ecstasy.

And, whew. We'd had great sex before, but this was a whole new level. The entire time, I felt radiant. Beautiful, even, and bonded to him in a way I'd never imagined possible.

Not that I was complaining. But I did worry that the huge, happy bubble I was floating around in was about to burst — and burst big.

The next time I checked the clock, it was almost nine. Which was all right since Anastasia wasn't due to call with her decision until noon.

I giggled. "At the risk of sounding like something Bene would say... Boy, are we on fire."

I expected Marius to chuckle, but he stiffened and went very, very quiet.

I turned in his arms, facing him. "What?"

He forced a smile. "We are. And it's great."

His tone left me hanging, so I waited. And waited.

"But?" I prompted.

He hesitated. "But this might be a good time to talk."

Uh-oh. That didn't sound good.

"That night by the canal in Paris..." he started haltingly.

My body heated at the memory, and my hand went to my neck in the new habit I'd formed since then. One guaranteed to set off all kinds of sensual imagery, even now, when my lust ought to have been more than sated.

Marius gulped, following the gesture.

I froze, then probed my skin in a more clinical way. "You mean that hickey you left me with?"

He shook his head. "Not a hickey."

After waiting an eternity, I hit him with my sternest teacher look. "Explain."

It took him a good minute to work up the nerve to begin, and when he finished, I practically shrieked.

"You what?"

He winced and patted the air, urging me to lower my voice.

"I marked you," he repeated. "By moonlight."

That part, I'd heard. I'd also caught that it was a form of staking one's claim to a future mate. But *like an engagement ring for supernaturals* sounded way too harmless for the pained expression on his face.

I sat up and crossed my arms sternly, though part of me loved the idea that he wanted me the way I wanted him. Forever.

"You don't sneak an engagement ring onto a woman's hand. You discuss it with her to see if she agrees."

"It will wear off with time," he tried.

"An engagement that *wears off*?" My voice hit the ceiling.

"I didn't mean to," he tried lamely.

I glared. "Oh, that makes me feel better."

"Don't get me wrong — I would love to mark you if the timing was right. But at that moment... Well, it was destiny."

I knew the man wasn't an ace with words, but I was losing my patience quickly. Did he want me or didn't he?

"So, destiny wants us together, but you don't want me?"

"I want you," he insisted. "More than anything."

"And yet you decided to wait for the mark to wear off. Without telling me."

"For your own protection."

I put my face in my hands. There we were, back at the P word. The man was obsessed with it. A fact I ought to be grateful for, but there was the *why* and the *how*, and his *how* was so messed up, I didn't know where to begin.

I waited until I thought my voice wouldn't exceed the decibel level of a dragon roar to speak.

"And you were going to bring this up. . . when?"

"As soon as I could." When I pinned him with a hard glare, he stuck up his hands. "Not soon enough. I know."

That was an understatement, but I didn't trust myself to reply.

Lucky for him, my phone rang.

"Yes?" I snarled into it.

"Um. . . everything okay?" Roux replied.

I pinched the bridge of my nose. "Next question."

Poor Roux. He sounded stressed himself.

"Did you catch the morning news?" he asked a little ominously.

Marius leaned in to listen, but I pushed him away. He could come close when he made up to me. . . somehow. Right now, I was still furious.

"Uh. . . no. . ." I said, watching Marius pull out his phone. He hit a few keys, then cursed.

I leaned in, and he let me, but that was only fair in my book. He owed me, dammit.

My jaw dropped as I skimmed the BBC headline.

Latvian art expert murdered.

Underneath, the subtitle screamed, *Hotel guests raised the alarm after hearing cries, but too late.*

I skimmed the body of the article. *Raisa Kepke, 59, pronounced dead at the scene. . . Signs of forced entry. . . Cause of death not yet officially established. . .*

"Get your asses over here, *tout de suite,*" Roux grunted.

∞∞∞∞

We did, though only after a thorough scrub in the shower to erase the scent of sex. But nothing dimmed the glow of my skin, and I grumbled at Marius the whole time we rode the Tube.

The nerve he'd had, secretly marking me! The gall! How patronizing!

185

Then again, if I were in his position, I might have done the same to him — and not just to protect him, but for entirely selfish reasons.

I glanced at him, going ramrod straight with a sudden thought.

"Wait. Did you say this marking thing you did is to claim a partner and keep others away?"

His throat bobbed. "Yes."

I thought of Bene, Roux, and Henrik. "Will the others be able to tell?"

He nodded slowly, and I panicked, tightening my scarf.

"Shit, I need a bigger scarf. And perfume..."

Then it hit me, and I gaped at him. The other guys had been making me wear a scarf for days.

I smacked Marius on the arm and yelped, "They already know?"

At least half the commuters in our carriage looked up. The other half looked carefully away.

My cheeks burned as Marius nodded miserably.

"They're in this with you?" I shrieked.

More looks while Marius squirmed in his seat.

"No. They just... They care about you, like I do."

I put my face in my hands. Very sweet — in principle. Yet all I felt was burning shame.

The minute we marched into the suite where the others had spent the night, I crossed my arms and glared.

"We'll be discussing this. Soon," I growled, motioning to my neck.

"Talk to him, not us." Bene pointed at Marius.

Roux shook his head firmly. "No time. We have a murder on our hands."

He was right, and I chastised myself for being so self-centered. A woman I'd met the previous day had been brutally murdered. It was awful. If I had said or done something differently, might she still be alive now?

A knock sounded on the door, and Bene muttered, "Please, don't let that be Gordon."

Roux looked through the peephole, annoyed. Then he stiffened and opened the door. "Good morning, Gordon."

I froze. Surely he was joking.

Roux shot us significant looks as he slowly opened the door. Bene winced, glancing at the empty takeout containers and paperwork littering the place. He backed toward the dining table, blocking Gordon's view of the worst.

"Good morning?" Gordon huffed. "Good bloody morn—" He spotted me, then caught himself. "Oh hello, sweetheart."

I hugged him, stepping sideways to make him turn toward the wall. "I'm so glad to see you. Such terrible news."

The truth of the second half of my statement helped cover the lie of the first, and my position gave Bene a few seconds to clear the table. God, I was getting as devious as the rest of them.

"Terrible, indeed." Gordon glared at the guys like they were to blame.

They gazed back with poker faces capable of winning millions in Vegas.

"Good to see you, sir," Roux said smoothly. "Glad you could make the trip so quickly."

Surprised was more like it.

It was close to ten a.m. When had Gordon learned about the murder, and how had he gotten to London so quickly?

Private jet answered the transportation part, but what about the rest?

"We were just discussing... Well..." Roux hesitated, looking at me.

Everyone's eyes followed, as if I were a child who hadn't yet figured out there was no tooth fairy.

"Discussing what to tell the police if they question what business we had with Raisa," I said flatly, looking right at Gordon. Unlike Mallorca, there was no need for secrecy about my involvement here.

He tugged at his collar. "I'm sorry to have involved you."

Was he, though? And how many times had he secretly involved me in much worse?

"We were also discussing how to proceed with the other buyers," Roux added.

Gordon motioned everyone to the table, then gestured to Bene. "Fetch Celeste, will you?"

I'd spent the subway ride considering possible murder suspects. Now I added one more. Celeste.

Then my imagination served up another suspect, and I stared at Gordon, my heart hammering.

Marius's dark eyes flashed, telling me he was thinking the same thing.

"Ah, Gordon. Thank goodness you're here," Celeste announced upon entering.

And wow, what a transformation. Around us, she was coy and cunning. Around Gordon, she was usually calm and efficient. Now, she played up *weak* and *helpless*.

I rolled my eyes. Obviously, she'd missed her calling in Hollywood.

"All right, everyone. Gather around," Gordon ordered, moving to the head of the table.

Bene's eyes went wide, and he lunged forward.

"Oh, Gordon?" I called sharply.

His head whipped to me while Bene snatched the pizza box Gordon had been about to sit on.

"Yes?" he asked sharply.

"Um... Would you like a coffee?" I answered a little meekly.

His brow furrowed, but he nodded. "Yes, please. Thank you, sweetheart."

I turned away to make the coffee, cursing myself. How had I never noticed the special treatment Gordon bestowed on me? He barked at the men, while I always got a soft, indulging *sweetheart*.

No wonder Celeste hated me. And, oh. An even uglier thought hit me. No wonder I'd never questioned what Gordon did for a living. My sweet, generous godfather would never get involved in anything murky, would he?

But the truth was, everything about him reached Loch-Ness-level murkiness. How could I have been so blind?

Still, I was in this now and just as invested as anyone.

My mind went over the situation. What if the police arrived to question us about the highly unusual, valuable, and secretive art deal we'd been attempting to broker? Neither Anastasia nor the buyers would wish to be named, and she certainly wouldn't want her painting to make the evening news. On the other hand...

Perfect opportunity to get The Tower of Blue Horses *out in the public eye*, the devious part of my mind noted.

I squirmed in my seat. Did I dare? Should I?

An uncomfortable hour passed, most of it taken up by Gordon blustering and thinking out loud. He hardly let anyone get in a word edgewise, and no one risked drawing his ire.

We'd barely settled on what version of the truth to share — and which details to omit — when another knock sounded on the door. Gordon frowned at Bene, who jerked a thumb at Roux, whose eyes flashed with a look that asked, *Why is it always my fault?*

I went to the door before they broke into another one of their fights. Then I peeped out and took a deep breath.

"Police," I whispered.

Gordon straightened his tie and motioned for me to admit them.

"Metropolitan Police, ma'am," the head officer announced as three others fanned out around the room. "We have a few questions."

Gordon greeted them calmly. "Gentlemen, good morning. What can we do for you?"

"Just a few questions, please," the constable said.

A major understatement, because as it turned out, he had *lots* of questions. Questions that grew more pointed with every passing minute.

"According to Ms. Kepke's diary, she had an appointment here yesterday. What was the nature of your business with her?"

Gordon did most of the answering, sticking largely to the truth, while the rest of us looked on solemnly. Celeste clutched at a handkerchief, apparently shattered by the news.

I pictured Meryl Streep opening an envelope. *And the Oscar for Best Supporting Actress goes to...*

"Celeste," Gordon barked.

She jerked her head up.

"Forward copies of my correspondence with Ms. Kepke to the constable," he finished.

Celeste took the officer's card and scurried out of the room.

They questioned Gordon, then each of us. We all stuck to the truth with certain omissions, as agreed. The last any of us had seen of Raisa was when she'd left the hotel the previous morning.

"And you, sir?" one of the officers asked Marius.

He looked up sharply. "Like they said — I last saw her when she left here yesterday morning."

The policemen looked at one another. "What about later?"

Marius's eyes went hard, and he repeated himself in a clipped, angry tone. "I last saw her when she left here yesterday morning."

"And where were you at approximately two a.m. this morning?" they demanded.

Gordon huffed. "What is the meaning of this? He said—"

"A man of his build was seen leaving Ms. Kepke's hotel in the early hours of the morning," the officer butted in.

That build was *dragon*, and boy, was he pissed.

Me too. Not every man in London had Marius's broad chest and shoulders, but it was a big city. There had to be dozens of other men of that general description.

Gordon shook his head. "That may be, but my associates all spent the night here."

My gut started to sink. Doubly so when the policeman shook his head. "Neither the night shift nor security cameras show Mr. Aecher returning after leaving through the rear entrance before noon."

I winced. So, a camera had caught us leaving. Or, wait. Judging by the constable's insistent glare, a camera had only caught Marius leaving. Which was possible, if his body had happened to shield mine from view.

My gut sank another few inches.

Marius carefully kept his eyes away from mine. "I didn't spend the night here last night."

Gordon nearly gave himself whiplash looking over. Henrik gritted his teeth.

"Where were you?"

"I took a room in Belgravia."

"Which they'll be sure to corroborate, along with your whereabouts at two a.m.?" the officer asked.

Roux shifted from foot to foot, looking at Marius, who remained stony.

"The room wasn't reserved in my name, and there was a lockbox," he said. "So, no. But there were probably cameras on the street."

He gave them the address, but they pressed on.

"So, no alibi?"

Marius whispered into my mind. *Do not say anything. I repeat, do not say anything.*

"I have not seen Ms. Kepke since yesterday morning," he growled.

The head constable looked at one of his men. A window opened in my mind, allowing me to read his thoughts clearly. Raisa Kepke was an associate of a prominent member of Parliament, I learned, who didn't want their dealings to go public. The constable's superiors wanted this case solved quickly and with minimal media attention. They needed a closed case fast, and Marius was as good a suspect as any.

The constable was already calculating where to position his men in case Marius resisted arrest and how many more squad cars to call in for backup.

"Backup?" I yelped.

The officer stared at me, and I coughed into my hand. "Let's back up, shall we? You haven't questioned me."

Gordon frowned. Roux's eyes went wide, and even Henrik made a cutting gesture.

Don't! Marius yelled into my mind.

"You don't match the suspect's description, miss," the officer reasoned.

Thank goodness, but yeesh. Talk about female privilege. Marius was being grilled, while I was assumed harmless. Which I absolutely was, but still. It was the principle of the thing.

"I had nothing to do with Raisa Kepke's murder, but neither did he."

"And you know that because...?"

Not a word! Marius barked into my mind.

Celeste looked on with interest. The others, in panic. My confession could get Marius off the hook with the law, but Gordon would be furious. An offense by one of the men would be held against all four of them, which they couldn't afford, especially now that they were nearing the end of their contracts. In a few weeks, they would all be free of their ridiculous arrangement with Gordon.

I took a deep breath, then spoke.

"Because he was with me."

Marius closed his eyes. Everyone went very, very still.

"At two in the morning?" the constable asked, and yikes. Never had five words been so loaded.

Heat flooded my cheeks as I nodded. Not because I was ashamed, but because the officer on the right looked from me to Marius and back, graphically picturing us in the act. I could tell because the special power that had slipped out of my subconscious was still turned on.

Magic was a bitch sometimes.

The officer stroked his chin. "I see."

Gordon's face turned red with fury. "Now, wait just a moment—"

"We left for the night," I cut in. "I booked us a room in Belgravia. Marius was with me all night."

Celeste looked half jealous, half triumphant, because trouble for me was her catnip.

"He could have slipped out," another officer pointed out.

I glared at him. "You seem very determined to place suspicion on the basis of a very general description of a man's build. Even when that man has an alibi." I paused, collecting myself before I started yelling. "And no, he did not slip out at two in the morning. I woke to hear a church bell chime at that time. And Marius was with me."

The first police officer glanced at the other. One thought I was covering for Marius, but the other two believed me.

This woman couldn't lie to save her life, one was thinking rather critically.

Celeste, I could tell, was siding with the first guy. A glance inside her twisted mind revealed her warring with herself. The more trouble for me or Marius, the better, but that risked irking Gordon, which wouldn't serve her ends.

What those ends were, I couldn't see. But the endless machinations of her mind chilled me.

Still, she kept her mouth shut, and the ranking officer lowered his little notebook with a ponderous, "I see."

They questioned us for another few minutes. Then, with stern warnings that they would be in touch, they departed, leaving the room as quiet as a graveyard at midnight.

Gordon glared at Marius, then shot me a look I'd never, ever seen before. One that said, *I'm deeply, deeply disappointed.*

It hurt. It actually hurt, though it shouldn't have, because he was the one with something to hide, not me.

Then he looked at Celeste, silently communicating, which spooked me. But exactly when it might have been most useful, my ability to read minds faded away. Great.

I added it to my list of magic to buckle down and learn as soon as I mastered shadow-walking.

Gordon nodded to Celeste, then checked his watch and grunted at the men. "We'll reconvene here in thirty minutes. No one leaves." He pinned Marius with a look that said, *Especially you, you bastard.* Then he turned to me and spoke in a scarily measured tone. "And you, Wilhelmina. I'd like a word. In the other suite. Immediately."

Chapter Twenty

MINA

Gordon stared out the windows of the neighboring suite while I sat at the dining table, silently squirming. I'd never, ever been hauled into the principal's office as a kid, but this was what it must feel like — only worse, because school principals weren't terrifying warlocks with a license to kill.

Well, Gordon didn't have that either, but he was hardly one to play by the rules.

I waited, wilting like the flowers in yesterday's bouquet.

Celeste was in the adjoining room that served as an office, fetching something for Gordon. And boy, did she take her sweet time.

My skin went clammy with sweat. My feet cramped. I cracked my knuckles, trying to remain calm.

I looked for the painting, then remembered it had been returned to Anastasia. Even that hint of beauty and innocence had been stripped from this room.

Finally, Celeste sauntered out of the office with a file in her hands. An honest-to-God, old-fashioned file full of printouts that said Gordon had been collecting dirt on someone for years.

She walked over to Gordon, swinging her hips with every step. An effect that was lost on him, because he stared steadfastly out the window. As she approached, he stuck out a hand without so much as turning.

"Thank you. That will be all," Gordon said gruffly.

Celeste headed for her room, but Gordon motioned to the main door with a quieter, scarier echo of his own words. "I said, that will be all."

She departed sullenly, closing the door hard enough to make a statement while leaving room to deny any such intent.

Gordon remained at the window for another full minute before turning with a hard look. He placed a file on the table and slid it over, looming over me.

"Have a look," he ordered.

I didn't have to ask what it contained. It could only be one thing. The file with everything he had on Marius.

And boy, was that file thick.

I raised my chin. That was Marius's past — or the parts cherry-picked by someone determined to document every misstep of a stubborn, rebellious dragon.

Well, there were two sides to every story, right?

I didn't touch the file. I didn't have to. I'd long since drawn my own conclusions about Marius, based on my experiences with him.

The man was no angel, but he was good to me and around me. And he was doing his damned best to build a better future, even if that meant playing by Gordon's twisted rules.

Then I frowned, thinking of the mark he'd left on me, and how furious that made me. Furious but also weirdly touched, because he wanted me. Sort of.

God, what a mess.

Steeling my nerves, I looked straight at my godfather.

"What are you doing, Gordon?" I asked evenly.

"I'm doing what your father would want me to do — protecting you."

I curled my hands into fists, recognizing another attempt to manipulate me by triggering my rawest emotions.

I gritted my teeth. "Maybe I don't need protecting."

He shook his head sadly. "Ah, but you do. There is so much you don't know."

"Maybe I know more than you think."

His brow furrowed, and a brief flash of concern crossed his eyes. But he shook it off, one hundred percent confident I couldn't — wouldn't — ever uncover his ugly truths.

"I don't doubt your expertise in some matters. But when it comes to understanding the ways of the world — and men who would take advantage of you..." He trailed off.

The world was full of patronizing older men, and the art world doubly so. But, wow. This took the cake. Did he think I lived in a château or a convent?

I was so angry, I nearly burst out with it all. *I know you've been taking advantage of me, Gordon. I know all that money you make doesn't come from legal means. I know the men you described to me as bodyguards are mercenaries coerced into working for you. I know you're using me to gain Anastasia's trust and that you're primarily concerned with your own profits.*

But somehow, I kept my big mouth shut and slid the file back to him.

"There's nothing here I need to see."

"Ah, but there is," Gordon insisted.

I shook my head. "You may be an expert in your field, Gordon, but I'm an expert in mine. And when new students join my class, I form my own judgments about them. I don't cloud that with the opinions of others."

Gordon gave me that face that said, *That might apply to a coddled school setting, but not the real world.*

I could have shaken him. School *was* the real world, raw and unfiltered. And kids weren't alien species — they were humans susceptible to the same behavioral dynamics as adults. They just weren't as good at hiding them yet.

"Mr. Aecher has his qualities, but many, many faults," Gordon said sadly, as if it truly pained him to see anything but the best in anyone.

"So do we all," I hinted, keeping my eyes firmly on Gordon's.

He frowned, then went back to principal mode. "And honestly, gallivanting off with him alone..."

Gallivanting? I nearly screamed. After spotting Szabo lurking around?

I nearly blurted as much but stopped cold. So far, I'd assumed Szabo was working alone or in cahoots with Celeste. But what if he'd been hired by Gordon?

As unlikely as that seemed, anything was possible, so I kept that to myself. All I said was, "I didn't feel safe here."

He snorted. "You couldn't be safer than in a place where I can protect you."

A place where he could also monitor my every move, I realized.

Gordon sighed tragically. "I blame myself. I made it clear to the men that I expected the highest standards of behavior, but I failed to communicate that to you." He went back to that disappointed look that added, *Frankly, I didn't think I had to.* Then he continued. "But this is business, which calls for strict codes of conduct."

Said the man who routinely resorted to manipulation, intimidation, and blackmail.

"Where I spend the night and with whom is my business," I shot back.

Gordon shook his head. "Not when you're on business."

"I don't work with Marius. In fact, I'm not working at all," I said icily. "I'm here to do you a favor, at your request."

Gordon's face clouded, like a man who'd been nipped by a docile lapdog.

"But this *is* business, my dear. And in business, there is no place for intimate relations. Especially when it comes to people in unequal positions of power."

Ah. Back to the patronizing, *you're so weak and ignorant* argument.

Oh, poor Marius, I nearly quipped. He was bigger, stronger, and more knowledgeable about Gordon's dirty businesses. But I was the big boss's favored goddaughter, which put me in a privileged position far, far above Marius and the others.

A sour taste registered in my mouth. How many other little privileges had I profited from that I'd never been aware of?

Not that that would interest Gordon. So I stuck to what would.

"A woman has been murdered. I have no idea what's behind that, but it's terrifying." I stuck up a hand before he decided to reassure poor, stupid me that he would keep me safe. "It could also frighten the other buyers away. Not to mention that a high-profile murder case puts Anastasia's artwork at risk of falling into the public eye. *Those* are the fires we need to focus on extinguishing."

Not me shagging Marius, in other words.

You have a point there, Gordon's pursed lips admitted.

I slid the file back across the table and stood, enumerating an actionable list that would get Gordon off my case.

"Right now, we have to reassure the other interested parties. We have to talk to Anastasia before the police do to make sure she doesn't say too much." I shivered, listening to myself. This felt all too *Al Capone.* But I powered on. "And we should consider putting the deal on ice until things settle down."

Gordon shook his head curtly. "Anastasia has a deadline. We must respect that."

I would rather Gordon respect the law and basic human decency. But sadly, I'd learned to lower my expectations.

He called Celeste back in and repeated most of my points as orders, making them sound like his own brilliant thinking. But the last point he made, I gave him full credit for.

"And keep tabs on the police," he ordered Celeste. "Anything they learn, we need to know too."

My jaw hung open. Did Gordon actually have the means to do that?

I slumped. Of course he did.

Celeste finished taking completely unnecessary notes, then gave the file on the table a pointed look.

Gordon frowned, then shooed her off. "Go. I'll take care of the rest."

My knees wobbled as I wondered what that meant.

Luckily, my phone rang then. Unluckily, it was our client.

"Good morning, Anastasia. How are you?" I said, looking at Gordon.

He listened to the beginning of our exchange, then strode into the office and closed the door, presumably to make his own calls.

I made soothing noises into the phone. "Yes, it really is terrible... Yes, the police were here... Of course, I'm available to come by any time you need me..."

A moment later, I practically squawked. "What?"

"Bogdan called to say he was no longer interested in the painting," Anastasia lamented. "You must do something. Immediately!"

I suspected she was more alarmed at losing a gentleman caller than a buyer, but I agreed to call.

I thought it over as I dialed. Surely an arms dealer wouldn't be put off by the murder of a competitor? What had changed his mind, then?

Bogdan was apologetic but vague. When I pressed him about why he was pulling out of the deal, he hesitated, and the sound of footsteps indicated he was moving to a more private location. When he stopped, his voice dropped, and his tone changed.

"You seem like a nice girl to me, Hermina."

Not exactly my name, but I was too anxious to interrupt.

"I would hate to see you fall down any harm," he went on ominously.

Any harm to fall upon you, I silently corrected, but boy, did I get the gist.

"So I suggest you remove yourself from this deal before the fan spreads the shit," he continued. "Leave the profits — and the risks — to others."

"Risks?" I gulped.

Silence was his only reply, and my imagination filled the void with graphic images of powerful hands choking the life out of poor Raisa.

"Do you think her death was meant to send a message?" I finally asked.

He laughed, though there was no humor in it. "The phone call I received was much clearer."

I gaped. "Someone threatened you? Who?"

He thought that over, then said, "I have made a fortune — and lived to a ripe old age — by recognizing when the reward outweighs the risk. And let me assure you, this is not one of those times."

I froze because, yikes. If an arms dealer found this too risky, I sure as hell should too.

The line went silent as we both chewed over our own thoughts — and fears, in my case.

A thought struck me, and I glanced at the office door. Still firmly closed.

I walked to the far end of the suite and whispered into the phone. "Will you answer one question, please?"

"It depends on the question," he chuckled.

I found myself admiring his ability to maintain a sense of humor in a time of murder and mayhem. Essential qualities for a man in his line of work, I supposed.

"What commission did Gordon say he would charge?" I whispered.

Bogdan huffed. "Twenty percent — on top of the selling price. Outrageous. But fitting, perhaps, given the risks."

Years ago, I'd interned at an auction house, and *risks* had occasionally come up, but never, ever the kind that left people dead. What had I gotten myself into?

Bogdan sighed, signaling the end of our call. "Give my best to Anastasia Nikolaevna. It was truly a pleasure."

"I'm sure she would be happy to hear from you," I threw in. It was a terrible time to play matchmaker, but I couldn't help myself. "Even if that might be some time from now and not in relation to artwork."

He chuckled. "You think so?"

I did indeed. And why not strive to create something positive amid all this shit spread by the proverbial fan?

"I believe so, yes," I said.

∞∞∞∞

The minute I could flee Celeste's suite, I did, heading next door to where the others waited. Everyone looked up when

I opened the door, and while no one said a word, I saw the question marks in their eyes.

Most of all, though, I saw Marius, looking more anxious than ever. More than I thought him capable of.

And just like that, all the unnecessary clutter around my emotions fell away, leaving what mattered most: love. Devotion. Respect.

My feet flew across the floor, and a second later, we were hugging tightly. Not just me hugging him but him hugging me like a dragon's greatest treasure.

He buried his face in my shoulder and breathed me in. I closed my eyes, clutching his back. His body warmed mine, and in the recesses of my mind, a single thought registered.

Actions speak louder than words.

So, to hell with Gordon's file. To hell with my own doubts. To hell with anything that stood between me and my man.

Yes, we would definitely have to work on our communication. No, he shouldn't have secretly marked me. But he was a good man at heart, and he loved me.

I sensed the others shuffling uncomfortably. Well, to hell with them too.

Then I caught myself and pulled away. I loved Marius, but I'd come to love the others too. Not in the same, desperately passionate way, but as friends. And maybe we hadn't been thrown together by chance. Maybe that was destiny too. From day one, we'd been in this together.

And now, on a day with all hell breaking loose, we needed one another more than ever.

I drew back and turned to the others.

"Nice to see you too," Bene quipped.

I did my best to look stern. "For the record, I'm still furious." I pointed at Marius. "Especially at you. But right now..." I stopped talking and switched to body language.

I opened and closed my hands in a chatting motion, then pointed around. *We need to talk.*

Next, I put a finger over my lips and pointed to the adjoining suite. *In a way they can't overhear.* Because it wasn't unreasonable to assume Gordon had tapped our room.

Finally, I raised my hands, palms up. *So, what do we do?*

What seemed hopeless to me was child's play to men trained in skills most law-abiding citizens had no clue about, let alone use for. Bene motioned Marius and me onto the small balcony off the far bedroom, while Roux turned the television to a sports channel and cranked up the volume.

Zoom! Zoom! Race cars sped around and around a course.

"Formula One," Bene murmured. "Perfect."

Roux and Henrik joined us, and we huddled together in that tiny, exposed space. Yet I felt safer and more comfortable than in Celeste's warm, enclosed suite.

My eyes met Henrik's, and his hit the floor. So, maybe vampires could feel shame. I wouldn't count on that to save my life, but I figured I was safe enough for now.

"What did Gordon say?" Bene asked.

I skimmed over the details and got to the point. "As I see it, we need to figure out how to protect ourselves from whatever goes wrong next — including whatever surprises Gordon pops on us."

Henrik frowned. "You think he has something planned?"

Roux chimed in before I could. "No, but he isn't above throwing any of us under the bus."

His eyes landed on Marius and stuck like glue.

"Everyone but her." Bene pointed to me.

I grimaced. "Maybe, but I have the feeling my immunity might wear out soon."

Henrik shook his head. "Worst case, he'll find a way to send you home and keep you out of trouble."

I hated the thought, but he was right.

"So, where do things stand now?" Bene asked. "With the art deal, I mean."

Roux rubbed his chin, thinking aloud. "Raisa is dead. That leaves the Bulgarian and the tech guy."

I shook my head. "Bogdan just pulled out. That leaves Jensen."

Briefly, I filled them in on what the Bulgarian had reported.

"Jensen was Gordon's top choice all along," Bene mused.

I shot Roux a look, but he just shrugged. "Gordon will always do what earns him the most."

I heaved an inner sigh. Clearly, I had to adjust my assumptions about Gordon from *bad* to *worse*.

"According to Bogdan, Gordon stands to earn twenty percent of the selling price," I murmured, doing a quick calculation. "Twenty percent of eighty-seven million…"

"Seventeen-plus million," Henrik supplied.

"On top of the selling price," I emphasized. "If Jensen doesn't cut Gordon out of the deal."

Marius snorted. "He can't be that stupid."

"Maybe he's that confident," Henrik mused.

I made yet another vow to cut ties with my godfather — soon.

Then I caught myself. Soon wasn't good enough. I needed a deadline.

As soon as this mission was over, I decided, and as soon as the guys completed their contract.

"Will Anastasia even sell the painting to Jensen?" Bene asked. "Will she agree to cutting Gordon out of the deal?"

"Someone killed Raisa and strong-armed Bogdan," I pointed out. "That someone could be just as 'convincing' to Anastasia."

"The question is, who is he?"

"Or she," I said.

We all looked in the direction of the adjoining suite.

Chapter Twenty-One

MINA

Ultimately, we agreed on four potential suspects in the murder of Raisa Kepke. Jensen's motive, we decided, would be to eliminate his competition in the sale. Gordon's, to secure the highest bidder and earn the highest possible commission. Or it could have been Szabo, working on behalf of Gordon. Alternatively, it could have been Celeste, working on behalf of Gordon *or* on her own behalf, to somehow profit from the ensuing situation.

"My money's on Gordon or someone working for Gordon," Bene decided.

"My money's on Celeste," Marius grumbled.

I agreed. It was always a safe bet to assume the worst about that bitch. Er, that woman.

Szabo, we all agreed, was unlikely, mainly because he wouldn't have passed up the opportunity to drink Raisa's blood. But we couldn't be sure, given the vagueness of the police report.

"No matter who it was, we have to protect ourselves," I insisted. "So, from now on, we all share everything we know. No secrets, no matter what Gordon swears any of us to."

Marius glared at each of the others, reinforcing my point. None of them were team players at heart, but we'd never needed transparency as much as now, when Gordon would happily sacrifice any of them to make his deal work.

And Marius, I knew, would be first on his hit list.

A problem I grappled with all morning and into the afternoon. We were all confined to the suite in a situation that reeked very much of house arrest.

Roux paced and paced until I was ready to scream.

Henrik sat at the table like a chess master, hands at his temples, thinking.

Marius went between pacing with Roux and close by my side, swearing hell and damnation to anyone who dared threaten me.

I doodled horses overlooking a mountainous landscapes framed by ominous clouds and dollar signs.

Bene was the only relaxed one, ordering liberally from room service and lounging on the couch, watching TV.

"It's on Gordon's tab, right?" He grinned.

Ah, to be able to switch off all worries about the future, just like that.

I went to my room, gazed out the window, and thought. Hard.

The problem, I concluded, was that I hadn't been thinking deviously enough. Gordon — and unknown enemies — had been plotting and conniving, and all I'd done was react.

Well, I was about to get proactive. To put myself in Gordon's — and Celeste's, Jensen's, Szabo's, and Anastasia's shoes — and think ruthlessly. Greedily. What were they likely to do, and how could I protect myself and Marius — plus Bene, Roux, and Henrik?

Yes, even Henrik. A little less out of loyalty than in hopes of having something to hold over him the next time an unexpected thirst struck.

At three o'clock, Gordon allowed me to visit Anastasia, sending Henrik and Roux with me as protection rather than Marius.

I nearly rolled my eyes. Did he think we would strip and screw in Anastasia's stairwell at a time like this?

The idea made my pulse skip, I had to admit.

I dragged myself out of the hotel, fearful that Gordon might try to bump Marius off. But Bene promised to look after him, so away I went, plotting the whole time.

No more Mr. Nice Guy — or Nice Girl, in my case. No more principles or ideals. No more hoping. Something much more precious than that painting was at stake, and it was up to me to save it.

In short, it was time to release my devious inner bitch.

So, when a fretful Anastasia asked my advice, I talked up Jensen over the bitter taste in my mouth. Oh, and Gordon too.

"It's essential to work through Gordon, and only through Gordon," I said. "Anyone trying to circumvent him is trying to circumvent you too."

A white lie, but hey. Jensen wanted exclusive rights to one of the most beautiful paintings on earth? Let him fork out another seventeen million for the privilege.

"But he's. . . he's. . . "

"Unfeeling? Unworthy?" I supplied. "Yes. But he's also rich. And he's willing to close the deal before your deadline."

Anastasia looked sullenly out the window, contemplating her Achilles' heel.

I looked too, contemplating mine — my ideals and my love for Marius.

Then I patted her dry, wizened hand and forced a smile. "You know what I suggest?"

She tilted her head expectantly.

"We take our tea upstairs and enjoy the painting for a little while."

I'd meant to say *you* take *your* tea, but my tongue slipped.

Anastasia flashed a bittersweet smile and led me upstairs, where we sat, quietly drinking in Franz Marc's masterpiece.

At least, that's what I did for the first minute. Then I gazed off into the distance, thinking. Scheming. Calculating.

∞∞∞∞∞

Roux and I departed, leaving Henrik with Anastasia. I was sure she would refuse a bodyguard, but Henrik had read aloud from a quote framed on one of the walls, launching a lively discussion about poetry — in Polish, from what I could tell.

Adam Mickiewicz, the vampire murmured appreciatively.

One of those world-famous-in-his-home-country figures, I gathered.

Anastasia lit right up. Henrik had Bogdan's old world manners, minus the charm, but that didn't bother her. Especially since neither Roux, nor I, nor most of London was capable of discussing that poetry at the same (or any) level.

We left them and made our way back to the hotel. On the way, I took my frustrations out on Roux.

"I can't believe you didn't tell me about this stupid mark," I grumbled, tugging at my scarf. "I thought it was a hickey."

He snorted. "No way. You're as bad as a dragon when you get angry."

I decided to take that as a compliment.

"And I can't believe Marius did this in the first place," I ranted.

Roux chewed on that for a moment, then surprised the hell out of me by whispering. "I would have done the same if love meant more to me than the mission."

I stared.

He flashed a thin smile. "Not that it does."

I had no illusions about Roux dedicating himself to anything but a job. But, wow. His words shed a whole new light on what Marius had done.

I chewed that over through the first half of the trip back to the hotel. Then I informed Roux we would exit the Tube one station early and walk the rest of the way. Slowly, because I was still deviously plotting.

I finalized my plan just as we turned the final corner to the hotel, where I took a deep breath. Roux held the door open for me, but instead of thanking him, I marched in without a word.

No more Mr. Nice Guy, I reminded myself.

I peeked into our suite to make sure Gordon hadn't killed Marius, or Marius killed Bene, or Bene Marius.

But, whew. Both shifters were hale and hearty, and not at each other's throats. Actually, Bene was in lion form and sporting a hell of a mane. When I walked in, he was stretching as only a feline could, but upon seeing me, he strutted around and tossed his golden mane in a gesture that said, *See what you could have had, baby?*

Marius growled under his breath.

Roux rolled his eyes. "Lions."

I didn't stop to belabor the point. I just popped back in to the hallway, steeled myself, and raised a hand to knock on the door of the neighboring suite.

"Wait!" Roux motioned urgently at my scarf.

I tightened it quickly, then cleared my throat and knocked sharply.

Celeste answered, but I marched past her and announced, "I'd like a word, please, Gordon."

My godfather rewarded me with a brilliant smile, looking hopeful that I would dump Marius, beg for his forgiveness, and run home to my château, where I would go back to being the sweet, manipulatable young woman he knew.

Well, that wasn't happening.

He sent Celeste out, and she complied, though not without a huff.

"So, I've done some thinking," I began. "A lot of thinking, and I've reached a conclusion."

"Yes?" Gordon smiled eagerly.

I took a deep breath, then started, "This art deal stinks."

Why mince words, I figured.

Gordon frowned.

"Everything about it stinks, from the secrecy to the manipulation and the total lack of morals," I continued.

Gordon's mouth fell open, but I plowed on before he could speak.

"You asked me to help evaluate a rare artwork. To ensure it found its way into good hands. And here we are, dealing with a murder, a police investigation, and a dwindling list of buyers — most of whom are highly questionable. Plus, that list was rigged from the start."

"Now, wait a second," Gordon protested.

I shook my head, because I'd already waited far too long.

"Now I find myself trying to salvage a sketchy backroom deal for you, and honestly, I've had enough."

And boy, was I putting it mildly.

Gordon's brows knitted together. "I never intended—"

I nearly cackled. "Oh, I think you did. I think you planned this all carefully. Not the murder, perhaps, but keeping Jensen at the top of the list and a number of other things. You planned to use me to get the deal done to your liking."

Gordon looked sour. "Are you asking for a cut?"

I stomped the floor. "No! I don't want a cut! I don't want anything to do with this, but it's too late, isn't it?" I gulped for breath, then hammered on. "All I want now is to get this over with and get back to my life. A life where I'm free to make informed choices about my involvement in anything."

Gordon reached for that damn file again and pushed it in front of me. "There. Inform yourself. He's held back plenty of information."

In my mind's eye, I saw myself shoving it back, sending papers flying everywhere. But I refrained.

"Keeping private matters private is different from hiding information pertinent to me, as you have done again and again."

"Now, let me make one thing clear," Gordon thundered.

"No, let *me* make something clear," I cut in. "If I choose Marius, that's my choice, and you must respect it."

"Your father would never approve," he spat.

"Maybe, maybe not. But my father would let me run my own life. My father wouldn't manipulate me into helping him with questionable deals. He wouldn't engage in questionable deals in the first place."

I sucked in a breath before my voice rose to a shout. I was that close.

Gordon's eyes flashed with anger, but he calmed himself with a deep breath.

"That couldn't be further from the truth." He shook his head. "I see what a mistake it was, allowing you to mix with men of their ilk." He gestured toward the neighboring suite.

And just like that, magic struck, revealing his thoughts to me. Thoughts of killing Marius. Punishing the others. Convincing my sister and cousin to believe I had lost my marbles and could not be trusted to lead my own life.

"Don't even think about it, Gordon. I'm warning you," I growled.

He stared. "Is that a threat?"

"It's a warning. Leave me alone. Leave all of them alone. You depend on me more than you think."

He snorted like I was a child and in way, way over my head.

Which I absolutely was, but I wasn't about to let that stop me.

"I can turn Anastasia against Jensen — who, by the way, will probably try to cut you out of the deal."

"Nonsense."

"Don't believe me? Check your own files," I snipped. "You'll find reference after reference to him delighting in cutting the middleman. But that's a moot point if Anastasia decides to look for another buyer. That de Mézières woman, for example."

"The influencer?" His face went all stormy. "You wouldn't."

"No, I won't, as long as you assure me of the following." I stood and stretched to my full height while he remained seated. "You declare the conditions of your contracts with Marius, Roux, Benedict, and Henrik met, to be replaced with normal — dare I say, voluntary — contracts that run to the end of their original term with you. So, nothing changes, except their pardons are guaranteed, effective immediately."

I'd had the past few hours to think it all over, and that's what I'd come up with. And yes, I'd been sorely tempted to leave Henrik off the list, but I'd decided not to stoop that low.

Lord knew I'd come close, though.

Gordon's eyes narrowed. "What do you know of their contracts with me?"

"More than I ever wanted." He was about to protest, so I hurried on. "If you want this deal to go through, you will agree to my terms."

He stared in shock. "*Your* terms?"

Ungrateful brat went through his mind, but I had prepared myself for that.

"I appreciate everything you've done for me, Gordon. For all of us, for all these years."

"And yet here you are, making demands of me," he said bitterly, like *I* was the one who'd used *him*.

"Not making demands. I'm defending myself and defending men whose lives you have no problem risking, again and again."

He shrugged. "They work in a risky business."

I banged my hand on the table. "That business is *your* business! Something you've hidden from us all these years."

He shook his head. "Again, you've been misled."

I had no desire to go down that rabbit hole of an argument, so I finished quickly.

"All these years, I've loved and appreciated you, Gordon. I've been able to do so much thanks to your support. But manipulation and deceit are not part of a healthy relationship."

"Which you hope to achieve with the likes of that dragon shifter?"

That rabble, his tone implied.

"None of your business, in the same way your personal choices are none of mine."

My teacher side tapped on my shoulder, telling me to end this while I was ahead. I'd said what I had to say. Going on would simply open the door to argument.

"What happened to you wanting the best for the painting?" Gordon snipped viciously.

I'd already turned to the door, but at that, I turned back. "A question I've asked myself a thousand times. But I think the answer lies with you, not me."

My heart raced, and every nerve in my body tensed as I marched out the door. But march out the door I did, leaving a dangerously disgruntled Gordon in my wake.

Chapter Twenty-Two

MARIUS

Every minute Mina spent with Gordon was an eternity. But
Celeste was in our suite with the rest of us, so I couldn't pace,
roar, or vow to kill Gordon in a thousand different ways. I
just stood by the window, my back to the room, trying not to
quiver with rage.

Go in there and help her! my dragon howled.

I burned to, but Mina was capable of handling Gordon.
More capable than I was, probably.

I stared out the window, my hands balled into fists. Somewhere behind London's gloomy skies, the sun was setting without any fanfare. It just drained away gradually, leaving us in
limbo.

Auberre is so much better, my dragon complained.

Which just went to show how much my priorities had
changed. Forgotten little towns in the countryside had never
really done it for me before. I'd grown up in one and escaped
as soon as I could. But now...

I closed my eyes, picturing the forest. The rolling vineyards.
Quiet nights in the drawing room.

Mina defending her grandmother's china, my dragon chuckled.

My lips curled in a faint smile, then went hard as Celeste
approached.

"Poor, poor Marius. So deep in love, he doesn't know what
to do with himself," she cooed.

Oh, I knew what to do. Throttle Celeste. Help Mina get
through this shitty job and back home, where I would leave her

just long enough to destroy every one of my enemies. Then we could live happily ever after.

I grimaced. Not a plan Mina would approve of.

Poor Celeste, Bene mocked, though only into my mind. *Nothing better to do than hang around guys with zero interest in her.*

Roux growled, warning him not to rile up the succubus. Especially when she was probably already plotting against us.

Bene grimaced and flicked through the channels. "Poor us. Ninety-nine channels and nothing interesting on any of them." Then he brightened, coming across a documentary set on a savanna. The camera panned to a pride of lions, and a narrator spoke in hushed tones about social hierarchy.

"Got that right," Bene murmured as the narrator gushed on about the alpha lion.

Celeste rolled her eyes.

I ignored her and did my best to emulate Bene — a first — by picturing myself gliding over the Alps with cold wind under my wings and bursts of heat from occasional spits of fire. I closed my eyes, reliving my favorite route. I used to zoom low over Lake Lucerne at midnight, then race up over the slopes of Mount Pilatus. The surrounding villages were usually asleep at that hour, but a few lights dotted the slopes. In winter, snow blanketed the landscape. In summer, a lush carpet of grass. I recalled the scent of mountain flowers and dairy farms and glaciers...

Then my nostrils flared, and I whirled as the door flew open.

Mina stormed in. Literally. The napkins on the table fluttered, and the air pressure dropped, the way it did when clouds rolled in to smother the mountains.

"Gordon wants you," she snipped to Celeste in a very un-Mina-like tone.

Roux's eyes went wide, and Bene shuffled to the far end of the couch.

Even Celeste was thrown off — enough that she slipped out of the room without comment. Mina slammed the door behind her.

"Did Gordon really want her?" Bene asked quietly.

"No." Mina slumped against the door.

Bene held up a little bag. "Here. Have a cookie."

The man had more brains than I thought.

Mina looked at the bag, clearly warring with herself.

"You deserve it," Roux threw in.

"Bet your ass, I do," she grumbled, snatching it. She sat at the dining table with her back to the room, munching aggressively.

I approached her... slowly.

Bene looked over, wincing. *Maybe not the best time...*

No, but I couldn't stand to see her like that. Plus, he and Roux might have learned a lot about Mina, but I knew her even better.

I stepped behind her, making enough noise for her to hear, and slowly wrapped my arms around her.

And, whoa. She was seething with angry energy. Pulsing with it, almost.

Calm down, my mate, my dragon crooned softly.

I squatted, getting as close to her as the chair allowed, gradually nudging my chin over her shoulder.

Every muscle in her body was tight as a wire and not in a good way.

I didn't bother asking if she was all right, because the answer was obvious. I was dying to ask what had happened, but I didn't. Still, one thing was clear. She'd finally stood up to her godfather — something I'd never dared do, and I was a goddamn dragon.

I leaned my head against hers and focused on deep, calming breaths. The way she'd done for me after all hell had broken loose in Mallorca.

Everything will be all right, my mate, my dragon whispered.

Mina laced her fingers through mine and squeezed. Her chest rose on a deep breath, and she slowly straightened, then turned to flash me a tight smile.

"Thanks. I needed that," she whispered.

My heart lifted, and my dragon crooned smugly. *Of course, you did.*

"Oh, check it out. Adorable lion babies." Bene pointed to the television.

Mina folded into a soft laugh — another thing she needed — and joined him on the couch. I sat between them and put up with thirty minutes of lions, lions, and more lions.

"Why not a documentary on tigers?" Roux grumbled.

Bene shrugged. "Ask the BBC."

"Or dragons?" I threw in.

"Baby dragons aren't adorable. I mean, look at those cubs!" Bene pointed smugly.

I never dreamed I would waste minutes of my life on a lion documentary — or in a conversation at that low a level — but somehow, it was just what we all needed.

The documentary went on to show a hunt, but the antelope got away, to Mina's relief and Bene's consternation. Eventually, it concluded with a few philosophical words about man and beast striving to live in harmony or some such fluff, and it closed on a montage of flicking, tufted tails and lions gazing off into spectacular sunsets.

Bene clapped. Mina joined him. I sat between them with my arms firmly crossed.

"Say cheese," Roux called.

We looked up as he snapped a picture.

"Wait. You have to be in it too," Mina insisted.

I grumbled under my breath as everyone squeezed together for a selfie no one needed, especially one with a tiger shifter in the foreground. That didn't stop Roux from sending it to Mina, who picked up her phone to admire it.

I frowned, thinking of the picture of the two of us in Mallorca. Thinking of my enemies.

"Oh." Mina's face fell as she scanned her messages.

We all looked over expectantly.

"Anastasia has agreed to sell to Jensen," she read stiffly.

"Won't Gordon be glad," Roux muttered.

I put a hand on Mina's leg in a sign of solidarity. Bene raised his to echo the movement, but I snarled into his mind.

Don't even think about it, asshole.

He reached for the room service menu instead.

"I say we celebrate — or drown our sorrows — in dinner and a good bottle of wine." He ran his finger down the list. "Now, which is the most expensive? After all, it's on Gordon."

Mina leaned in for a look. "Filet mignon for me."

"Lobster for me," Roux snickered.

"I'll take the Argentinian steak," I said.

Bene laughed. "With side orders of truffles for each of us."

Throughout the wait for the food and then dinner, we managed to keep the mood lighthearted and conversation to a minimum. Happily, neither Gordon nor Celeste interrupted.

"Good, but nowhere near Madame Picard's cooking," Bene decided.

"God, I wish we were home now," Mina breathed.

We. My heart tightened.

"Me too," Bene echoed the sentiment.

Roux didn't speak, but a faint sigh said he agreed.

I looked into my wineglass, wondering where destiny would take us. Sorely tempted to do a little more steering.

Then Roux's phone pinged. When he read the message aloud, our fair moods dissipated.

"Gordon says the deal is going through. We'll all convene at nine in the morning." Then he frowned at the screen. "And he says, tell Mina he accepts her terms."

"Terms? What terms?" Bene asked.

Mina ignored him, swallowed hard, then nodded to herself and told Roux, "Tell him I want to see it in writing, in the morning."

My eyes went wide. That did not sound good.

"Um..." Roux hesitated.

She pointed to the phone firmly. "Tell him." Then she softened, back to the Mina we knew. "Please. Thank you."

As he typed, she stood, stretched, and yawned. "Well, it's been a long day." She headed toward her room.

My heart crumpled as I considered reality. No Belgravia hideaway for us tonight. I resigned myself to a lonely, pensive night on the couch.

But she stopped at the door to her bedroom and looked back at me.

"Will you come? Please?" she asked softly.

It was all I could do not to sprint in.

She blushed as the others observed. "We need to talk."

Bene snorted. "Talk. Right."

"What about...?" Roux jerked his thumb in the direction of Gordon in the next suite.

"To hell with Gordon," Mina muttered, echoing my thoughts exactly.

Bene chuckled. "That will be my motto the day we finish our contracts."

Mina opened her mouth, then closed it.

I slid past her, into the bedroom, as she called to the others before closing the door.

"Goodnight."

"Goodnight," they echoed — Bene cheerily, Roux less so.

We stood in silence for a while, gazing out the floor-to-ceiling windows. Eventually, Mina drew the curtains and sat on the edge of the bed, pulling off her shoes and socks. Then she stood again and pushed down her pants. I stared as she pulled her shirt over her head next.

"Uh... no talking, I guess?"

"Oh, we're taking, all right," she grumbled, turning her back to slip her bra off and toss it on a chair. Just as quickly, she pulled on a white T-shirt that came to mid-thigh in place of pajamas.

I froze, because that was my shirt. One I'd left at home — er, at the château.

She turned back and stuck her hands on her hips, catching my expression.

"Yes, I have been sleeping in your shirt, because I missed you. Because I love you. Yes, I've been going to bed every night wishing you were beside me." Her voice trembled just a little. "But I will not play by your rules any more. So, time to decide. Stay with me now and make good on that mark you left on me, and stay for real this time. Not for a few nights between jobs or whenever it suits you or when you judge it safe enough. I want one night after another and then another, not for weeks or months, but for decades." She took a deep breath.

"The other option is backing out and letting your mark fade. Forever. Is that clear?"

Wow. This really was a new Mina.

And she wasn't done yet.

She stuck a finger at my chest. "You marked me. Well, consider this my mark on you. One that says, this man is mine, and everyone else needs to stay the hell away."

My dragon glowed, nodding *yes* to every statement.

She punctuated each word with a fierce tap. "But you have to do your part — and I don't mean protecting me. I mean, you commit to making this work, or you leave." She gulped for air. "There. Your turn to talk."

I opened my mouth, then closed it. What the hell to say?

Say yes. To her. To us. To forever, my dragon grumbled.

She softened slightly. "What does your heart say?"

"Stay. Forever," I said without the slightest hesitation.

"So how does this even require deliberation?"

"It shouldn't. But I don't want to see you hurt."

She rolled her eyes. "That again."

That was her life. Did she not know that?

She took my hands. "I think you're looking at this from the wrong perspective."

I frowned. There was another perspective?

Her eye roll said, *Stupid dragon.*

"Picture us back at the château. Picture a nice, normal life. No Gordon, no secret missions, no bad guys," she started. "Just you and me fixing up the château and running a business."

Yes, please, I wanted to yell.

"Do you want that or don't you?" she demanded.

I dipped my chin. "Yes." Then I corrected myself. "No." Mina looked ready to punch me, so I hurried to clarify. "I mean, that would be nice, but all I really want is you. Everything else is a bonus."

Her eyes warmed, and her clenched fists loosened. "That's what I want too. You. So, the question is, how do we get there?"

Hunt down each of my enemies and kill them didn't seem like the appropriate answer, but it was all I had. I scoured my mind for something better.

"We... uh... get this deal closed for Gordon," I tried.

She nodded. "Then what?"

I scratched my chin. "Then we figure out who sent that picture and why."

Bingo, her eyes said.

"And then what?" she prompted.

"Well, it depends on who. Why. Where..."

She squeezed my hands. "That's what I'm saying. One step at a time. But we do it together. You don't get to make secret decisions for both of us."

Now that she put it that way...

"This is where you tell me yes, you love me, you need me, you want me," she whispered after a few tongue-tied seconds ticked by. "Where you say *I'm in* or *I'm out of here.*"

"I'm in."

Her eyes lit up. "Really?"

My brain caught up with my heart, and I nodded. "Really." I took her hands and kissed them.

She didn't just grin — she basked in the moment. "Oh. *Really* really?"

I nodded. "Really really."

Her grin grew, then faded. "Well, then. All we have to do now is finish this deal for Gordon, solve whatever problems are sure to arise at the last moment, vanquish any lurking enemies, and we're done."

I nodded slowly. Now she was seeing things from my perspective.

Which, now that I considered it, was a pretty gloomy perspective.

"One step at a time," I whispered, dropping down beside her.

She rolled to her side, looking at me, then spooned up next to me. I wrapped my arms around her and closed my eyes, telling myself to live in the moment.

Which wasn't all that hard to do with her rose-and-lilac scent filling my soul with carefree butterflies or with the heat radiating from her body. Heat that said, *Come to me, my mate.*

Slowly, I moved my hands over her sleep shirt. It was mine after all.

She hummed and snuggled closer.

I kissed her shoulder, then pulled off her scarf. And, wow. Her skin radiated in the darkness.

"Now, suppose I wanted to leave a moonlight mark on you," she whispered as I nuzzled her skin. "How would I do that?"

I thought it over, then shrugged. "Let destiny guide you."

She lay quietly, then wiggled her rear against my crotch. "Destiny says, you need to lose those layers."

A smile curled over my lips. "Yes, ma'am. Or do I say yes to destiny?"

"*Yes, ma'am* will do," she said primly.

I laughed and did as I was told, stripping out of everything. Then I cuddled up again, my chest to her back.

I exhaled. God, that felt good.

Maybe she was right. Maybe I had been making things too complicated.

"Oh." She tensed suddenly. "What if there's no moonlight to mark you by?"

I kissed the curve of her shoulder. "Then we make our own."

She chuckled, twisting around to come face-to-face. "And how do you suggest we do that?"

I snuck a hand along her ribs. "Let me show you."

Her breath caught, and she arched, making space for me to kiss...touch...explore. Everywhere.

"Oh..." she murmured as I worked my way down her body.

My hands roved, as did my lips, eliciting happy sounds from her. From me, too.

We touched until we were breathless, until the weight of the world slipped away and there was only the hush of the city outside the window and her warmth beneath me. She tugged me closer and wrapped her legs around my waist. I followed her cue and slid inside with a low groan of need. Slowly. Quietly. A little spitefully too, with Gordon next door.

We moved in a slow dance, not wild or frantic this time, but sure and steady, weaving a vow words never could. Every sigh of hers, every growl of mine, was a declaration of love and defiance.

"Yes..." she hummed, clutching my back as I rocked deeper and deeper.

The more we moved, the more the glow of my mark intensified, filling the space between our bodies. It tickled over our shoulders, creating a faint halo.

Claim, a voice in my mind chanted quietly. *Claim your mate.*

At first, I put that down to my dragon. But it wasn't. It was coming from Mina.

Her eyes glowed as she bucked to meet me intently, that chant echoing in her mind.

My back heated as her nails scraped my skin, and magic swirled around us.

My breath caught, and it was all I could do to keep up my steady rhythm. Mina was doing what I'd done that night in Paris — marking me by moonlight. But in this case, she drew upon her inner glow to provide the moonlight, or at least, a reflection of the moonlight that had stayed with her since that night.

"Tell me you want this," she rasped between breaths, giving me the choice I'd never given her.

I'd never felt so guilty — or so blessed with something precious.

"I want this," I assured her, over and over.

As we built to a crescendo, the words slurred together, and it was all I could do not to shout them. Then she cried out in ecstasy, clamping down around me. I exploded a moment later, and we catapulted through time and space.

I saw us our first time together. I saw that night by the canal in Paris. I even caught a glimpse of the future, but that view was a little hazy. Hazy enough to hint that destiny still had some tricks up its sleeve.

I collapsed over Mina and held her tightly, daring destiny to try delivering anything but a happy ending.

Gradually, our pants slowed to deep breaths, and Mina curled up comfortably in my arms.

"So good..." she murmured. Then she turned in my arms and touched my neck.

I chuckled at the ticklish sensation. "What are you doing?"

Her eyebrows knitted together. "Looking for my mark. Tell me I didn't screw that up."

Only Mina would worry that a high this good could somehow be a failure.

I shook my head.

"But there's no glow. No mark..." she fretted.

I wrapped my hand around hers, then held both against my chest. A faint glow appeared around our interwoven fingers.

"Oh," Mina breathed.

"I guess it manifests itself differently when a shifter mark mixes with magic," I whispered as the glow spread up our arms and connected with the shimmer around her neck.

"Wow," Mina breathed, looking down.

When I lifted our hands away from my chest, the glow faded. But when I pressed them down again, the glow illuminated the space between us like candlelight, and my blood heated. So much, we found ourselves slipping into another round of slow, hungry lovemaking.

At some point, when we were spent, Mina lay curled against me, absently running her fingers over my forearm.

"Do you think tomorrow will go smoothly?" she whispered.

I would have loved to say yes, but that would have been a lie.

"Guaranteed not to," I murmured, holding her closer.

She thought it over, then kissed me. "Well, a good thing that's not until tomorrow. Until then, I guess all we can do is get some rest."

Rest, not *sleep*. A critical difference.

I nuzzled her shoulder, then started working my way lower. At some point, we would sleep. But we were too keyed up for that yet, and there was only one antidote to that.

"Mmm," Mina murmured, wrapping her legs around me.

Chapter Twenty-Three

MARIUS

Mina and I managed a few hours of sleep, but not enough. Intense, emotional sex wasn't entirely the reason (but okay, partly) because we were too keyed up to sleep even when we tried. Mostly, we'd settled for curling up together and staring off into the darkness.

"One more night after tonight, and we can go home," Mina whispered at one point. Then she sighed. "Back to stripping paint."

Ha. Even stripping paint would beat what we were in London for.

A million things could intervene, but I played along in a more upbeat tone. "Don't forget fixing the roof."

"And hosting weddings..." Mina said, then rushed to explain. "I mean, for other people. I mean, for money. I mean..."

I chuckled, holding her tighter. If she thought I would bolt at the W word, no. But I needed to be sure she was safe first. So, if she spent the night obsessing about the painting, I spent it worrying about how to keep my past from catching up to us in the worst possible way.

Szabo, my dragon hissed in my mind. *Or that son of a bitch Etienne.*

They were my top two worries — the vampire and the wolf shifter I'd tangled with a few months ago. I'd turned a blind eye to most of the illegal activities in Etienne's bar/fight club, and I'd even picked up a little cash through a string of wins in his subterranean fight pits. But in the course of hounding him for my prize money, I'd discovered that sex trafficking — of minors — was another keystone of his business, and there was no way I could turn a blind eye to *that*.

A verbal spat had turned into an all-out fight, and I had been well on my way to ridding the world of one wolf-size packet of evil when his minions intervened. We'd both ended up before a tribunal of supernaturals who handled such things, all in a hush-hush way that protected the many pies they dipped their dirty fingers in.

All that had led to my involvement with Gordon, but that had also brought me to Mina. So, maybe I owed Etienne in a weird, twisted way.

In my half sleep, I pictured his ruthless, mud-colored eyes. The flash of his bright, long teeth. The nick in his right ear from some long-ago fight...

"What?" Mina asked sleepily.

I forced myself to relax, other than the tight wrap of my arms around her.

"Sorry. Just overthinking," I murmured.

She brought her lips to mine, whispering, "Try overthinking this instead."

∞∞∞∞

At nine the next morning, I jutted my jaw and listened to Gordon drone on about the timeline for the day. He was furious with us — well, me — and it showed in each of his growly, bitter statements.

Last day of this piss-poor mission, Bene murmured into my mind. *By this time tomorrow, we should be back at the château.*

As desperately as I wanted that, I would believe it when I saw it.

Back at the château for as long as Mina lets us, Roux added glumly.

There was that too — something she and I hadn't gotten around to discussing. But I was committed to the *one thing at a time* plan now, and that item was much, much farther down the list.

Next, Gordon outlined the final details of his plan. Then he checked his watch, muttering something about keeping his pilot waiting.

I rolled my eyes. Of course. The pilot. Of his private jet. Such an inconvenience.

"Mina and Roux will go to Madame Petrova's and oversee the transportation of the painting to the drop point," Gordon instructed.

I kept my lips sealed, though my dragon raged inside.

"Afterward," Gordon continued, "Mina will take the train home."

She gulped. "Home?"

"Home," he said firmly.

We all froze. Bad news, because that meant Gordon expected the shit to hit the fan. But good news too, because I wanted her safe.

Her wide, anxious eyes met mine.

Gordon held up a hand. Celeste pressed an envelope into it, which Gordon handed to Mina.

She blinked. "What's this?"

"Your train ticket," Celeste snipped.

Mina peeked inside. "I see," she said, looking up slowly. "Will Szabo get a matching one this time as well?"

Gordon looked genuinely confused, but Celeste...

For the briefest of instants, she flashed an *oops, caught-in-the-act* expression. If I hadn't been looking for it, I would have missed it. But I didn't — and neither did Mina.

"What do you mean?" Gordon demanded, unamused.

It meant we'd been right to suspect Celeste. But why would she hire Szabo to go after us?

Mina held Celeste's gaze. "Never mind. Back to arrangements."

Gordon grumbled under his breath and stuck up his hand again. When Celeste didn't move, he snapped his fingers. "The contracts, dammit."

Celeste jolted into action and handed him four more envelopes, which he distributed — one each to me, Roux, and Bene, with a fourth for Henrik, which he entrusted to Mina.

Then he begrudgingly pulled a pen from his breast pocket —
one of those fancy pens that cost as much as a compact car —
and handed it to me.

I stared at the pen, then the envelope. "What's this?"

"Your new contract," he spat. "Take it or leave it."

Roux's eyebrows jumped up. *New what?*

I glanced at Mina, but her gaze aimed steadfastly out the
window.

Roux tore open his envelope and began reading, moving his
lips silently. Bene's eyes went wide as he skimmed his. Gordon
crossed his arms and tapped his foot. I started reading, then
trailed off in shock.

Bene flipped between the front and back of his document
several times, gaping. "Is this for real?"

Gordon huffed. "Of course it's real." He checked his watch.
"You have three minutes to accept the new terms — or not."

Bene snatched the pen out of my hand. Roux's brow knotted as he reread his carefully. I did the same, looking for a
catch, but couldn't find one.

Why would Gordon grant us our pardons early? Roux asked
into my mind. *Why offer us new contracts on more favorable
terms?*

I stared at him blankly. Then we both turned to Mina,
remembering the message Roux had relayed the previous night.

Gordon says to tell Mina he accepts her terms.

My mouth dropped open, and Roux muttered an expletive.

I read mine again.

*The above pardon takes effect immediately. Penalties for
prior offenses have been deemed sufficiently met, and the signee
has no further obligations to Monsieur Clervaud, nor to any
other party, now or at any time hereafter, in perpetuity. This
contract supersedes all previous contracts, which are hereby declared null and void. By signing below, you agree to the following new terms...*

I couldn't move. I couldn't think. What had Mina risked,
traded, or promised to gift me my freedom?

"Mina," I murmured.

"Just sign," she growled, keeping her eyes away from Gordon.

No *I'll explain later,* no private message whispered into my mind. Just a dogged determination that scared me. So much, I considered not signing to spare her whatever she'd promised Gordon.

But something told me it was too late. Plus, she would be furious.

Roux took the pen from Bene, signed, and handed it to me. I scribbled my name at the bottom of my contract, and Roux snapped pictures of each before handing them over. That prompted Gordon to make outraged sounds, which we ignored, because for the first time ever, we could.

I tried organizing my thoughts, but they flopped around like slippery fish.

"What about Henrik?" Mina held up his envelope.

Gordon grimaced while countersigning the others. "He can hand his copy to Celeste later today."

Right. Later. When I would drag an explanation out of Mina and do my damnedest to protect her from the fallout of all this.

Gordon stepped toward the door with an ominous, "I expect everything to run smoothly."

Another veiled threat, but that was nothing new.

"Celeste will, as usual, report to me on your progress," he went on.

She smiled, baring her teeth.

"Yes, sir," Roux barked in an effort to hurry him out the door.

Gordon stopped to glower at me, then glance at Mina, who averted her eyes. To his credit, he genuinely looked sad.

Still, I kept my guard up, fully expecting Gordon to try to off me in a tragic "accident." So far, he hadn't. No shove out the window, no poisoned drink, no stab in the back...yet.

He was sure to try at some point, though. That, I was sure of. Anything to get me out of the picture so Mina could end up with a more suitable partner.

I thought of Clement, that ass of a wolf shifter. I hated the cop, but talk about poetic justice — if I got offed, Mina could end up with him, and wouldn't Gordon just love having a nosy police officer in the family?

I had to chuckle at the idea.

Everyone exhaled when he exited, letting the door slam behind him.

Then Celeste's heels clicked over the floor, and we all tensed again.

"Well, isn't that nice," she cooed dangerously. "New contracts for everyone."

Except me, her tone said, as if she'd ever worked by the letter of the law.

No one said a word, and no one moved.

"Well, don't just sit there," she snipped. "Get to work. As Gordon said...I'll be watching."

∞∞∞∞

We had hours before the eight-p.m. handover, but time flew. We were that busy making arrangements and reconnoitering the location Jensen had named — a Docklands warehouse — according to the schedule Gordon had outlined.

"Convenient that he'll be out of the country by the time the trade is made, isn't it?" Roux observed as we climbed the stairs to Anastasia's apartment.

I didn't comment. I didn't need to.

Then again, Gordon's absence made it easy for us to adjust his arrangements, such as who accompanied Mina to Anastasia's. Henrik and I had come along with Roux, while Bene remained in the vicinity of Jensen's warehouse.

Boxing up the painting went more or less to plan, especially since the plan anticipated delays in getting Anastasia to part with her masterpiece.

And boy, did she delay, touching and weeping over it. She'd donned black clothing for the occasion and dabbed at her eyes with a handkerchief — a white one with the red teddy bear logo of the 1980 Moscow Olympics.

230

"Just wait for the cash to come through," Bene whispered. "She'll be dancing through the house in a cha-cha."

She and Mina locked us out of the study for some kind of private service, and when they finally opened the doors, the place looked and smelled like an Orthodox church. Anastasia had even moved a couple of icons into the room and burned incense for the occasion.

There was one bright side to all this. No Celeste. She was back in the hotel, ostensibly coordinating things. Which couldn't have amounted to much since we kept communication with her to a minimum.

Mina patted Anastasia's hand as Roux and I slid the painting into its crate.

Henrik murmured solemnly. "Our time on earth is limited. But art is eternal."

Pretty rich, coming from a vampire, but Anastasia didn't need to know that.

"You will always be a critical part of this painting's story," Mina assured Anastasia.

"Immortal, in a way," Henrik threw in, somehow keeping the irony out of his voice. And, hell. Maybe he meant it. He was that hard to read.

Anastasia brightened. Having already kissed the painting (leaving no lipstick smudges, to Mina's relief), Anastasia kissed the crate and finally allowed us to carry it outside. She followed us every step of the way, hugged and kissed Mina on the sidewalk, and finally disappeared inside. When I glanced back up, she was gazing down from the study window. No cha-cha. In fact, she looked more like a widow than ever.

Mina sighed from beside me. "I'll have to help her find something to put in its place." She forced a rueful smile. "Or get Bogdan to."

I rubbed a thumb over her cheek, wiping away Anastasia's lipstick. "You are too good, you know that?"

She frowned. "Not so sure."

"For once, the dragon is right," Henrik said quietly, patting the pocket he'd slipped his contract into. "You are too good."

He and Mina locked eyes for a long time. I stood on guard in case the vampire tried to pull anything, from sucking her blood to kissing her hand — or any other part of her. But he didn't. He just stood there, looking sincere.

"Oh, you know." Mina shrugged. "Someone's got to make up for all the shitty people in the world."

Henrik digested that for several quiet seconds before murmuring, "I'm deeply indebted to you."

"We all are," I added, while Roux nodded solemnly.

Someone like Celeste would have pounced on that, but Mina just squirmed uncomfortably. "Don't we have a painting to deliver?"

Roux, Henrik, and I did, but Mina was supposed to catch a train to Paris. She refused, of course, so I nodded, looking forward to getting this all over with. "We do."

We sat three across the front seat of our rented van, with Roux driving, Mina in the middle, and me at the window. Henrik rode in the back with the painting. At a stoplight along the way, my phone pinged, and I checked it, expecting another of Celeste's demands for an update.

But the avatar that came up was blank, and the message included a photo. One of Mina and me that had been taken outside our hotel that morning, judging by the clothes and van in the background. Our hands were clasped, our eyes locked.

A nice shot, but terrifying too.

Remember, those who love, lose, the caption said. *And even a moonlight mark can't stop that.*

I whipped my head up to scan the area. Someone knew we were in London together. Someone who hated me enough to want Mina dead. A shifter — or vampire — who could recognize the mark I'd left on her.

My mind scrolled through a long list of suspects. Szabo. Celeste. Etienne. Gordon.

No, scratch Gordon. He would hurt me, not Mina. But that still left plenty of suspects.

I turned my head left and right, cursing nightfall.

Mina touched my arm. "What is it?"

I nearly stuck my phone in my pocket and bluffed. But we'd sworn to come clean, so I turned the screen to Mina.

She stiffened, prompting Roux to look over.

"What?"

Mina glanced at me, probably just as tempted to lie as I was. But lying to Roux might imply that I might someday lie to her, so I gave him the short version.

He cursed and ran a hand through his hair. "Now?"

I scrutinized every vehicle and pedestrian in the vicinity. Windows and roofs too, in case our unseen enemy lurked up high, sniper-style. But nothing. Not a hint of him — or her — in the darkness.

A car behind us beeped, and Roux cursed, then drove slowly onward.

"What now?" He tapped on the steering wheel.

Mina pointed ahead. "We stick to the plan."

Roux glanced over at me. I didn't like that either, but I didn't have an alternative plan. So, we drove on, keeping our senses piqued.

We were nearly at the warehouse when my phone rang again, and Bene came over the line.

"Caution. Repeat, caution. Jensen's security people report a man in the vicinity whose description matches Szabo."

For once, he didn't sound like he was kidding.

Roux hit the brakes, and Mina stuck out a hand to brace herself.

"Where?" I growled, looking around.

"Corner of Manchester Road and Stewart Street, moving south."

Mina tapped her phone, pulling up the location, with ours showing nearby as a blue dot. Making a split-second decision, I motioned for Roux to continue, then pull over two blocks later. Popping the door open, I slid out, ready to tear the vampire to pieces.

"What are you doing?" Mina protested.

"Going after Szabo. This ends now," I grunted.

"But—" Mina started.

I flicked my eyes to Roux, who nodded to say, *Of course we'll take care of Mina.*

I gritted my teeth and backed away from the van. "I'll catch up."

With that, I forced myself to slam the door shut. Mina's shocked expression haunted me, but what could I do?

I turned and sprinted down an adjoining alley, every sense on alert, ready to hunt down a vampire.

Chapter Twenty-Four

MINA

I craned my neck, but Marius had already disappeared into a dim alley. Roux revved down the street, racing from one pool of light to another.

I cursed both of them, but it was halfhearted.

"Will he be all right against Szabo?" I asked.

Roux tightened his hands over the steering wheel. "He should be."

Should be? I wanted to scream.

I had a lot of faith in my dragon shifter, but he had a tendency to act impulsively. And given the state he was in, not to mention the darkness...

I peered down the next alley, catching a view of lights glittering over the Thames. The river was that close.

A sea gull's haunting cry pierced the night, and I caught a glimpse of white overhead.

"Don't worry," Roux tried.

I grimaced. "I'm worrying."

His mouth settled into a tense line. "This is how teams work — by trusting each person to do their job."

True, but teams usually operated according to game plans, and taking off after Szabo had not factored into ours.

My hands formed fists. Damn that Szabo! He had come after me at home. He had stalked me on my first trip to London. Now he was back again. Why?

Roux pointed into the darkness ahead, past the headlights. "Focus. We have to complete this mission."

Easier said than done, with my heart roaming the Docklands with Marius. Was he all right? Where was all this leading?

Roux pulled up in front of a tired old warehouse on the banks of the Thames — one that hadn't yet been converted into upmarket condos or torn down to make way for modern construction, like the buildings around it. Four men in dark suits separated from the shadows to open the doors, and Roux coasted in.

The hair on my arms stood as we slid out of the vehicle. Bene and Henrik flanked the rear doors of the van, while I followed Roux toward a bright circle of light in the center of the dark, empty warehouse. The place smelled of salt, slime, and the ocean, much like the nearby river.

Jensen closed the laptop he'd been hunched over and stood. "Good of you to be punctual."

"Of course," Roux said smoothly.

Standing beside Jensen was Celeste, who glanced behind me, then looked away quickly, hiding a smug look. What did that mean?

Briefcases cluttered the floor around Jensen's feet, making me even edgier. Everything about this screamed *Mafia! Cartel! Illegal!*

And there I stood, right in the thick of it.

I shifted my weight from foot to foot, once again reviewing my life choices. But ultimately, I knew I'd made the right decision. My friends' freedom was worth helping Gordon finish this distasteful art deal.

Jensen motioned to the briefcases, and his men opened one after another for our inspection.

"Three million British pounds in cash, as Ms. Petrova requested."

I stared at stack upon stack of bills. Wow. Maybe I didn't have to feel all that sorry for Anastasia.

A svelte woman — Jensen's personal assistant — took notes on her tablet.

Jensen checked his watch. "The remainder is scheduled to appear in that account in the Cayman Islands right...about...now."

Celeste's tablet pinged, and she scrolled through a message, then nodded primly. "Confirmed."

Bene and Henrik opened the crate and slid enough of the painting out to satisfy Jensen, along with papers declaring the work genuine, signed by Gordon's weasel of an art authenticator.

Jensen didn't look too concerned. In fact, he barely glanced at the painting.

I felt as sick as I would be turning live horses over to a negligent new owner. Would he take good care of them? Would they be all right?

No, my gut told me.

Jensen would ensure that the canvas remained in good condition. But the art on it, and what it represented — that would be neglected.

"Good doing business with you," he said, shaking Celeste's hand.

She held his a little too long and smiled a little too coyly.

And just like that, it hit me. Somewhere along the line, they'd found time to sleep together, hadn't they?

Bene rolled his eyes, signaling, *Duh.*

I hung my head. Of course they would. And of course, I was the last one to figure out the obvious. Celeste was a manipulative succubus, and Jensen had the two things she most coveted — power and money. Even more than Gordon.

A vague, uneasy feeling came over me, but I couldn't quite place it. I was too worried about Marius — and too disgusted by the expressions Jensen and Celeste flashed at each other. *Triumphant,* like that was all sex amounted to. Not a revelation or a step toward something deeper. Just a contest. A victory.

"Good doing business with you," Celeste echoed, flashing a seductive smile.

For a few seconds, Jensen stood in her spell. But he was enough of a tech nerd to eventually lose interest and turn away.

"Well, that's that." He clapped with an air of finality. "Thank you, gentlemen. And you, Miss Durand."

I ought to have stepped back like the others, but I couldn't help myself.

"What will you do with it?" I asked.

"Map its every feature," he said proudly.

"I hope you'll consider loaning it out for exhibition when you're done," I said, giving my (probably lost) cause one last-ditch effort.

"Oh yes. I'll consider it," he said with little conviction.

Outside, a ship churned past. Two ships, maybe, passing each other on the dark river.

At Jensen's signal, his men loaded the crate into a dark van and drove off. I watched them go, but he didn't. He just started packing away his laptop.

Bene and Henrik carried the cash to our van. Then Bene slipped away to help Marius. That gave me just enough headspace to press on with my crusade.

"Loaning a work comes with many benefits," I tried.

"Such as?" Jensen paused on the way to his limo.

I followed, sensing an opening. "Well, I'm sure any gallery would be extremely grateful to secure a loan. For example, the Tobler Arts Foundation. In *Switzerland.*"

I named the country with such emphasis, I practically trampled it.

Jensen looked at me sharply. "A random example?"

Not at all, because my research had turned up a number of interesting tidbits about Nils Øren Jensen and his rapidly expanding tech empire. Rapidly expanding, that was, except in one key location.

"Just one possibility," I bluffed. "Many foundations there are very well-connected, and they would be extremely grateful for the opportunity to exhibit such a painting. I imagine many influential people in the country would be grateful too."

I didn't add, *Like the ones currently blocking your efforts to expand into their tightly controlled market,* but I didn't have to.

Ice-blue eyes narrowed on me, and I felt a hell of a lot like the antelope stalked by the lions in that documentary.

"Interesting," he murmured. "Very interesting."

Celeste tugged on his sleeve. "Didn't you mention another appointment?"

He frowned, and the svelte assistant piped up, checking her tablet. "Yes, sir. That call from Buenos Aires."

Briefly, I wondered what a billionaire followed up an eighty-seven million dollar art deal with. Did he partner with an oil company to drill in Antarctica? Buy off the head of a major South American country — or plot to overthrow one?

He considered, then motioned toward his limo. "I'd like to hear more. Why don't you join me? It's only a short ride, and my captain can bring you to any location you wish afterward."

Captain? As in a boat?

Another sea gull cawed, reminding me of our proximity to the river.

Roux shook his head curtly. "Maybe another time."

I shook my head back at him. Any moment now, Jensen would be distracted by a phone call or a new idea for world domination. This was my chance — my only chance — to make the painting available to the public, just as my father would have wanted.

My mind warred with a dozen contradictory commitments. Marius. Getting this deal over with. My own safety.

But Bene had gone to assist Marius, and there was little I could contribute to a confrontation between a vampire, a dragon, and a lion. And when it came to my own safety...

Henrik stepped forward. "I'll accompany her."

I gulped, then nodded.

Celeste huffed as if to say, *Lucky you. Always a man around to protect you.*

It's called friendship, I wanted to say. *And friends help each other.*

But she did have a point there. And, yes — my friendship with Henrik had been more than a bit strained lately, but he was finally coming through for me.

Roux looked at the van unhappily. The plan called for all of us sticking together to bring the cash to Anastasia.

His phone pinged with a message, and he brightened upon reading it.

"Bene and Marius are on their way back."

I didn't know what that said about Szabo's fate, and I didn't want to know. I was just relieved that they were safe.

"Coming?" Jensen beckoned from his limo.

I hurried over with Henrik, promising Roux I would call soon. The river was just a short drive away. Henrik and I would be free to rejoin the others in no time.

The limo driver took off. I found it strange, sitting in a space that small — well, big, even for a limo, but still — with people I didn't relish spending time with. Henrik. Jensen. His stunning personal assistant. And Celeste.

Not exactly time to turn up the music and party.

I focused on my mission. The clock was ticking.

"As I understand it, you've hit certain...hurdles in your efforts to...um..." I waffled for a minute, trying to think of a better way to say *Your efforts to put local enterprises out of business and steal as much data from innocent customers as possible*. Finally, I came up with, "Your efforts to offer your services to the people of Switzerland."

Jensen nodded, and I went on with my pitch. But the limo stopped less than a minute later. We were already at the river.

A sleek speedboat with tinted windows awaited Jensen — of course — and he headed straight up the gangplank, asking me questions. How long were paintings typically loaned for and on what terms? Had I been speaking broadly, or was I actually in touch with high-level players in Switzerland?

"I'm not, but I'm sure Gordon is," I said truthfully.

I gave myself a mental pat on the back, because I was finally learning to stay out of trouble. If Jensen wanted to pursue my idea, he could do it through Gordon, and I would have no part in it.

I hurried up the gangplank, ignoring Henrik's muted protests, because boats didn't just shoot away from docks. I'd once joined friends for a day trip on a canal boat, and even the smallest maneuver had taken us ages.

Except, oops. This crew proved a lot more adept, and we zoomed away from the dock faster than you could say, *Watch out, Switzerland.*

"Just to the other side of the river," Jensen said, catching my wild-eyed expression. "Go on, then."

I continued my spiel as we rounded a bend in the Thames. Minutes later, the boat bumped up against the dock in Greenwich. I chased Jensen off the boat in the same hurried manner as I'd boarded, desperately making suggestions and fielding questions.

Amazingly, he actually paid attention. He even eschewed his waiting limo (because who didn't keep at least two limos in each city?) in favor of walking, and I tagged along, trying to keep pace with his long, clipped strides.

It was only when we were four blocks inland, approaching a row of swanky townhouses on a side street, that he dismissed me.

"Well, thank you, Miss Durand. A fascinating proposition."

I pursed my lips, tempted to correct him. I wasn't proposing anything — nothing that involved me anyway. I was just... er, insistently suggesting.

"I'll let Gordon know if I decide to get in touch with such a foundation," he finished.

"Just one thing," I blurted.

Jensen waited impatiently.

I flashed my meekest smile. "I was just wondering... As a person who admires your success in the world..."

A lie, but heck. My soul was probably already on its way to the devil.

"...why go with a middleman in this instance? Given your oft-cited advice of avoiding them, I mean."

Jensen flashed a smug smile that said how adorable I was for hoping to learn from him.

I tried not to gag as I waited.

"I was tempted, believe me." He shot a glance Celeste's way.

And oh, if I'd only had a body cam to report *that* to Gordon! That was proof — okay, strong circumstantial evidence — that she was working behind her boss's back.

"But one has to consider whether certain middlemen might prove useful on a later occasion," Jensen finished.

That meant the prospect of future collaboration with Gordon was worth more than the seventeen-million-dollar commission. Yikes. That said a hell of a lot about what my dear godfather was capable of.

My mind spun around that terrifying thought like a hyperactive bumblebee, and I slumped in defeat. What chance did a person like me have to do any good in the world, no matter how modestly?

"Goodnight," Jensen called, disappearing into the building with his entourage — and Celeste, who left me with a sneer.

"Goodnight," I echoed quietly.

A long minute later, I was still standing there, processing it all.

Henrik shuffled behind me. "All right. Enough saving the universe for one day. It's time to say goodbye to London."

There was nothing I wanted more. I turned away from the building and headed toward the river.

"Do you think Celeste will spend the night there?" I asked a few steps later.

Henrik made a face, no doubt reliving the night he'd spent with her.

"She'll try."

I walked on, thinking. Celeste was definitely operating behind Gordon's back. But what was her endgame?

I stumbled over a cobblestone, then looked around. And oh. It was dark and quiet. Uncomfortably quiet.

A creepy feeling set into my bones, and I walked faster, eyeing every dimly lit cross-street. Greenwich wasn't a bad neighborhood and I had Henrik with me, but neither was of much comfort.

Henrik hung back as I stormed on. "You're not going back to Jensen's boat, are you?"

"Absolutely not. There's a stop for the public ferry by the *Cutty Sark.*" I pointed to the masts towering over the row of buildings closest to the water.

I knew, because I'd stopped by the tall ship on my last trip to London, revisiting a sight from a family vacation we'd taken when I was ten. We had a lovely family photo of the occasion, showing my sister, my mother, my father, and me, all happy and blissfully unaware of what the future would bring.

Like the car accident that had killed my father, I couldn't help thinking. Like my recent discovery that my doting godfather was deeply mired in criminal activity.

"Does the ferry run at this hour?" Henrik asked.

I picked up my pace. God, I hoped so.

Henrik pulled his phone out of his pocket and dialed — Roux, I imagined.

Everything will be okay, I told myself. No reason to panic.

But the square beside the *Cutty Sark* was empty, and creepy strands of mist drifted over the cobblestones. Worse, my skin prickled in warning.

"Dammit, Roux..." Henrik muttered when no one answered.

I ran my finger down the posted boat schedule, noticing the chilly night air for the first time. Then I checked my watch.

The good news was the next stop was Docklands, where our friends waited.

The bad news was the next ferry was forty minutes away.

I swore and looked around. There was no reason to freak out and no sign of trouble.

Until footsteps sounded, and a shadow stretched from a streetlight behind us. I froze, watching a tall man approach calmly. Confidently. Quietly.

Henrik hissed, recognizing him.

"Szabo," he grunted as his eyes burned bright red.

My knees wobbled, and I backed away.

Szabo and friends, I thought, when more figures separated from the shadows.

Henrik scanned the area in alarm. I did too, then pointed. "There! The tunnel!"

A small pavilion marked the entrance to a century-old river crossing from Greenwich to the north bank of the Thames, where we'd started.

I took off at a sprint and charged into the pavilion, then down a wide flight of spiral stairs. Around and around, around and around. We were nearly four stories down when feet clanged over the steps above us.

I stopped, staring up in fear. Then Henrik shoved me. "Go! Get moving!"

I jumped down the last few stairs, then raced down the long, sloping tunnel.

Chapter Twenty-Five

MINA

My footsteps echoed along the length of the tunnel. The air was damp and stuffy. The ceiling wasn't all that high, and the walls weren't too wide on either side of me. Just wide enough for a pedestrian lane in either direction.

I raced along, wondering how fast Szabo could run. Praying Henrik could reason with him. Hoping Henrik would be inclined to.

A big if.

Henrik followed a few steps behind me — so close, we nearly crashed when I screeched to a stop.

"Dammit, woman," he cursed, in as much of a hurry as I was.

I pointed a shaky finger at the figure trotting toward us from the other end of the tunnel.

Moments ago, the tunnel had been empty. Now, we were sandwiched in between two groups of strangers. I squinted ahead, praying for a friend, not a foe.

I didn't recognize the language Henrik spoke in next, but I knew it was a curse.

Foe, then.

"Stay close," he murmured, turning sideways to peer in both directions.

Never had I imagined I would voluntarily follow such a command coming from him. But I did, brushing his side as we stood trapped in the middle of the tunnel.

Henrik's eyes shone bright red. His fangs and fingernails extended.

"Over there," he instructed.

We shuffled over to a small construction zone. I leaned over the low fencing and grabbed a length of metal pipe. Then I yanked out my phone and checked for a signal. Nothing.

It was me, Henrik, and three feet of metal against the two...four...six figures prowling closer, three from one end of the tunnel, three from the other.

"The moment you spot an opening, run," Henrik whispered.

A noble plan — truly — with zero chance of successful execution. Not with a trio of supernaturals blocking me from either direction.

Marius! I screamed in my mind, half hoping for a miraculous rescue.

But he'd been delayed by a vampire, and all I had for protection was Henrik and my own shaky capabilities.

I sniffed long enough to ascertain that the men on the left were vampires and those on the right shifters. Wolves, their musky scent indicated.

"Henrik." One of the vampires grinned from a few steps away.

"Szabo," he spat back.

Szabo bent into a bow, addressing me in an accent much thicker than Henrik's. "And the lovely Miss Durand. A pleasure to finally meet you."

His face was all angles, as if his creator had kept moving the ruler when sketching his outline.

"I believe we've met," I said icily. "Though you turned your tail and ran rather quickly."

The man behind him snickered, but Szabo kept up his arctic smile. "Perhaps, but you are the one running today."

Not any more, unfortunately. Not now that they'd cut us off in either direction.

Then he switched to...Polish? Romanian? and spoke rapidly to Henrik. Something along the lines of *Join us or perish,* I guessed.

My knees wobbled. If Henrik did...

But even if he remained loyal, what hope of escape did I have?

Three pairs of vampire eyes lasered in on my neck, and I imagined their mouths watering.

A thousand questions raced through my head. Was Szabo the one who had threatened Marius with those pictures? How had he reached the south side of the river when he'd been sighted on the north side a short time ago? And yikes. Would these men suck the life out of me slowly or end it all quickly?

My palm sweated against the pipe, and my mind screamed. *Escape! Escape!*

It wouldn't feel right to leave Henrik behind, but living life as a coward beat dying nobly.

Still, that was a moot point. I had no way of sneaking around these killers.

Then it hit me. Actually, I did.

Shadow-walking.

I gripped the pipe hard, doubting I had the skill to pull it off around so many highly sensitive supernaturals. But given my lack of alternatives...

I took a deep breath and started cataloging my position. The lighting. The cracks in the asphalt beneath my feet, and the pattern of tiles covering the wall beside me.

The wolf shifters prowled closer, eyeing me greedily.

"You sure you want to kill her, Etienne?" one called to the stockier man beside him in French.

I froze. The one Marius had tangled with?

Brown eyes, long white teeth, nick in one ear. This was Etienne?

He rubbed his chin. "I'm starting to rethink that."

The words *sex* and *trafficking* paraded through my mind like thugs in a police lineup.

I looked at my feet, trying to find a position that wouldn't appear too odd for a terrified woman to remain in, unmoving, for several minutes. I was too panicky to pull off a walking, talking illusion.

Rolled up in a pathetic ball would be easiest — but a little too meek, even for my ego. So I kept my eyes on my feet and my shoulders slumped, letting my chest rise and fall as little as possible. Then I closed my eyes, duplicated exactly that image, and stepped away.

I forced myself to snap my eyes open and check the illusion. Not bad, really.

I inched toward the wall and started moving sideways.

The men continued conversing, shifters in French, vampires in Romanian, as I decided it must be. My shoe scuffed, and I froze, but no one looked over.

Slow. . . steady. . . I told myself.

I peered ahead, memorizing the look of each cubic foot of unoccupied space before slipping into it. One hint of my shadow on the wall, one line out of place, and I would be busted.

My mind ached with the effort of maintaining two parallel illusions.

"Now you've really scared her, Etienne," one of the wolves laughed. "She's like a block of ice."

I focused all my attention on moving my illusion's elbow and bowing the neck to appear even meeker. But I forgot to let the hair on fake me sway, and the effect was a little jarring.

A good thing Henrik changed position just then, covering my mistake with his shadow.

I thought it was a coincidence at first, but then he did it again, and I realized it wasn't. Henrik had caught on to what I was doing, and he was doing his best to help me.

I'd never felt more grateful to a vampire. I also prayed I would never have to be.

I readjusted the angle of fake me's neck and continued tiptoeing along. This was the really tricky part, because the three shifters had spread out across the width of the tunnel.

I flattened myself against the wall and continued, holding my breath as I pulled level, then past, Etienne, who was just inches away. His buddy stood half a step behind him, closer to the center of the tunnel, giving me more space to maneuver. I took another step, then another.

The wolf shifter frowned, and his nostrils flared.

I froze.

He looked around, then turned back to the others and asked Etienne to repeat whatever he'd just said.

Heart pounding, I moved faster. Still a snail's pace, but a frantic one. Any second now, they would be onto me.

"Hey, you," the closest shifter barked to fake Mina. Once. Twice. Then he whistled sharply for my attention.

Shit. He was definitely onto me.

I moved faster, a yard past him now. Two yards...

He turned his head, following my movements with his nose instead of his eyes.

"Wait a minute..." he muttered.

I broke into a jog, doing my best to replicate the empty space before me. But my nerves were too shaky, and my shadow jumped in and out of view instead of remaining invisible. The flickering overhead lights helped mask the effect, but—

"Shh," the wolf shifter ordered.

Everyone went quiet. Even Henrik, dammit.

I halted a moment too late, and the slap of my foot echoed down the tunnel.

Muttering, one of the vampires reached for the illusionary me, which was now leaning strangely and weirdly out of proportion. Henrik moved to block him, but it was too late. The vampire's pale, bony hand swept through the air, and—

I released the illusion and sprinted for the far end of the tunnel. Chaos erupted as the men gaped at the empty spot my illusion had occupied a moment earlier.

"She's over there!" someone yelled.

"Get her!" Etienne shouted.

I ran for my life.

The pipe slipped out of my hand, and the man closest to me swore and leaped sideways. The sound of metal bumping over cement echoed through the tunnel, and a lightbulb went off in my head. I was moving too fast to shadow-walk in a convincing manner. But I might be able to cast simple illusions to trip them up.

I tried a pipe first, because the feel of one was fresh in my mind. Still running, I formed an illusionary pipe in my hand, then threw it behind me.

"*Merde*," the shifter cursed, dodging it.

He could have run straight through it, but he didn't know that, and the metallic bumping sound I cast — a first ever for me — helped maintain the illusion.

The tunnel sloped gently upward.

I raced toward the far end, hurling a stream of hastily created illusionary items, starting with things I'd had practice with. A newspaper. A hat. A book. Another book — a big, thick one.

"What the...?"

The men chasing me darted from side to side, dodging the barrage. Growing bolder — or more desperate — I started throwing more elaborate illusions. Flying bats. Darts. Hailstones. None were real, so they couldn't trip up those in hot pursuit. Still, they formed enough of an obstacle course to keep the men from running at full speed.

One of my creations — a crooked frying pan — was so bad, they halted to stare at it.

"What is this?" one muttered.

I dropped the illusion before they tried grabbing it and ran on. The spiral stairs leading to the north bank of the Thames were only a few steps away now.

A scream rang out behind me. I cringed, picturing an innocent bystander caught up amid vampires and shifters. But a quick glance told me that was Henrik, sinking his clawlike nails into one of the vampires.

My steps faltered, because it was three vampires to one. Surely I shouldn't leave Henrik to fight them alone?

Then I decided I definitely should. Especially when the three shifters stopped, hunched, and started morphing into wolf form. I gasped as fur broke out over their backs and their faces stretched into snouts.

I rushed on, taking the stairs two at a time. The ring of my shoes over metal echoed through the tunnel. Moments later, those echoes were joined by the swift, soft pad of paws. Growls followed, and I nearly cried out in fear. They were gaining, and I had no hope of throwing illusions at them while running in a spiral.

Marius! I screamed, if only in my mind. *I'm sorry. So sorry...*

Never, ever had I imagined that it was my destiny to be ripped to pieces by a pack of rabid wolves in a tunnel in London.

It isn't, the back of my mind insisted. *Keep running!*

I pounded around three more stairs, and my next gasping breath was of fresher, drier air. I was nearly there!

A snarl sounded as one of the wolves tried to overtake another on the narrow stairs. They tangled and snapped at each other, letting me gain a few precious seconds.

I burst out onto a wide, grassy park. The night sky was shrouded with clouds, and the lights of skyscrapers shone behind a lower row of buildings nearby.

Another scream sounded from the tunnel, and I winced. Was that Henrik?

I didn't stop to turn, though. Not even when snarls sounded behind me.

The faces of my loved ones flashed through my mind. My mother. My sister. My cousin. I pictured the château and everything I had hoped to achieve there. But most of all, I pictured Marius and the future we wouldn't have.

A roar split the night, and I cringed, picturing more shifters closing in. God, they were everywhere. Even in front of me.

I squinted as a bright light flared between two buildings, then fizzled. Another roar sounded, and the light flared again.

I nearly stumbled, because that wasn't a light. It was fire. And behind it...

A huge shadow swooped toward me, bulky in the middle, with narrower protrusions at each side.

Wings, I realized. Dragon wings.

It roared again, and my heart lifted. Marius?

Behind me, the wolves halted.

"Marius!" I croaked between gasping breaths.

The dragon raced in, skimming over the closest rooftops, then over the ground.

Get down! his roar burst into my mind.

I waited until the last possible second, then threw myself down.

Whoosh! Marius sliced the sky over me. The downdraft tossed my hair, and the air heated as a long line of fire scorched the park. The wolves scattered.

Keep running! Marius urged.

Rolling to my feet, I ran toward the buildings. Then two shapes burst out of the shadows ahead, and I halted.

Shit. This was it. I was finished.

But the beast on the left ran directly past me, snarling. I stared at the blur of dark stripes. The one on the right sprinted past too, and I spotted a thick, flowing mane. A lion?

Then I cheered. "Bene! Roux!"

Mayhem ensued, and I backed away from the snarls and screams. When things died down, I rushed closer, gesturing toward the tunnel.

"Henrik is in there fighting Szabo and two other vampires!" I yelled.

Bene flew into the pavilion and down the stairs, his long, tufted tail streaming behind him. Roux followed. I was of half a mind to follow, but Marius roared.

Don't even think about it.

So I didn't. I just stood there, listening as snarls and curses broke out in the tunnel.

Marius circled overhead, studying the ground. I turned, following his gaze. The earth was singed, and three lumps lay still on the grass. Marius lifted his mighty dragon muzzle and roared into the sky.

So, Etienne and his cronies were dead. But what about Szabo? What about Henrik?

Chapter Twenty-Six

MARIUS

My heart pounded as I circled the riverside park, peering into the shadows. Fortunately, Mina wasn't hurt, but I wasn't about to relax. Not when another foe could appear at any moment.

I dipped for a closer look at Etienne's lifeless body... or the ashy remains of it. Then I exhaled, but only slightly. One bitter enemy eliminated, but others remained. Like Szabo.

After another tight turn, I swooped down. The ground rushed up at me, and I stuck out my claws for landing. At the last possible moment, I braked by catching the wind with my wings. Touching down, I took a few skipping steps, then stopped, gazing at Mina.

She stood a few steps away, startled yet stubbornly holding her ground.

"Marius..."

My heart thudded as she stared at me, wide-eyed.

"Are you all right?" she whispered.

I snorted. She was the one who'd tangled with Etienne and his gang.

I grunted quietly. *I'm fine. What about you?*

She nodded. "Thanks to you."

My dragon preened.

A snarl drifted up from the tunnel entrance. We both whirled, and I opened my wings, forming a protective wall before her. The next vampire who showed his pale face would be toast — literally.

"Not if it's Henrik," Mina yelped.

I grumbled. She might be ready to forgive him, but I never would.

I flared my nostrils, analyzing the mixed scents drifting out of the tunnel, then growled quietly.

Szabo, my dragon rumbled, more on the basis of his preferred cologne than his actual scent.

Mina nodded. "He turned up in Greenwich with two other vampires. I guess Jensen's men were wrong about sighting him near the warehouse?"

I growled under my breath. More like a deliberate false alarm, though I couldn't understand why Jensen would cooperate with Szabo, nor how Etienne fit in with any of this.

"Bene…Roux…" Mina fretted.

Footsteps sounded from the pavilion, and I opened my mouth, prepared to spray it with fire. Two figures appeared — one man leaning heavily on a low, sleek animal.

I prefer "King of the Jungle," Bene muttered into my mind.

Yes, that was him, helping Henrik limp out of the tunnel.

"Henrik! Bene!" Mina rushed over. "Are you all right?"

Henrik croaked something about being just fine, though he looked terrible. Bene played up his own injuries by limping and whimpering.

"Poor baby," Mina cooed, stroking his mane.

Asshole, I grumbled.

He snickered into my mind. *I always knew she liked me.*

I let out a thunderous roar. Mina's hair and Bene's mane flattened, but Henrik's slicked-back hair didn't so much as flutter.

Bene crouched, muttering a weak, *Just kidding.*

"Please do make sure to alert all of London to our presence," Henrik muttered.

Stupid dragon, Bene grumbled, moving away from Mina.

She shot me one of those sharp, teacher looks that asked, *Was that really necessary?*

I glared at Bene. *Yes.*

Roux appeared next, sporting a gash on his striped shoulder that looked painful, though not serious.

Everything all right here? he asked.

Only if the dragon refrains from torching us along with the rest of the Docklands, Bene grumbled.

Roux sighed. *Let me guess. You provoked him.*

Bene licked his paw and touched up his whiskers. *Maybe a little.*

Henrik brushed at the blood seeping through his torn sleeve, then looked at Mina.

"That was quite the trick you pulled back there." For once, his voice was a little awed.

I tilted my head. What trick?

Mina slumped, looking ashamed. "You mean, running for my life while you fought three vampires? Thank you, by the way. They would have killed me... or worse."

I fought away horrible images of vampires drinking from Mina.

Henrik shook his head. "Running was your only option. But that shadow-walking... Well done."

My eyes went wide. A compliment from Henrik was like a twin moon — it never happened. But Mina just shook her head.

"They figured it out, though."

Henrik shrugged. "Only after a while, and in close quarters. If we'd been out in the open, they might never have caught on."

Mina brightened a little. "Really?"

Henrik looked genuinely impressed. "I haven't seen anyone create that convincing an illusion in decades."

I wasn't surprised, but Mina just looked back at the tunnel. "Are they... ?"

Henrik's clothing was splattered with crimson that turned to ash and fell away as he plucked at the fabric.

"Szabo and one other are dead. The third..." He looked at Roux.

The tiger flexed his claws and dipped his head in a nod.

Is that all of them, then? Just three? I asked.

Henrik shot me a hurt look. "Just?"

Not what I meant, I muttered.

Mina rubbed her arms in the night chill. "So, what now?"

Henrik straightened, wincing, but already healing. "No cleanup necessary in the tunnel. But out here..." He gestured at the slain shifters with disdain, implying something like, *At least we vampires have the grace to go cleanly.*

Yes, conveniently. They left nothing but piles of ash, which wouldn't be noticed in the tunnel. But shifters...

Bene tilted his head at the river, and Roux nodded. I held up a wing, trying to distract Mina as they disposed of the bodies. Still, she peeked around the edge, grimacing.

"I can't even bring myself to feel bad for them. God, I really am going over to the dark side," she lamented.

I snorted. Etienne deserved no pity, and neither did the other two, whom I'd recognized as a couple of thugs from his fight club. The world was truly better off without them.

I led Mina over to the van Roux had parked nearby and quickly shifted into human form. Mina watched, rapt, as I did so. Scrutiny like that from anyone else would have felt invasive, but I loved it.

Roux and Bene joined me, and we all pulled on the workmen's jumpsuits Roux had packed along with an assortment of equipment.

"Let's go," Bene urged, sliding the van door open.

"Where to?" Mina asked.

Roux waved. "I'm not sure, but let's start by getting out of here."

∞∞∞∞

We were on edge all the way to Anastasia's, where we dropped off the cash — all three million pounds worth.

"Are you sure you want this much cash sitting around your apartment?" Mina asked, as ever looking out for others. She was a lot better at that than looking out for herself.

Good thing she has us, my dragon declared.

Yes, but I wasn't counting my baby dragons before they hatched. I would only relax when we got home to Château Nocturne and put all this behind us.

"It will be fine," Anastasia assured her.

256

Bene snorted once we'd extracted ourselves. "Did you see the way she grabbed the cash? She didn't even ask about the painting."

We piled back into the van, with Roux, Mina, and me in the front, as before, and Bene and Henrik in the cargo area.

"I don't get it," Mina gazed glumly out the window as we drove away. "What happened to principles?"

"Not sure she ever had any," I said.

A few seconds ticked by. Then Mina murmured, "Maybe I should pose the same question about my principles."

I took her hand. "Just asking shows they're right where they ought to be." Then I managed a little smile. "Then again, I am biased."

We drove the rest of the way in silence. Roux's eyes constantly roved the streets, but we made it back to the hotel without further incident. Once there, we all flopped into chairs or the couch.

"I still don't understand what happened," Bene said. "With Szabo, I mean. And what the hell was Etienne doing in London?"

"Celeste," I grumbled. "It had to be. In both cases."

Bene stirred the air with his hand. "Explain."

I looked at Mina, then laid it all out. The threatening photo. The grudge Etienne held against me. Szabo following Mina to London...

"But how would Etienne have taken that photo in Mallorca?" Roux asked.

"He didn't," I said, having finally figured it out. "That had to be Celeste's doing. But she passed it on to Etienne, probably hoping we would take each other out." I grimaced, squeezing Mina's hand. "And maybe take Mina out too."

Her eyes met mine, grim but grateful.

"Why would anyone want to off Mina?" Bene asked.

To her credit, she didn't glare at Henrik, but I did.

"I think Celeste is a bit...jealous," Mina said carefully. "You know, of the château. Of the preferential treatment I get from Gordon."

Roux snorted. "The preferential treatment that nearly got you killed?"

"Also, the château is kind of a money pit," Bene said. When Mina grimaced, he threw up his hands. "No offense."

She sighed. "None taken."

Henrik rubbed his chin, thinking. "So, that report of Szabo lurking around the warehouse..."

"Celeste," I grunted. "Again. I'm sure she came up with that."

Mina grimaced. "Was Szabo there at all, or was it all a false alarm?"

"He was there," I said, "But only long enough to lure me away."

"Why?" Bene asked.

Roux had an answer to that one. "To give us one less man on the job. You know — divide and conquer."

And to get me away from Mina. I was sure of it. The clincher was Szabo and Etienne working together to trap her in that goddamn tunnel. There was no way those two would ever have cooperated on anything...unless Celeste put them up to it, promising a reward she may or may not have delivered in the end.

I glanced at Henrik. I'd never thought I'd feel indebted to him for anything, but hell. I was. If he hadn't been there to help Mina...

I shook that ugly scenario away.

Everyone remained silent for a while, digesting all that.

"God, what a night," Roux muttered, summing things up perfectly.

"Not over yet," Bene pointed out. "We still have to call Gordon."

Everyone groaned, but Mina raised her hand. "I'll be happy to do it."

Roux side-eyed her. "Not sure that's a good idea."

It was a *terrible* idea, but Roux wasn't as blunt as I was.

But Mina, of course, pulled out her phone and began dialing.

Everyone tensed.

"Uh, Mina..." Bene started.

She put the phone on speaker mode, muttering something that sounded like *No more Mr. Nice Girl.*

Roux and I traded looks. What the hell did that mean?

"Clervaud here," Gordon answered the phone in a clipped tone.

Mina motioned to Roux, who leaned in to say, "Anand here, calling to report."

"Yes?" Gordon asked eagerly. "How did everything go?"

Roux thought that over, then spoke in a tone as dry as the Sahara. "Jensen has the painting, and Anastasia has the money."

Definitely an abridged version of events.

"Excellent, excellent," Gordon said.

Then Mina leaned in. "Hello, Gordon."

The line fell silent before he recovered. "Mina?"

"Yes, it's me," she said, waiting for him to put two and two together.

"What are you doing in London? You should have left hours ago."

"Irrelevant," she said curtly. "The question is, what is Celeste doing with Jensen?"

Boy, was she good at deflecting.

"With Jensen?" Gordon parroted, clearly caught off guard. Then he put the obvious together. "Listen, my dear. Celeste is a woman with certain...er...peculiarities."

Mina rolled her eyes. "Do you mean the insatiable sex drive of a succubus or something else?"

Gordon was speechless. I was fairly taken aback myself. I was the blunt one. Mina was the one who found a nice way to put things.

Not this time, my dragon chuckled.

"How is *that* relevant?" Gordon finally sputtered.

Mina rolled her eyes. "I seem to recall a lecture about no place for intimate relations in business."

"Yes, well..." he hemmed and hawed. "Celeste is a rather special case."

"So special, you're willing to put up with her trying to cut you out of your own deals?" Mina asked.

"What?" Gordon's voice spiked.

We all listened as Mina explained what she'd witnessed in Greenwich.

"She tried to convince Jensen to cut you out of the deal. And that's just the tip of the iceberg."

"Are you saying—" Gordon fumed.

Mina cut him off. "I'm saying, I think you ought to have a closer look at your assistant's comings, goings, and secret connections to the likes of Szabo."

"Szabo?" he growled.

"Szabo," Mina affirmed then addressed the rest of us. "Does anyone have something to add?"

Henrik smirked. "I believe that sums it up nicely."

"Well, I think that's all we have to report for now," Mina told Gordon in a voice flatter than one of Madame Picard's crêpes. "Congratulations on another profitable deal."

"But—" Gordon started.

"I'll brief you the moment we return to Paris," Roux hurried to assure him.

"Right now, I suggest you follow up with Celeste. If she's not too busy with Jensen," Mina snipped.

I hid a grimace. If I knew Celeste, she was keeping Jensen *very* busy. The question was, how did that fit into her master plan?

Mina hung up, and no one spoke for a long time.

It was Bene who finally broke the ice. "I vote we put Mina in charge of all future calls to Gordon."

She shook her head vehemently. "No thank you."

"Well, then I vote we order dinner." He held up the room service menus. "And a nice bottle of champagne to celebrate with."

I closed my eyes, not too inspired to celebrate. A lot had gone our way, but things could have just as easily ended in disaster.

Roux echoed the sentiment. "I'd rather go home."

Everyone fell silent, and one by one, we looked at Mina.

Roux's throat bobbed. "Home to Château Nocturne. I know it's a lot to ask, Mina. And I know we already owe you more than we can ever repay, but... Would you reconsider?"

Mina bit her lip, thinking.

"I think you should," Henrik said next.

I nearly spat fire at him. Was he serious?

But then he went on, and I shut my mouth. Or rather, let it hang open in surprise.

"I mean, I think you should consider accepting the others back. I shall find alternative accommodations."

Mina's lips parted in surprise.

"Just consider," Henrik continued, more humbly than I'd ever seen him. "You would have your own in-house workforce, and Gordon would continue to pay for boarding costs. At least to the end of our new contracts, if I read the document correctly."

Mina gulped. "I *need* Gordon's money, but I don't *want* it."

"Why not?" Bene butted in. "At least it will go to a good purpose that way."

Mina looked at her hands, stuck on an issue that would take a lot longer than tonight to resolve — as in the future of her relationship with her godfather. But when it came to the issue of who lived where...

I looked at her, my heart filling with hope.

She looked around, contemplating each of us in turn, leaving me for last. I met her gaze, wary and hopeful at the same time. What if she'd changed her mind about me? About all of us?

"Like I said, I need Gordon's money, but I don't want it," she started. "But I do want *you* back." Her voice broke a little. "I missed you."

Bene shot her a winning grin. "I knew it."

"She means all of us, dumbass," Roux grumbled, then pointed to me. "Especially him, for reasons beyond comprehension."

Mina smiled. "I did miss Marius. But I missed the rest of you too." Then her face fell, and her eyes drifted toward Henrik.

"As I said, I shall find alternative accommodations." He moved quickly to the liquor trolley, where he poured himself a scotch and gazed silently out the window.

Still, Mina looked pained. "There is the issue of the police championships. . ."

I groaned, picturing that ass, Officer Clement.

Bene's eyes twinkled mischievously. "I promise, we'll be on our best behavior."

Mina shook her head. "How about, you'll be taking that weekend off somewhere far, far away from Burgundy?"

Bene opened his mouth to protest, but Roux smacked his shoulder.

"Anything it takes is fine."

Mina nodded, and just like that, our futures were secured. At least for the next few weeks, which was about as far as any of us planned ahead.

Well, that was how it had always been. But for once, my mind revved much farther ahead. As in years. Even decades.

Bene smacked his hands together and grabbed the room service menu. "Deal. Now, I think we deserve to celebrate."

"I'd rather catch the next train to Paris." Roux checked his watch, then groaned. "Tomorrow, I guess."

"No problem. It's a big menu," Bene chirped, not quite getting the point.

"One more night here. . ." Mina looked around bleakly.

A sudden brain wave struck me, and I stood, reaching for her hand. "Come on."

She rose hesitantly, her eyes full of questions.

"We'll meet you here in time for breakfast," I told the others, towing Mina toward the door.

"Where are you going?" Roux demanded.

I flashed Mina a hopeful smile. "Well, there's this little place in Belgravia. . ."

Mina broke into a wide grin and looped her elbow through mine. "Sounds perfect." She waved to the others. "Have a good night."

Bene sighed. "At least you two will."

In the spirit of teamwork and a successful mission, I decided not to kill him. But it was a close call.

Mina pulled me toward the hallway. "See you tomorrow, everyone. And thank you again. For everything."

Her eyes lingered on Henrik, who raised his glass in a silent toast.

Roux shook his head, echoing her words on everyone's behalf. "No, thank *you.*"

Then we were out the door and on our way to what I hoped would be the first night of many. Maybe even a lifetime.

Chapter Twenty-Seven

MINA

I had a mile-long list of things to do when I got home — topped by *kiss the ground* and *block Gordon's number* among more mundane things, like *follow up with plumber and roofer.* Eventually, I would also have to get to a few really big burning issues, such as Celeste and Gordon.

But the first thing I *actually* did...

"Are you sure?" Marius panted, pausing in mid-sex above me.

About a mating bite? Hell yes.

"So, so sure," I mumbled, though it came out a little slurred.

My body was on fire, pulsing with ecstasy and an insatiable yearning for more. *More* that only a mating bite could quench.

I'd fantasized about it all the way over from London, to the point that the faint glow around my body — and Marius's — had amped up to a high-wattage radiance. Only supernaturals could see it, but oops. We'd turned plenty of heads on the train ride back under the English Channel. Who knew so many supernaturals made the early morning commute from London to Paris?

Roux and Henrik had moved two rows away, with Roux muttering something like, *Please, do us all a favor and get the mating bite over with. All this sexually charged energy is killing me.*

Bene had mimicked scooping a handful of something out of the air. *Maybe this could be harnessed as an alternative to nuclear energy.*

Marius had bared his teeth, and Bene had skittered over to join the others, chuckling.

We'd practically burst through the front doors of the château and sprinted upstairs to my bedroom, where Marius had uttered the first of a half dozen *Are you sures?*

The man was definitely overcompensating for marking me without asking.

"You want to protect me? What better way than making me into a dragon shifter?" I shot back, because that was one of the effects of a mating bite.

He couldn't fault that logic, so there we were, turning my bedroom into a steam bath. We'd already powered through one round of sex — a warm-up, one might call it — and were now well on our way to the main event.

"You're really sure?" Marius asked, hanging on by a thread.

(Well, a lot more than a thread, considering how. . . er, *thoroughly* the man filled me.)

"Ask me again, and I'll be the one biting you," I growled.

His eyes sparkled. "Nothing I'd like more."

All well and good, but I was happy to wait until I could extend the right set of teeth for the job. Namely, dragon teeth. Until then, I would leave the honors to him.

I tightened my legs around his waist, but he withdrew. Drat the man!

"I said, I'm sure," I groaned, clutching at him.

But those rippling abs won out, and he shuffled back a little.

"Not stopping. Just repositioning," he promised, nudging my hip.

We could be tied upside down in a pretzel shape, and I would have been perfectly happy as long as he stayed deep inside me. Since when were dragons so picky?

"You'll see," he said.

I didn't want to see. I wanted to feel, dammit.

"Is dying of lust a thing?" I groused.

He chuckled. "If it were, I would be long dead. Ever since the day I met you."

He was trying to butter me up, and it was working.

I rolled to all fours and wiggled my rear. "Happy?"

The rumbling sound he replied with assured me he was *plenty* happy.

Gripping my hips, he slid up behind me, whispered, "I love you," and powered back into me.

My vision blazed as he moved, deeper and harder. As soon as I caught the rhythm, I moved too, bumping back to meet him.

There was a fair chance I was yowling like an oversexed cat, but my ears were too filled with a roaring sound to tell. At first, I thought that was Marius's dragon, but no. It came from deep in my soul.

I'd always pictured my mixed supernatural heritage as a ball of cast-off yarn in dozens of different colors. The original strands were forever tangled, and no amount of plucking would ever separate them.

But now, a single, golden thread glittered in the darkness, telling me one tug would pull it free. My dragon heritage?

Marius scraped his teeth along my neck, and I arched up into him.

Yes! Yes! my soul cried in eager anticipation.

Twin points of fire sliced into my neck as Marius bit down — a quick flash of pain, followed by blinding pleasure. I groped around and pulled my lover's head closer, urging him to bite deeper.

Supernatural energy zapped and hummed inside me, a thousand times more intensely than ever before.

Marius inhaled, sealed his lips around the bite, and—

Whoosh! Flames raced through my veins.

A dragon kiss. I'd heard the stories, but nothing came close to describing that dizzying, sensual heat.

Marius rolled his hips, powering into me one more time, then exploded.

I cried out, deaf and blind to everything but the forces inside me. Suddenly, space and time jumped, and wind breezed past my ears. Cool air tickled my skin. A thousand countryside scents filled my nostrils. My eyes were closed, but I saw the château and its grounds from an aerial perspective.

I was flying — at least in my mind — beside a huge, dark dragon. He looked at me with sparkling eyes and shot a plume of fire into the sky just for the joy of it.

At first, it was terrifying, because that fire could incinerate everything around it — including plain old me.

Then I realized I wasn't a plain anything any more. I was a dragon, like him.

The massive dragon at my side swooped, rolled, and loop-de-looped around me, showing off like an elite fighter pilot.

Much better than a fighter pilot, Marius growled.

My eyes snapped open, and I was back in bed, skin tingling, heart pounding.

Whoa. Had I really been flying? Was I really a dragon?

No, but you will be soon, Marius murmured into my mind.

He'd collapsed behind me and lay there, as limp and breathless as me.

I touched my neck carefully. It was warm and tingly, but there was no wound or blood, just a humming undercurrent of magic inside me.

We'd done it. The mating bite. We were bound together — forever.

Mess that I was, I rolled around to face him. Hug him. Hold him. Trying to process it all.

"I didn't know you had that much dragon in you," he whispered, running his hands over my back.

"I didn't know I did either."

It occurred to me that if I had ended up with anyone else — say, Clem, a wolf shifter — then that side of my DNA might have been activated. But boy, did I like the idea of being a dragon shifter.

I hugged Marius fiercely. Shifter species aside, he was the only man I wanted. The only one I would ever live a truly happy, satisfied life with.

And if that meant living on the edge from time to time — say, another art caper or a brush with another dangerous supernatural — it would be worth it. I'd never felt as alive as I did with Marius, and I'd never felt as eager to embrace my supernatural side.

"You're going to have to learn to control it, of course." Marius warned.

"Ha. I've taught middle schoolers for years. If I can handle thirty of them at a time, I can handle one measly dragon."

In truth, I worried about a dragon running amok with my actions, words, and emotions. But I'd done pretty well handling Marius, Roux, Bene, and Henrik. I could do the same with the dragon that would eventually emerge from within me.

"The trick is to keep that side of you in a separate compartment and only let it out when you need to." That sounded ominous, but Marius shook his head and framed it more positively. "I mean, when you want to. Like when you want to fly, just for the fun of it."

"Only if I get to do it with you."

He grinned. "Believe me, that can be arranged."

He kissed me, slowly at first, then more urgently, and soon, we were back in the throes of passion. Not that I was complaining.

Afterward, we cleaned up, straightened the bedding, and lay spooned together.

"So, you're stuck with me now," I whispered.

He shook his head. "Not stuck. Delighted."

I nuzzled the arm he'd looped over me, gazing at nothing in particular. Slowly, the row of paintings on the wall came into focus, and I considered them, one after another.

There were a few from my grandparents' collection, plus the one I'd painted of the château on a misty morning, with all my friends represented. A lion sauntered across the lawn, a tiger blended into the bushes, and a bat flew between the chimneys. Best of all, two figures stood at in the windows of my suite, one tall, the other a little smaller.

I wove my fingers through Marius's, thinking back to the morning I'd lain here, fearing I had lost everything.

Then my eyes wandered to the Van Gogh we'd brought back from Mallorca. Having *The Painter on the Road to Tarascon* on my wall was a privilege I would enjoy for months before finding a way to anonymously slip it into the hands of a museum. As always, I asked myself, *How did I get this lucky?*

But part of me couldn't help sighing a little. If only I'd succeeded in finding a more fitting buyer for *The Tower of Blue Horses*. But it was Jensen's now and would probably remain locked away from the public for another generation.

Marius must have picked up on the sentiment, because he kissed my shoulder, then rolled away.

I protested, but he only chuckled.

"I'll be right back. I have a present for you."

"Well, in *that* case..." I joked, watching him step across the room to the clothing we'd left strewn by the door.

He found his pants and rooted around in the pockets, giving me a prime view of his ass. Another kind of masterpiece, in my humble opinion.

Then he walked back. I lifted the blanket to let him slide in, then stopped.

"Wait. Your phone?" I protested. The damn thing had only ever brought us bad news.

"Just for a moment," he assured me.

I let him back in bed, not all too enthusiastically. What could he possibly have on there that would add to this perfect moment?

He scrolled through his pictures — not that he'd taken many — then stopped, grinning at one.

I cocked my head. "Yes?"

He looked up, then set the phone on the dresser.

"Nah. You're right. This is no time to look at pictures."

He was teasing, of course, and I was hooked like a prize marlin.

"But my present..."

He grinned and reached for the phone again. "All right, already." He located what he wanted, then motioned to me. "Lie back. Get comfortable."

I frowned. Just to look at a picture?

Still, I complied. Otherwise, he would draw out the suspense *forever*.

"Now close your eyes..." he murmured.

I did, going all warm again. Even if his present turned out to be a dud, this position was awfully convenient for other activities. And we were both naked, so...

I drifted deep enough into a sexual fantasy that I didn't open my eyes when Marius told me to. But when I did...

I stared at the picture, then at Marius.

"No way."

He grinned. "Yes, way."

I jackknifed up into a seated position, grabbing his phone for a closer look.

"Where did you get this?"

"At Anastasia's, that first time we went there."

I stared and stared. The picture showed me from the back, gazing at *The Tower of Blue Horses.*

"I know you said a picture couldn't capture the painting, but I thought one might capture the moment," Marius said quietly.

"Pretty sneaky, mister," I joked over the lump in my throat.

He shrugged. "I don't always play by the rules, you know."

Oh, I knew. And boy, was I grateful. And not just for this picture.

"Thank you," I whispered. "Thank you so much."

The image blurred as tears sprang to my eyes.

"It's beautiful," was all I could manage.

For years, the only image art scholars like my father had of Franz Marc's masterpiece was a grainy 1940s photo, plus a postcard-size copy the artist had sent to a friend. And for years, my father had investigated what had become of the original, to no avail.

It has to be out there somewhere, I recalled him saying.

It is, Dad, I wanted to whisper. *And I saw it. In person.*

I held Marius's phone tightly. Why was I the lucky one who got to glimpse the painting, instead of my father? And would he celebrate the discovery or mourn my failure?

Sometimes, I had the feeling destiny enjoyed tying up loose ends. Other times, the universe seemed cruel and random.

I lay there, feeling a mixture of both. Lucky yet guilty. Happy yet yearning.

Then I wrapped my arms around Marius, reminding myself what the real masterpiece was. Love. Commitment. The chance to build a future together.

"Good present?" he asked, wiping away my tears.

I nodded quickly. "Best present ever."

Chapter Twenty-Eight

One week later...

I'd never appreciated Auberre as much as I did in the week after we returned from London. No crowds. No traffic. No criminals waiting to ambush me. Just a sleepy little town with one bakery and acres of peaceful forests and vineyards. Best of all was Château Nocturne — a safe, private world of its own where I got to make the rules and invite or exclude whomever I wanted.

But the week since we'd returned — and my first week of mated bliss — hadn't been as peaceful as I'd hoped. First, because my dragon side had emerged much more quickly than expected, and it was all so new to me.

"Feet out. Wings back. Back!" Marius roared as I plunged toward the ground in what was sure to be a disastrous landing.

And, yikes. I was still reeling from the fact that I'd managed to get aloft in the first place. I'd only meant to shake out my wings after my first shift, but my inner beast had had other ideas, taking off for several out-of-control loops over the château. If Marius hadn't shifted and caught up to coach me, I would have died in the first few minutes.

At one point, I nearly crashed headfirst into the château's central tower. Then I'd come within inches of clipping a chimney. Now, I was plummeting to certain death.

Whee! my inner beast squealed happily.

"Steady out! Tail straight! Steady!" Marius hollered in dragon-talk that my mind immediately translated.

Steady would be great, but I was wobbling like an albatross.

Then, *thump!* My teeth jarred as I touched down — to put it mildly — and tumbled head over heels over the south lawn. When I finally came to a stop, it was just inches away from the ballroom windows. Big windows with arched frames that cost a king's ransom to replace.

I picked myself up off the ground, cursing every bruise on my leathery body.

"Amazing — shifting *and* flying only one day after the bite. Must be a new record," Marius had announced proudly when the dust had settled.

A day later, my landing was a little smoother, and the one after that was even better. Encouraging enough that I let out a victorious roar afterward. I wasn't just a mixed-up relic with magic that came and went unpredictably. I was a dragon shifter too, and those skills came to me quickly, even naturally. So much that I started to believe I might be able to harness more magic if I really put my mind to it.

But that would have to wait, because adjusting to the new me wasn't the only thing on my mind that first week back at home. The police championships were rapidly approaching, and we had a hell of a lot of work to do to get ready.

On the plus side, that kept me from worrying about Celeste. Word was, she'd returned from London, acting innocent as a lamb, then departed Paris — quickly — once Gordon started asking her hard questions. Where she was now, and what Gordon planned to do about it, I had no idea. But it worried me.

For now, though, I decided to focus my nervous energy on the police championships.

"Today's the big day!" Bene announced cheerily that morning.

I was anxious as hell — hence the lecture I delivered over an extra-early breakfast.

"Swear to me you'll all be good," I demanded.

Marius and Roux nodded earnestly. Henrik made a face.

"Goes without saying," Bene promised.

I didn't believe *any* of them. Well, maybe Marius. Possibly Roux. But not Henrik, and *definitely* not Bene.

I pointed at him fiercely. "I mean it, Bene. Do not mess this up. Don't even show yourself — in human *or* lion form."

He stuck up his hands. "Not in my self-interest. Not when the place is crawling with police officers."

His tone suggested roaches rather than Burgundy's finest, so I pinned him with a hard look.

"Please. I need to get this business up and running, and this is an important first step."

Bene looked doubtful. "Sports business?"

I rose to put away the dishes. "Any business! And this is free advertising. People will come away from this event talking about what a great place this is for weddings and other events."

Roux scratched his cheek doubtfully. "Police weddings?"

I stamped my foot. "Normal people's!"

Bene cocked his head. "Define normal."

Simple question, yet I came up totally blank. Six weeks of living with these men — and two missions for Gordon — had warped my sense of normalcy forever.

I gritted my teeth. "It will also give me a sense of how well logistics will work for future events. Road access, parking, toilets. . ."

A slight exaggeration, because the event organizers had trucked in dozens of portable toilets. But any detail they let slip would reflect poorly on the venue, and my hopes for future business could be marred forever.

"Oh God." I grabbed for my clipboard. "Spare toilet paper—"

Marius touched my shoulder gently. "Already taken care of, remember?"

Was it? Over the past week, we'd made more runs to the *hypermarché* than I could count, and it was all a blur to me.

"We have enough toilet paper to survive the apocalypse," Marius assured me.

"Or the next pandemic," Bene threw in. "Whichever comes first."

Henrik looked smug, the only one of us immune to both those events.

I carried the plates to the kitchen, then hurried back to the dining room. The event organizers would be here any minute, and hundreds of contestants and spectators would follow.

"Now, listen," I instructed them. "Roux has a list of jobs I need you to do today..."

Roux leafed through the pages with a dry expression. Yes, *pages* — plural.

"As soon as you finish one job, you're to start right on the next," I went on.

That was my strategy — to keep them so occupied indoors that they wouldn't find time to sneak outside and mingle with our visitors.

"That's not a list. That's a goddamn manifesto," Bene protested.

"Don't like it? Move out," Marius growled.

Bene made a face but held his tongue. That was the nice thing about our new arrangement — I still had something to hold over them. I also had Marius as the ultimate enforcer.

Joy trickled through my veins, and I reminded myself to maintain a sense of perspective. I'd survived a combined vampire/shifter attack and my godfather's latest sketchy scheme. I could survive hosting a sports event too.

"We really, really can't afford any trouble today," I admonished for the last time. "So, please. Stay out of sight. No exceptions — not even for you, Henrik. Not until the last police officer leaves the premises. Understood?"

He shot me a sullen expression but nodded. "Understood."

Back in London, he'd volunteered to find his own accommodations. At the time, that sounded like a great idea, and I hadn't asked any questions.

That was before I realized he would go and rent a house on the edge of my property. Now, I had *lots* of questions. Had he had that in mind all along? Had he chosen that particular property to spite me, or could he genuinely not bring himself to part ways with our motley little crew?

I was grateful for what he'd done in London, but that didn't exactly make us besties.

As for the house he'd rented... Oh, the irony. Years ago, my grandmother had sold the roomy caretaker's "cottage" on the edge of the property to a friend to help pay expenses. That friend had sold it to a friend and so on, until it ended up in the hands of a complete stranger. Their plans to renovate the place had fallen through due to unexpectedly high expenses (an all too familiar theme), and the house had stood empty for years. It was still run-down, but that hadn't stopped Henrik from moving in.

He'll feel right at home with all the dust and cobwebs, Bene had joked.

The thought had saddened me. Didn't Henrik have anywhere better to go?

On the other hand, I was still stuck with an unpredictable vampire, and I had less oversight of him than ever. Over the past few weeks, he'd both threatened *and* saved my life. What would he do next time?

Another problem for another day. For now, I had to get through the next twelve hours.

"And on no account should you let anyone into the house," I reminded everyone.

I had a priceless Van Gogh upstairs, and I didn't want to have to explain that to anyone. *Especially* a police officer.

The doorbell rang, and I steeled myself, expecting the event organizers. I hurried to the door and opened it. But instead of the four nice officers who'd stopped by before to discuss logistics, I found my sister.

"Geneviève?" I squeaked.

"Surprise!" she chirped. "I'm here!"

I didn't know whether to clap or cry, because wow. Talk about timing.

Gen threw herself into a tight hug, which was a good thing. Otherwise, I might have keeled over.

The floorboards creaked behind me, and I knew without looking that my houseguests had found us. More importantly, they'd found Gen.

Like me, she had blue eyes and long, straight hair, though hers had an auburn tint. She was a little shorter, a lot prettier, and *much* more outgoing.

If I'd had some police tape to cordon them off from her, I would have.

"Dammit, guys. I said, stay out of sight!"

"Of the police," Bene said, flashing my sister a dazzling smile. "Nice to finally meet you."

She blinked, confused but delighted. I would have felt the same if I had turned up to her house and found four strikingly handsome houseguests.

I introduced everyone through gritted teeth, and the guys practically swooned over her. Henrik kissed her knuckles. Bene turned up the charm. Roux's nostrils flared like she was the best thing he'd scented in a long time.

Marius was the only one who was more guarded.

Now? his eyes asked me.

I had no words. After months of delays, my sister had somehow picked exactly today to turn up.

"Gordon says hello," she said, all blissful and ignorant.

Boy, did we have a lot to discuss.

Then we all looked up, hearing cars coming down the drive. Three, to be exact, all adorned with police logos. The event organizing committee, no doubt.

I gulped. This had all seemed like a good idea a few weeks ago. Now, I wasn't so sure. But at least they weren't here to arrest me.

Hopefully.

"We have to go," I ordered Gen, propelling her outside with me.

"But—" she protested.

"But—" Bene and Roux mourned at the same time.

What a fool I'd been to imagine my life might regain some semblance of peace and quiet. Instead, I was facing a potential love triangle.

I whirled back to leave the guys with one last order.

"Not a peep from any of you. Now, please, please get to work, and please don't ruin this."

With that, I slammed the door.

Gen stared. "Ruin what?"

I sighed. "I'll explain in a minute."

Behind me, the door opened a sliver, and Marius handed me my clipboard.

"Thank you." I grabbed it and blew him a kiss.

He gave me a thumbs-up and closed the door.

Gen went bug-eyed.

"Oh my God. You're sleeping with a dragon shifter?" she squealed exactly as Clem drove up.

I put my face in my hands, wishing for a hole to crawl into. If only Gen didn't share the supernatural genes that allowed us to identify all kinds of supernaturals.

Then I took a deep breath and faced Clement.

His face was stony, as it had been ever since I'd come home with Marius.

"Good morning, Clem," I said.

"Good morning." His dejected murmur suggested all light had been sucked out of the universe and darkness had swallowed the galaxy.

Wolf shifters did not take rejection well.

I'd tried to let him down gently, but no go. Now, I really, really needed to find him a new love interest.

Then I brightened because, oh. As it so happened...

I motioned toward Gen. "You remember my sister, Geneviève."

Clem removed his hat and nodded politely.

"Good to see you," he said unenthusiastically.

"Good to see *you*," Gen breathed, like her world had just exploded with sunshine, unicorns, and rainbows.

I cringed, rethinking my logic. What was a love triangle with four parties called?

I greeted the other officers and led them away from the house, along with my sister. There was no way I was leaving her unsupervised with three shifters and a vampire.

"So, the arrangements..." I started, bracing myself for a very long day.

∞∞∞∞

Soon, the grounds were inundated with athletes and spectators, most of them members of France's finest.

Clem only had eyes for me, while Gen couldn't take *her* eyes off *him*. Luckily, he left us quickly, having duties as a marshal of the cross-country running competition. Also, Gen had worked enough events to make herself useful. The event organizers had sworn they could handle everything, but the inevitable issues arose, from desperately needed extension cords to garbage bags and — as I'd guessed — toilet paper.

"Wow. This looks amazing." Gen stopped in her tracks when we entered the stables.

Rackets blurred and balls flew. We turned our heads, watching them pinging and ponging.

"Table tennis is one of three events we're hosting today," I explained.

"I mean, the stables," Gen said.

I looked around. Weeks ago, junk had filled the place from floor to ceiling, and cobwebs had shrouded the windows. Now, everything had been cleared and cleaned, and the fairy lights I'd strung up helped inch the space past *functional* toward *stylish*. I'd even had flyers printed, optimistically listing all kinds of events the château could be hired for, from weddings to anniversary parties and even car shows. (Roux's idea. The man had high hopes for our vintage Jaguar.)

Being involved in the nitty-gritty of that work had blinded me to the big picture, but now, I looked around with fresh eyes.

"You'd done so much!" Gen enthused.

"We have," I whispered, proud and amazed. "All of us."

I yearned to share the moment with Marius and the others. To celebrate what we'd accomplished, and to seeing the grounds brought to life again.

In my grandmother's day, the château had always been a lively place, hosting parties, concerts, and soirées. And while the police championships were a far cry from teatime and games of croquet, it was a step in the right direction.

"Grandma would be proud," Gen decided.

My heart swelled as I looked around. I thought so too.

"This just shows how much more we can offer, and not just here in the stables." Gen pointed to the gazebo where the officials had set up tables, then to the tiny chapel out by the duck pond. The roof had caved in, but that didn't stop Gen's vivid imagination.

"Either of those would be perfect for weddings, and receptions can take place in the stables or in the ballroom."

My thoughts went there. With any luck, the guys were feeling cooperative and working on it at that very moment, spackling cracks in the plaster.

"Guests can book suites in the west wing..." Gen went on.

Yes, but we would have to figure out where to put the guys first. Marius had moved in with me for good, but the others...

My mind spun. So much to do, and we'd only just gotten started. But for once, the scale of it didn't discourage me. I had my man now, and he wasn't going anywhere. Neither were the others. So maybe, a year or two from now...

"We should be able to host our first guests next spring!" Gen announced, as happy and ignorant as I had once been.

I decided not to burst her bubble. Not on her first day anyway.

Shortly after, I slipped away from the event to check on the guys. The ballroom was empty — but wow. Every crack had been smoothed over, every wall prepared for a fresh coat of paint once the plaster dried.

I checked the dining room next, then the drawing room, finding no one. Where were they?

My mind filled with doomsday scenarios, like Henrik sucking the blood out of a spectator or Bene out flirting with female police officers.

But, whew. I eventually found them on a rooftop balcony, overlooking the action.

Marius swept me into a kiss worthy of a movie poster, while the others rolled their eyes and went back to critically micro-analyzing each athlete's performance.

I broke away from Marius long enough to chastise them. "Like you could do better."

"I could," Bene declared, and Roux nodded too. "Running — easy. Mountain biking — I could cover the same terrain faster without a bicycle."

I pictured him bounding along in lion form. Okay, maybe he had a point there.

"What about table tennis?" I challenged.

"How is that a police event?" Marius chortled.

"Maybe they use rackets to subdue very weak criminals," Bene joked.

"Well, it requires quick reflexes," I tried.

"There is a lot of back-and-forth, like an interrogation," Roux deadpanned.

Bene collapsed into chuckles, while Henrik groaned.

"I don't see Officer Dulaire competing," Marius said a little snidely.

I smacked his arm. "Be nice, please. He's officiating."

Marius opened his mouth, caught my look of warning, and closed it again. The man was definitely learning.

"Ah, yes. Officer Dulaire," Roux mused. "I've been wondering about him."

I frowned. "Wondering what?"

"Oh, you know. How it is that he happened to get posted to exactly this little town?"

I shook my head. "Nothing unusual about it. Clement grew up here."

Roux snorted. "So he ought to know how dead this place is on the weekends."

"Even deader, when you consider Henrik," Bene threw in.

Henrik flashed his fangs, but Marius thrust out a hand. "Don't start. Either of you."

I stuck my hands on my hips, facing Roux. "What are you getting at?"

"I'm getting at the question of why an ambitious alpha wolf would accept a transfer from Marseille, where he can make a name for himself fighting real crime, to a dead-end post like Auberre? And why with that particular timing?"

"You mean, the same time I arrived?"

Roux shook his head. "No, I mean the same time Gordon sent *us* here."

That's ridiculous, I nearly said. But maybe it wasn't.

"You think he's here to bust us? Or Gordon?" Bene asked.

Roux shrugged. "I don't know. But we need to be careful around that guy. All of us."

My gut dropped to about the level of my knees. Just when I thought I was on my way to living a quiet, normal existence...

But Clem would never snoop on me. He would never deceive me.

Would he?

A cheer went out, pulling my attention to the scene outside. The first runner had just crossed the finish line, and I spotted Clement step over to congratulate her. More people milled around them, and he slowly separated himself from the crowd. Smiling, he turned and fixed his eyes directly on us, up on that rooftop balcony.

His smile melted.

I gave a meek wave, while Marius muttered, "Is he keeping an eye on the event or on us?"

Clement waved back stiffly, gritting his teeth.

Then Gen skipped up to him, gushing enthusiastically about something, and Clem turned to face her.

"Thank goodness for Gen," I murmured for maybe the second time in my life.

I loved my sister, but she tended to be high-maintenance. Right now, though, I cheered her on. After all, I'd misjudged Marius at the beginning. I could be just as guilty of misjudging Clem. And if he and Gen found happily-ever-after together... Well, that would be nice for everyone.

Hopefully. Probably. Maybe?

"Back to work, everyone," Roux grunted.

Footsteps sounded as the men followed. All except Marius, who wrapped his arms around me and kissed me softly.

"Back to work now, but later..." he murmured.

I grinned, turning in his arms to kiss him.

Our lips moved in tandem, and soon, the police championships, Clement, and other worries faded away, leaving just my mate to focus on.

Because the *later* Marius referred to didn't just mean tonight or next week or next year. It meant a lifetime.

Sneak Peek: Touched by Magic

Genevieve "Gen" Durand is in France after another disastrous romance, determined to breathe new life into her family's crumbling chateau. She's sworn off extracurricular activities of any kind. No intense, overprotective shifters. No experimenting with magical powers. And absolutely no favors for her wealthy godfather, whose businesses all come with a secret, shady side.

But when an art case involving an irreplaceable painting emerges, she can't say no. Before she knows it, Gen is navigating a maze of murder, shifting supernatural alliances, and frenemies who are impossible to read. Luckily, a certain broody shifter insists on protecting her...whether she likes it or not. As secrets unravel, magic reawakens, and passions ignite, Gen will have to decide what she's willing to risk — and who she can truly trust.

Don't miss the magic, action, passion, and suspense of Touched by Magic! *Get your copy today!*

Books by Anna Lowe

Château Nocturne

Brushed by Moonlight (Book 1)

Marked by Moonlight (Book 2)

Touched by Magic (Book 3)

Spellbound in Sedona

Wind Whisperer (Book 1)

Fire Dancer (Book 2)

Dream Weaver (Book 3)

Sherwood Forest Shifters

Tempting the Sheriff (Book 1)

Tempting the Outlaw (Book 2)

Tempting the Maiden (Book 3)

Aloha Shifters - Jewels of the Heart

Lure of the Dragon (Book 1)

Lure of the Wolf (Book 2)

Lure of the Bear (Book 3)

Lure of the Tiger (Book 4)

Love of the Dragon (Book 5)

Lure of the Fox (Book 6)

Aloha Shifters - Pearls of Desire

Rebel Dragon (Book 1)

Rebel Bear (Book 2)

Rebel Lion (Book 3)

Rebel Wolf (Book 4)

Rebel Heart (A prequel to Book 5)

Rebel Alpha (Book 5)

Fire Maidens - Billionaires & Bodyguards

Fire Maidens: Paris (Book 1)

Fire Maidens: London (Book 2)

Fire Maidens: Rome (Book 3)

Fire Maidens: Portugal (Book 4)

Fire Maidens: Ireland (Book 5)

Fire Maidens: Scotland (Book 6)

Fire Maidens: Venice (Book 7)

Fire Maidens: Greece (Book 8)

Fire Maidens: Switzerland (Book 9)

The Wolves of Twin Moon Ranch

Desert Hunt (the Prequel)

Desert Moon (Book 1)

Desert Blood (Book 2)

Desert Fate (Book 3)

Desert Heart (Book 4)

Desert Rose (Book 5)

Desert Roots (Book 6)

Desert Destiny (Book 7)

Sasquatch Surprise (Book 8)

Desert Yule (a short story)

Desert Wolf: Complete Collection (Four short stories)

Blue Moon Saloon

Perfection (a short story prequel)

Damnation (Book 1)

Temptation (Book 2)

Redemption (Book 3)

Salvation (Book 4)

Deception (Book 5)

Celebration (a holiday treat)

Shifters in Vegas

Paranormal romance with a zany twist

Gambling on Trouble

Gambling on Her Dragon

Gambling on Her Bear

Gambling on Her Panther

Serendipity Adventure Romance

Off the Charts

Uncharted

Entangled

Windswept

Adrift

Travel Romance

Veiled Fantasies

Island Fantasies

www.annalowebooks.com

About the Author

USA Today and Amazon bestselling author Anna Lowe loves putting the "hero" back into heroine and letting location ignite a passionate romance. She likes a heroine who is independent, intelligent, and imperfect – a woman who is doing just fine on her own. But give the heroine a good man – not to mention a chance to overcome her own inhibitions – and she'll never turn down the chance for adventure, nor shy away from danger.

Anna loves dogs, sports, and travel – and letting those inspire her fiction. On any given weekend, you might find her hiking in the mountains or hunched over her laptop, working on her latest story. Either way, the day will end with a chunk of dark chocolate and a good read.

Visit AnnaLoweBooks.com